I LOVED YOU IN ANOTHER LIFE

David Arnold

VIKING

VIKING
An imprint of Penguin Random House LLC, New York

First published in the United States of America by Viking,
an imprint of Penguin Random House LLC, 2023

Visit us online at PenguinRandomHouse.com.

Library of Congress Cataloging-in-Publication Data is available.

ISBN 9780593524787 (hardcover)
ISBN 9780593691014 (international edition)

1st Printing

Printed in the United States of America

LSCH

Design by Lucia Baez

Text set in Joanna MT Pro

To Wingate, whose heart reflects my glow.
To Stephanie, whose love is my Lofoten snow.
And to Steven Spielberg, whose answer to me was "No."

This book contains references to
panic attacks and alcoholism.

Please read with care.

PART ONE

REQUIEM

EVAN
a bird in a tree at night

MY LITTLE BROTHER PREFERS CORNERS. He likes sitting quietly in them, and I just wish people understood that sitting quietly in a corner is not universal code for *I am sad, I am lonely, please save me.* All it means for sure is that the quiet kid in the corner would like to sit quietly in the corner, and can we not ascribe our own sets of values to quiet kids in corners the world over? It's not like it costs us anything. It's not like we were using that corner to begin with. And look, I'm sure there are *some* quiet kids in *some* corners who are sad and lonely and need saving. All I'm saying is, let's not assume they *all* are. Silence and sadness are not the same things. And I wish more people understood that, is all.

"Okay," says Ali, and she holds back my hair so I don't get vomit in it, and even though I can't see her, I know she has that look in her eyes, the soft one, the one she saves for when she wants me to know I am seen. And so I ramble about quiet kids, and she knows I'm talking about my brother, Will. She knows this because she sees me.

"You won't love me after this," I say.

"Eh."

"There's no way you love me after this."

"I mean, it's mostly you who loves me, anyway."

I laugh between heaves and feel the sudden urge to plant character flags. "This doesn't mean anything, you know."

"I know," says Ali.

"I'm a responsible adult, basically."

She says, "Just breathe, Evan," and I wonder if she was in the basement back at the party when Heather said that thing about all the important stuff in life being easy. Like how our bodies breathe on their own, even when we sleep, and how our hearts keep beating no matter what, and that's when I had to leave the party. Were you there, Ali? Do you know why I had to leave the party? I left because the heart is a muscle. I left because of what happens to muscles that don't get used over long periods of time, and even though that basement was packed with people, all I could hear were mottled voices, all I could feel were cruel hands, all I could see were hungry eyes.

Do you understand, Ali? I left the party because of atrophy. And if I think too hard about it now, I'm afraid I'll stop breathing. If I think too hard about it, I'm afraid my own heart will stop beating, and then whose heart will glow to Will?

"Mine," Ali says. "And anyway, that's not why you left the party."

"It's not?"

"No. You left for the same reason you drank three and a half vodka tonics. Which, for a constitution as delicate as yours, is roughly the equivalent of injecting a shrew with enough sedative to fell a baby moose." Ali gathers a loose strand of my hair, gently tucks it into her fist behind my head. "You got shit-faced and ran because of what Heather said about Will."

I wipe my mouth with the back of my hand and stand up

straight. We're in the park down the road from Heather Abernathy's house, which is as far as I could get before my stomach attempted to annex my internal organs.

"Heather Abernathy is a sack of shit," says Ali. "And her name should be illegal, it's impossible to fucking say."

O, Ali Pilgrim! She of the soft eyes and quick wit, whose heart is pure, whose amity is fierce, and whose hammer never missed a nailhead. No one understands us, what we have. It's not in books or movies. I've never once heard a song and thought, *Oh, that's Ali and me.* When two people spend most of their time together, misinterpretation is inevitable, though not surprising, given the world's preoccupation with the Horny Teen. It's like it never occurred to anyone that I might love my best friend simply for being awesome. (And to be clear, I am routinely horny, just not for Ali.)

Anyway, they don't write about us, even though we exist all over the place.

"You okay?" she asks.

"I feel like my stomach punched my throat in the dick."

Ali nods. "I find your biologically acrobatic metaphor appropriate."

In addition to the tears, the throbbing head, the furious retching, it's also late August in Iverton, Illinois, a uniquely miserable combination for anyone prone to crotch sweat (yours truly), so yeah, I'm a blessed mess, basically.

The park is silent.

A bird sits quietly in a nearby tree, watching us.

"Have you ever seen that?"

Ali turns to look. "Yes, I have seen a bird before."

Right, but I read this thing once about a scientist in the seventeenth century who believed birds migrated to the moon, because all he knew was that his favorite birds disappeared at the same time every year. He even calculated how long it would take to get to the moon, which apparently coincided with migration cycles, and since science in the 1600s wasn't exactly flush with cosmic data (vis-à-vis atmospheric pressure in space), when he theorized that birds were sustained by excess fat on their interstellar voyage, and when he said they slept through most of their two-month journey to the moon, everyone was like, *Yeah, probably, that's it.*

"You're a chatty drunk." Ali looks from the bird to me. "Though most people get *less* articulate."

"I've just never seen one like this. At night. Sitting like that."

I imagine this bird soaring through the outer reaches of space, alone and asleep, and it's the most peaceful thing.

A song plays from one of the houses surrounding the park; it's quiet but full, a beautiful kind of sad. I close my eyes and listen to the woman singing, imagine the notes floating from a nearby window, bouncing around the playground equipment, the trees. Her voice is a whispery echo, intimate and tortured, and even though the lyrics are imperceptible, you don't need to perceive them to know her pain.

With some songs, the scar is obvious even if the wound isn't.

"I am concerned about you, Evan."

I want to tell her she should be. That my old life is a building collapsed, my new one a sad composite fashioned from rubble. But before I can get the words out, nausea roils again, and I must return to the bushes. Ali resumes her posture of protection, pulling back my hair as I let my insides out, and I think of the ways Heather Abernathy was wrong: breathing isn't easy, not for me; maybe I don't have to tell my heart to keep beating, but it's a runaway train these days; mostly, Heather Abernathy was wrong when she said that thing about my brother. "Heather Abernathy is a sack of shit," I say, and now I'm crying as I vomit, and Ali sort of hugs me with one arm, guards my hair with the other.

The song echoes through the park; the bird sits quietly on high.

"I'm a responsible adult, basically," I say.

Ali says she knows, and I wonder how it's possible to love someone so absolutely and hate them so entirely for seeing me so completely.

SHOSH
an otherwise uneventful morning

THE SUMMER SUNRISE WAS ESPECIALLY vibrant, an explosion of pinks and purples so bright, anyone lucky enough to be awake right now must feel its colors in their teeth. Or at least, that's what Shosh thought, standing by the pool, taking it all in. It was the kind of sunrise to conjure vast ideas of one's place in the course of history, of purpose, of life and death and life again: the kind of spectacle wherein an existential brooder such as herself might see the entire timeline of the universe and, upon closer inspection, recognize her own infinitesimal place in the order of things; the kind of sunrise that—

"Greta fucking Gerwig, amirite?"

Pulled from her sunrise reverie, Shosh turned to find a girl wearing a bikini and a look of perpetual indifference. "What?" said Shosh.

The girl had a phone in one hand, a beer in the other, which she sipped with the measured authority of a true sunrise beer drinker, as if to say, *Yeah, I know my way around an aluminum fucking can.*

"*Lady Bird*," said the girl. "*Little Women.* I mean, I prefer Winona's Jo to Saoirse's, but let's be honest, we're all here for Chalamet's hair." She clinked her can into Shosh's bottle as if the two were partners in crime. "You're into mumblecore, yeah?"

"I don't know you," said Shosh.

"Oh. I'm Heather."

Shosh calculated the odds of multiple Heathers at this party. "Abernathy?"

The girl smiled down at the pool. "Yeah."

Before Shosh could think of what to say, the one and only Heather Abernathy—whose pool they were standing next to, and whose party Shosh had effectively obliterated only moments ago—began to pitch her original screenplay. "I mean yes, it's dragons and thrones, but it's more like if Wes Anderson invaded King's Landing. Total fucking edge."

The Abernathy house (not unlike Heather herself) was an orchestrated display of flash: everything was over-the-top luxurious, symmetrical to the point of obnoxious; the pool, a wide figure eight, was lit from the bottom up; there was a double-deck pergola, a garden gazebo, a cascade fountain. Most everyone had gone home by now, but there were still a few stragglers in various stages of undress, passed out or asleep like soldiers fallen in the world's least noble battle. Shosh's sister, Stevie, used to call them the three-step hangers . . . Those who beg to hang out try to hang on, only to wind up hung over.

A brief smile at the memory, as Shosh raised her bottle to the sunrise—cheers—and downed the last drop of whiskey.

"I mean, look at you," said Heather, reaching out, rubbing the hem of Shosh's coat sleeve. "You'd be perfect for it."

"For what."

"The lead." Heather's hand drifted up the sleeve of Shosh's waterlogged coat. "In my movie."

"Right. The Targaryen Tenenbaums."

"You're even funny. Plus, you look the part." Heather's eyes navigated Shosh like eager tourists. "Who wears a coat in August and gets away with it?"

If styles were climates, Shosh Bell was tornado couture. Currently, she wore a T-shirt that said FUCK GUNS tucked into high-waisted cutoffs, Sperry duck boots, and her favorite checked wool coat, an oversize Stella McCartney deal she'd snagged last year from a secondhand shop that didn't know what it had. Like any reasonable human, having discovered the perfect coat, Shosh considered the item more of an appendage than a garment. As such, it would obviously remain attached to her body for the duration of her time on earth. The way she saw it, if you couldn't say who you were with your clothes, there wasn't much sense getting out of bed in the morning, was there.

Unfortunately, at the moment, the entire ensemble was a sopping-wet mess.

"Heard about your sister," said Heather, turning back to the pool. "Fucking sucks."

Shosh held up the now-empty bottle. "Is there more booze in the house?"

Heather handed her the rest of her beer. "I'm serious about my movie. We should talk. Lemme get your number."

"I don't really do that anymore."

"Give out your number?"

"Act."

Heather said that was too bad, and then something else about following each other on social, how it felt like the night had brought them together, but Shosh had stopped listening. A bird had caught her eye, flying straight for the sunrise, and it wasn't the bird itself that demanded attention so much as the impression of the bird, the way its wings stretched out, not flapping, just a completely effortless soar. Time slowed, and the bird felt like beauty multiplied, elevated into something sacrosanct. Watching, Shosh felt herself elevated with it.

"You know Chris called the cops, right?" said Heather.

"Yeah."

When it was clear this was all Heather would get, she said, "Okay, well. Good luck, I guess," and then turned for the house.

"Hey," said Shosh.

"Yeah?"

Dripping wet, more hurricane than tornado, Shosh said, "Why do you think I did it?"

"I don't know. But you're a fucking legend now."

Only after Heather had disappeared inside did Shosh spot the small horde of faces huddled around the bay window. Mere months ago, she'd been in school with these jokers, back when her life was a rising star with LA on the horizon. But then she'd graduated, and her star had collapsed, her life a cloud of dust hovering aimlessly in space. She raised a hand as if to wave to the horde, then flipped her hand around at the last second, raised her middle finger.

Stumbling toward the pool, she could feel what a mess she was. You hit a wall, though, don't you. Reach a point where you're as much a mess now as you'll ever be, so why stop? At the edge of the pool, she crumpled into a sitting position, dangling her duck boots in the water. On the horizon, the sun was higher now, a little less rainbow fire, a little more ho-hum sun.

The bird was gone, and she felt the sadness that follows the absence of beauty briefly known: "Melancholy," she said. Sadness never sounded so lovely.

She tossed the empty whiskey bottle into the pool, watched it float for a few seconds before water began to fill it, drag it down. Someone in the house had turned on music. It floated through an open window, found her here by the pool, a song so perfectly sad, she thought the singer must understand her melancholy on a molecular level. In time, other voices rose over the music, stern ones carried by heavy boots. *Let them come*, she thought. The cops could inflict no punishment worse than the one fate had already doled out.

As she waited, she watched the bottle sink to the bottom, where it came to rest beside the front tire of Chris Bond's Chevy Tahoe, which, moments ago—just as the sun had begun its explosion of pinks and purples—Shosh had driven directly, and with great velocity, into the Abernathy swimming pool.

"It looks better down there, don't you think?" she asked the officer as he pulled her to her feet. "All lit up in the underwater lights."

EVAN
the dichotomy of Will Taft

I DON'T WAKE UP SO much as detonate in slow motion.

Whatever thunder I'd unleashed in the unsuspecting park bushes last night is nothing compared to the lightning in my skull this morning. Slowly—ever so gently—I inch my way to the edge of the bed, swivel, get my feet on the floor. The clock on the bedside table reads noon. The sunshine through the window is borderline belligerent. Downstairs, Mom is either cooking or constructing a small metal house, I honestly can't tell which.

O, vodka plus tonic! Siren of Night, why must you torment me so?

Truth be told, this is my first hangover, and I have to wonder why anybody ever has a second. Like—your first hangover, okay, you don't know what you don't know. But every hangover thereafter, that shit's on you.

My phone buzzes on the floor. I pick it up to find a slew of texts from Ali . . .

> Ali: G'mornin! Hi-ya! Top o' the day!
> Time to hop outta bed and sing odelay!
> The sun is shining, the birds are chirping
> The world is an oyster primed for slurping
> Get up, get up, come out and play!

Evan: OMG
WTF is wrong with you

Ali: EVAN, m'boy!
Let me guess—you woke up this morning
and immediately wished you hadn't

Evan: My head feels like a roaring
gorilla party

Ali: How fun for you
At least your mom isn't taking you to Target
for . . .
Wait for it . . .
BACK-TO-SCHOOL SHOPPING

Evan: Non

Ali: Oui

Evan: Be sure to get extra scotch
tape 😆

Ali: I am a perpetual 3rd grader in her head

Evan: You always think you have
enough scotch tape and then it's
gone

Ali: I could split an atom and she'd give me
a popsicle

Evan: Hey
Thank you

Ali: ??

> Evan: Last night was a disaster
> But my hair is delightfully vomit-free

> Ali: 💜

> Evan: 💜

> Ali: Have fun with your gorillas

> Evan: Two words: ECONOMY PACK

· · ·

Sharing a bathroom with a seven-year-old means plunging the toilet at least once a week. This morning's clog is especially resilient, and only after I get it to flush do I find the Post-it note on the counter. Scribbled in Will's handwriting is a single word—*sorry*—and two arrows: one points to the toilet; one points to the dried toothpaste in the sink.

In some ways, my brother is every bit the stereotypical seven-year-old: he is criminally disorganized, his room a shifting tectonic plate of toys; everywhere he goes, there's a trail of wrappers and snotty tissues in his wake; he leaves the house with the door wide open, leaves the lights on in every room, forgets to do his homework, forgets to take off his muddy shoes.

He's seven. So it goes.

But in other, more-difficult-to-define ways, Will is an absolutely singular human. And maybe this bathroom, more than anywhere in the house, encapsulates that dichotomy. He may leave a mess in the sink and a floater in the toilet, but he'll damn sure leave a note apologizing for both. Our trash can is usually full of Band-Aid wrappers, but (a) he paid for those Band-Aids with his own allowance, and (b) the Band-Aids are a self-identified coping mechanism, so I'll flush down a wave of floaters, and I'll scrape a mountain of toothpaste from the sink before I utter a word of complaint.

I brush my teeth, take a quick shower, and by the time I'm downstairs, Mom is scraping the remnants of what might generously be called "breakfast" into the garbage, mumbling under her breath. "I got greedy, is what happened. Those waffles last week were a hit, and I got too big for my britches."

Aside from the Mary Taft staples—taco casserole and spaghetti with spicy meatballs—Mom is a notoriously awful cook, though it never seems to stop her from trying. Gently, I remove the skillet from her hand, set it on the counter, wrap my arms around her.

"Hi, Mom."

It's a strange thing, being taller than the person who literally made me. I don't know when it happened, and it doesn't seem right, but here I am, feeling my mother's breath on my shoulder as her body deflates in my embrace. The word hug, as a verb, feels inherently lonely: you can hug someone who doesn't hug you back. But the same word as a noun implies mutual participation.

She takes a breath—

I feel her arms on my back, slowly turning the verb into a noun.

"You okay?" I whisper.

She nods, pulls out of the hug, wipes her eyes. After our talk a couple nights ago, I wasn't sure either of us would have any tears left, but I was wrong.

"I tried to make breakfast." She points to the trash can.

"Okay."

"I know you had a late night. Thought it might be nice."

I shrug. "Breakfast is overrated."

She opens the fridge, stares blankly inside. "How was the party?"

I consider the variety of analogies I might use to convey my heroically shitty night: Cheese-dust-on-your-fingers awful? Preface-your-Facebook-post awful? If someone calling when they could have texted were a night out, that was my night.

Instead, I answer with the only positive thing I can think: "Ali was there."

"Good," says Mom, and even though it sounds like a throwaway response, I know she gets it. Ali is the kind of friend who is also an answer.

I sit at the kitchen counter while Mom makes sandwiches. She asks about the Headlands application, if I've gotten a good start on my essay, which I haven't, so I deflect; I suggest she quit one of her jobs, given the circumstances, but she won't, so she deflects. When it's clear neither of us is willing to budge, she says, "Can't believe my baby's gonna be a senior," and I wonder at this apparent epidemic of adults not being able to deal with the passage of time.

"Guess where Ali is right now?" I say.

"Where?"

"Target. Her mom took her back-to-school shopping."

Mom smiles for a second, and then—"Oh shit! Shit!"

"What?"

She spins on a dime, puts both hands in her hair. "I forgot about school supplies. They sent the list, and I just—*damn it*—I have to be at work in an hour—"

"I can take him."

"—it's my only morning off this week—"

"Mom. I can take him."

Her hands fall to her sides, and her face tilts. "Yeah?"

"We'll go today. No problem."

She leans across the counter, puts a hand on my cheek, and gets that look on her face like her tears called and they're on their way.

"It's no big deal, Mom."

"You shouldn't have to be this good."

"Okay."

"But I'm glad that you are."

"Mom? I literally have nothing else to do."

"Thank you."

"He's in his room?"

"Disappeared into his spaceship this morning," she says. "Took his cereal with him. I haven't seen him since."

"You get ready for work. I'll clean up here and take him."

After another full round of hugs and thank-yous and lost-without-yous, Mom heads to her room. Alone in the kitchen, I text Ali to see if she's still at Target.

Ali: OMG yes
Mom won't let us leave until we find
something called a "trapper keeper"
WTF and FML
WTFML

Evan: Grab us some tape, we're on our way!

• • •

Mornings like these are why I question the Headlands gap year. Applications and finances aside, I can't very well fly from Southeast Alaska to Iverton, Illinois, every time Mom double-books or forgets a shift. One thing I've learned since Dad left: when you're a single parent, the duties aren't just doubled, they're multiplied exponentially. It hardly matters that I've had my eye on the Headlands program for years, that I've been obsessed with the idea of the north for as long as I can remember, or that every time I see a photo of snowcapped mountains, I feel the unstoppable urge to draw them on everything I own. It hardly matters that Dad offered to pay for half if I get in. An absent dad who pays for everything is like a mathematician growing a tomato: Tomatoes are great, but how about you solve for fucking x? However lacking our financial situation (and it is *lacking*), no amount of money solves the problem he's created by not being here.

Enter: the Headlands dilemma. Even if I get accepted—even if I qualify for the most generous financial aid package—I cannot envision a world in which I head off to Glacier Bay, Alaska, next spring, leaving Mom alone with Will for six months.

And that was *before* the bombshell two nights ago.

I put away the sandwich stuff, wipe crumbs off the counter, and when I pop the lid to the trash, the remnants of Mom's attempted breakfast greet me like some sluggish crustacean. Our house is small; I can hear her in her bedroom now, music blaring, drawers opening and closing as she gets ready for a job she shouldn't have to keep. And it occurs to me that the cooking, the loud music, the second job—all of it—are great ways to avoid the darker corners of the mind.

Halfway upstairs, I realize the song coming from her room is the same one I heard in the park last night.

The park where I vomited because I'd had too much to drink at a party I never wanted to attend.

Maybe Mom's not the only one avoiding dark corners.

SHOSH
namesake misnomer

"THIS PLACE SMELLS LIKE A hot shoe. Like that summer foot smell, you know? Peel off your socks and just . . ." Shosh made a little pfffff sound, exploding one hand—to demonstrate a cloud of noxious odor released into the air—while propping her phone on her knee with the other. "At least last time, I had one of those interview rooms to myself. You should see this waiting room, it's a shit-show."

"But you're not under arrest?" asked Ms. Clark.

"No," sighed Shosh. "Just detained."

Aside from the smell, her main gripe with the Iverton police station was the seating situation: the leather padding stuck to her legs so every time she shifted, it sounded like a low-key fart, and even though she was entirely innocent, she could hardly blame the chair, as doing so only made her more culpable in the eyes of the room.

And oh how they roved.

Onscreen, Ms. Clark helped her kid—an adorable three-year-old named Charlie—crack an egg on the rim of a bowl. "And you're okay? Other than the hot-shoe thing."

"I am okay. Other than the hot-shoe thing."

There was no word for what Ms. Clark was to Shosh. From day one in freshman drama, when she'd walked into the room to find her teacher standing on a chair in the tree pose, eyes closed, chanting the word *balance* over and over again like some bizarro Benedictine monk, it was clear Ms. Clark wasn't a typical teacher. And whether because of Shosh's talent, drive, or something else altogether, Ms. Clark took her under her swanlike wing for the duration of high school.

Part of Shosh was there still.

"I haven't seen a poem in a while," said Ms. Clark.

Shosh raised one eyebrow, then slowly rotated the phone a full 360 degrees. "Yeah, I've been a little preoccupied. Or maybe you hadn't heard."

"Frost says poetry is a way of taking life by the throat."

"You hear the one about the Jedi poet?"

Ms. Clark eyed her over the large mixing bowl. "Metaphors be with you?"

"So that's a yes."

"Shosh—"

"*Okay.* I'll post another one, God. They're barely even poems, just mindless little—"

"Anything you make is part of you. That's sacred, okay? While the masses may belittle—"

"We be big. Got it."

As a student, Shosh's life had been theater. How appropriate then that most of what she'd learned in theater applied to life, an education her ex-teacher seemed dead set on continuing from her kitchen across town. "You'll have enough critics without adding yourself to the pile," said Ms. Clark. "But critics aren't makers. They can't touch it, not really." Then, to Charlie: "Not yet, honey, the batter is still raw."

Baffled and betrayed, Charlie said, "You let me wid cookieth."

If cuteness were a buffet, little Charlie's plate would be piled high. Between his cheeks and his lisp, the kid was a complete menace to society.

"What are you making, Chuck?" asked Shosh.

Charlie stuck his face right up to the phone: "Blueburry flip-jackth!" And Shosh wanted to melt into the screen, become part of this tiny, beautiful family.

"Et voilà!" said Ms. Clark, popping the tray in the oven as Charlie disappeared from the room, a cloud of flour in his wake.

"Listen—" Ms. Clark relocated the phone to another part of the kitchen. "You've got plenty of people in your life to point out your fuckups. So I'm just going to be here for you. But don't think for a second that means I endorse your behavior or that I'm not going to urge you to get your shit together, Shosh. Speaking of which, I'm still in touch with the dean at USC—"

"No thank you. I told you, I'm done with that."

Ms. Clark sighed, and it killed Shosh to think how much time her teacher had invested in a future that was now nonexistent. Letters written, phone calls made, relationships formed, all on Shosh's behalf—all for nothing. Shosh sometimes wondered if her decision to forgo USC hurt Ms. Clark more than it hurt her.

"One thing about her?" said Ms. Clark.

Neither of them could remember when it started, but their calls always ended with Shosh recalling a specific memory about her sister.

"She named me," said Shosh.

"I didn't know that."

"I came home nameless from the hospital. Mom and Dad

couldn't agree what to call me, and after a day or two, Stevie was calling me Shosh. She was two, it's not like she was stringing full sentences together. When they asked where she got the name, she said she dreamed it."

Silence for a second, as Ms. Clark's piney-green eyes began to water, and just as she opened her mouth to say something—

"Stevie Bell?"

Shosh's phone slipped to the floor—"Shit." She bent down, grabbed it, and looked up to find a police officer scowling at her.

"Are you Shosh Bell?" the officer said.

In life, Stevie and Shosh had often been confused for each other. Since Stevie's death, that confusion seemed to have seeped into Shosh's brain: it wasn't the first time she'd heard her sister's name when someone said her own.

"Yes," she said. "I'm Shosh Bell."

"Your CDW's here. Also, your mother."

Onscreen, a worried Ms. Clark said, "What's a CDW?"

"Court-designated worker," said Shosh, wondering when she'd learned the shorthand of this place. "Gotta run. I'll text you."

Shosh followed the cop to the desk up front where two women awaited with faces like shadows: Audrey the social worker (or Aubrey, she could never remember which) and the one and only Lana Bell.

Shosh looked at the social worker. "Hello . . . Aubrey?"

"It's Audrey."

"Hmm, but what if it isn't?"

Audrey was not amused.

Shosh turned to her mother. "And . . . you are?"

The day before her sister died, Shosh stared down a grocery aisle, eyes glazed. "Everything looks the same."

"The illusion of variety," said Stevie. "No matter how many options we think we have, it's just different versions of the same crop." She grabbed a box of granola off the shelf, reviewed the ingredients on the back. "Corn."

"Wait, really?"

Stevie tossed the box in the cart and, in a feat of lackadaisical virtuosity, waved her arm in the air like a ringmaster presenting lions jumping through hoops of fire. "Corn! Far as the eye can see."

"How do you know this shit?"

Quietly, as if the lower the volume, the more legit the claim: "I saw a documentary."

Stevie and Shosh Bell were two years apart and entirely inseparable. From the soccer fields of their youth, where Stevie had lied about her age so she could play on Shosh's younger team, to every dance floor since middle school, which they'd proudly attended as each other's dates, they were a package deal, and everybody knew it. Where one went, so went the other—including a grocery run.

"What is this?" Stevie reached into their cart, pulled out a wedge of cheese wrapped in red wax.

"What is what," said Shosh.

They'd been walking up and down aisles for the last fifteen minutes, tossing items in the cart, checking things off as they went, trying (and failing) not to think about corn, how the corn had been transported, transformed, transmogrified into literally everything everyone everywhere ingested, so by the time they reached the cheese section in the deli, it was as if they'd been stumbling through a corn-swept desert, only to arrive at a sensible, nutritious oasis.

"This." Stevie held up the cheese wedge like a prosecutor presenting an incriminatory piece of evidence. "What is this?"

"Gouda."

"Um. No."

Shosh held up the list. "It's in your handwriting. See?"

"I meant no, as in this isn't gouda."

Shosh grabbed the cheese from her sister's hand. "It literally says gouda on the label."

"It's soft." Stevie picked a different wedge from the display, carefully reading the label. "Gouda isn't soft."

"I forgot you're a cheese expert."

"In another life, I may have been a fromager."

Shosh looked around the store, as if someone nearby might help explain what the hell was happening. "This feels like a dream—"

"A cheesemonger, if you will."

"—where nothing is as it seems."

"Though fromager has the added onomatopoeic appeal."

Shosh squinted. "I'm not sure you can do that with that word. Anyway, you're back at Loyola tomorrow. What do you care what cheese we eat?"

Stevie took the cheese from Shosh's hand. "We'll just put this back here for some other poor sap."

"Maybe I like soft gouda."

"First off, you don't, even if you think you do." Stevie studied the stacks of wedges with a glimmer in her eye, as if picking out a wedding ring or a luxury sedan. "And second, I care enough about my family to not let them eat cheese that isn't cheese."

"You know, you could probably stand to get laid."

"Here we go." Stevie picked up a long wedge of something under a label reading EXPLORE THE NETHERLANDS. "Cave aged for a thousand days."

"Why do you have to go back so soon?"

"Feel that. See?"

"It's summertime, Stevie. It is the time of summer."

"*That's* how gouda should feel."

"We are young and fetching and it is the time of summer."

"Perfect crystallization."

"You know what you should do? Blow off summer sessions. Hang with me instead. Let's be young and fetching together, in this, the time of summer."

"Rock hard. A mature, nutty flavor that melts in your mouth. And you know what the secret ingredient is?"

"Thinly veiled sexual innuendos?"

With more reverence than was necessary, Stevie placed the gouda in the cart. She turned to her sister, put both hands on either of Shosh's shoulders, and aside from the hair—Stevie's leaf-brown curls, Shosh's explosion of dark waves and sharp bangs—their faces were mirrorlike.

"*Time,* sister."

Digging deep, Shosh found the only true thing: "Don't go."

"You know I'd love nothing more than to spend my summer with you. But summer session means early graduation. Which means I can join you in LA sooner rather than later. Right?"

In the next aisle, Shosh tossed a can of Cheez Whiz into the cart, and Stevie called her a barbarian, and thus they proved the primary tenet of the charmed life: it's only charmed so long as you don't know it is.

The following day, Stevie loaded her Prius with freshly washed clothes and a pan of their mother's lasagna, and when the sisters hugged, they said, "Love you," and that was it. There was no need to say goodbye; they would of course talk on the phone that night . . .

According to the police report—which had been given to her parents, and which Shosh had snuck into the bathroom, snapped a photo of, and memorized soon after—the man's name was Phil Lessing. Having been fired from his job that day, Phil Lessing had decided his best course of action was to get hammered at the local bar. There, he wove for himself a sad little cocoon, until, ready to emerge a fully formed hazard, Phil picked up his keys, stumbled to the parking lot, and climbed behind the wheel of his built-to-last Ford F-150.

Shosh never knew if the details helped or hurt. Did she *want* to know that the F-150 had proved its slogan, not a scratch on it, while Stevie's Prius sat in the median like a crumpled ball of tinfoil? Did she *want* to know that her sister's eighties-fab Velcro watch had somehow landed a solid fifty feet away from the accident? Did she *want* to know that first responders couldn't immediately differentiate between blood and marinara from the exploded pan of lasagna?

Without her sister, Shosh devolved into something aimless. Like one of those bioluminescent bristle worms floating around in the pitch-black of the seafloor: if there was purpose in life, she couldn't feel it; if there was direction, she couldn't see it; her sister had been her natural habitat, and when that was taken away, she was forced to create a new one. And so she spun her own sad cocoon. Her father had quite the collection of whiskey in the basement. Their freezer was an oak tree, bottles of vodka stashed like acorns in winter. She was far from the only imbiber in the family; these medicinal nooks were forever replenished, and if her parents asked questions of her, they'd have to ask questions of themselves.

She could still feel Stevie's hands on her shoulders, the way each of them got lost in the eyes of the other. "*Time, sister.*"

Caves, cocoons, crystallization: time changed things on a molecular level. Maybe Shosh just needed a place to spend a thousand days, and like a Dutch gouda or a birdwing butterfly, she could emerge some extraordinary new thing.

Or just whole again would be enough.

Shosh leaned her head against the passenger-side window of her mother's car. Her hair was only half-dry from this morning's plunge in the Abernathy pool; her clothes and coat still smelled of chlorine. Through the window, downtown Iverton passed in a blur, and she imagined some other version of her life, one where she lived in a cabin in the mountains, by water, under snow, Finland or Norway maybe, somewhere cold.

The radio was on. The same sad song she'd heard this morning by the pool.

"I came a different way this time," said her mom. "Cut across Pasadena, shaved five minutes off the drive. Isn't that funny?"

"What's funny."

"I know the fastest route from our house to the police station. What a hilarious joke."

If Shosh was tornado couture, it was no secret where she'd inherited the tornado: Lana Bell had always been a bit of a mess, prone to leaving things behind and forgetting to shower for a few days. She was a first-grade teacher, though, so it had always been a schtick that worked. Her class was exactly the quirky house of whimsy you wanted for your first grader. But ever since Stevie's death, that whimsy had soured into something darker, the kind of empty-eyed volatility that compelled people to cross the street.

But then, the Bells were a family of shadows now, weren't they. Human negative space.

"I don't know what to do with you," said the shadow-mother.

Forehead against glass, Shosh watched a bird drift high in the sky.

"Are you going to tell me why you drove that boy's truck into your friend's pool?"

"She's not my friend," said Shosh, trying to decide if this was the same kind of bird as the one she'd seen at sunrise.

"Do you have any idea how bad this could have been? If someone had been hurt, or if someone else had been with you in the car? Aubrey says we're lucky they're not pressing charges—"

"Audrey."

"Whatever! Damages are coming straight out of your account, you can bet on that. I don't even—we're all dealing with it, you know? It's not just you, Sho, we are all fucking hurting here, and I just can't—why would you do a thing like that?"

No. Definitely not the same kind of bird.

"I want to live in Norway," Shosh said quietly.

A beat, and then: "Are you drunk?"

Shosh said yes, most likely she was, and as the shadow-mother railed, the juvenile delinquent bird-watched, and this was her life now, not a logical scheme but a bizarre convergence of beings doing things. You got blood on your hands, a bird would be better, sang the voice on the radio, apparently omniscient, and it didn't matter if she was sober now, later, or ever. How could it? How could anything matter when she'd never gotten a goodbye?

This word nobody wanted, but everyone needed. This word that apparently hurt to say, but she knew the truth: you only think goodbye is painful if you've had a chance to say it.

That evening, as the Bell family ate takeout in front of the TV, Lana Bell asked Jared Bell if they could switch cars the following weekend. "I have that teachers' conference in Milwaukee," she said, and Shosh's dad agreed without comment.

"Is something wrong with your car?" Shosh asked her mom.

"Sound system's been out for months. No way I'm making that drive in silence."

Later that night, Shosh lay awake in bed, staring into the rotating blades of her ceiling fan. And as she imagined soaring songbirds and Norwegian snowdrifts, she hummed the melody of a song that had followed her all day, a song that fell over her now like a warm quilt. A song she was beginning to think might exist only in her head.

PARIS

· 1832 ·

SHE CAME FROM THE NORTH with a song in her heart and blood on her hands. The former was a steady murmur of revenge; the latter, proof of sins committed in its name.

All around, pushing and vying, porters and coachmen shouting in garbled tongues. Watching those around her, she understood the men were asking about luggage and passport. Sølvi stretched out her empty hands. "Paris," she said, that great dream of a word her only possession.

A coachman shook his head, pointed to the ground—"Le Havre"—then pointed to some vague spot on the horizon. "Paris."

Exhausted, penniless, Sølvi turned to face the endless ocean, the port abuzz with people boarding and deboarding monstrous vessels. She stood in the shadow of the ship that brought her here—its constant sway sure to haunt her sleep for years to come—opened her mouth, and draped the cold commotion around her in the warm quilt of song.

Étienne often wondered if he was alone because he painted, or if he painted because he was alone. *Tant pis*, he thought. *Je peins parce que je peins.*

I paint because I paint.

Mornings found him in the galleries of the Louvre, working on copies with other students. Étienne lived in a comfortable one-bedroom apartment near the Sorbonne, left to him by his deceased parents. Where he'd once found gusto in life—lunch in the Garden of the Tuileries, sunset strolls across the Pont Neuf—he'd recently succumbed to a deepening sense of aimlessness. The most mediocre work of art could hold his interest far longer than any person he knew; he was bored of everyone. And when you are bored of everyone, it is only a matter of time before everyone is bored of you.

Boredom was impossible on an empty stomach. Having smuggled herself to Paris in the back of a stagecoach, it had only taken a few days for Sølvi to discover that the one she'd come to kill—her horse's ass of a father—had been dead for years.

She spoke no French, had no money, but she was a quick study. Soon, she was singing in the streets, learning which cafés abided her presence, which hotels catered to those who might flip her a coin. At night, she huddled among the rats and itinerants, but during the day, she sang. No longer a song of revenge, hers was a song of the north, of places frozen and familiar, of dancing lights in the sky, and though no one understood the lyrics, her songs haunted the hearts of all who heard them.

One night, quite late, Sølvi found herself following a bird out onto a bridge. A northern bird like her, she'd decided, entirely at ease in the cold. Careful not to disturb the creature, she hopped up onto the ledge beside it, thinking nothing of the height or the freezing Seine below. "Hej," she whispered, reaching out a hand, and whether she began singing then, or had been singing all along, she wasn't sure. It was a song like no other, a birdsong, a wildsong, as if she were many Sølvis, singing various parts in harmony.

They sat like that, bird and woman, muse and originator, their voices carrying across the river, until—

"Aimez-vous aussi les oiseaux?"

He hadn't meant to startle her. Drawn first by her voice, then by her appearance—perched on a ledge, clothes tattered, white-blond hair whipping around in the wind—Étienne was utterly beguiled for the first time in recent memory.

Sølvi searched his eyes. His face was pleasant enough, but the eyes of men were synopses: she could read them and know exactly what they were about.

"Aimez-vous aussi les oiseaux?" he asked again.

Days later, she would translate his question using the book he'd bought for her. Aimez-vous aussi les oiseaux? *Do you like birds too?* And she would smile and stumble through her response in French: "Oui," she would say. "J'aime les oiseaux."

But for now, she pushed her hair out of her face, touched her chest. "Sølvi."

He smiled; the bird flew. "Étienne."

In the coming weeks, they spent every moment together. He painted her in his apartment, the contours of her body alive in his brush. She sang as she posed; songs of the north melted into songs of love surpassing language, and in this way, they learned the language of each other's bodies: nights became days, they slipped in and out of bed, in and out of clothes, and as they painted and sang, their plural became singular, each soul more itself in the presence of the other.

Their love was a strange new metallurgy: before, they were iron unrefined; in each other, they found fire.

The tattoos were Sølvi's idea. She'd seen a few in prison, though Étienne would never know this. (Some places, you don't return to, even in memory.) His most recent painting of her—standing naked by the window, giant feathered wings sprouting from her back—had put the notion into her head. Her French was better now, though still rudimentary; when she told him the idea, he'd asked why they should brand their bodies, seeing as they were neither criminals nor royalty. To this, she threw off the bedsheets, climbed on top of him, leaned into his ear, and said, "C'est pourquoi."

It was reason enough for him.

They found a man in a cellar who possessed the proper tools and training. He warned of great pain and long healing. In response, Sølvi opened the book she'd brought—Histoire des oiseaux—and pointed to the bird she'd chosen for them.

"Ç'est de la folie," said the man.

"Oui," said Étienne, sitting in the man's chair, placing his hand on the table. "Une folie à deux."

That spring, as Sølvi's French continued to improve, and the tattoos were almost healed, she fell ill. What started as cramps and vomiting turned to convulsions and unbearable agony. Étienne rushed her to the Hôtel-Dieu, a hospital on the Île de la Cité, and by the time they arrived, he also was unwell. For months, whispers of cholera had spread through Paris like wildfire; now that the disease was here, it spread even faster. From adjacent beds, Sølvi and

Étienne grew sicker by the hour, as all around, the Hôtel-Dieu filled with those like them.

"Sølvi." Étienne reached toward her, flapping his hand weakly. A single wing trying to fly. She met his hand in the middle. The two wings joined, the bird became whole. Étienne smiled—then dropped her hand suddenly, turned, vomited on the floor.

In quiet, broken French, she told him the story of a girl who'd been abandoned, abused, locked up. She told the story of a high window, birds perched between the bars, and how this girl imagined herself in their company, coming and going as she pleased. Each night, the girl drowned the wailing misery of that place in song, swearing revenge on the ones who'd left her there to die. And when a chance came her way, she took it. And when a boat came her way, she took that too. She knew little of her true past, but there was a word, a place, tucked in the depths of memory: *Paris*. And so the girl had come to kill her father, only to find that he was already dead. And the place in her heart that was once filled with vengeance had been filled with surprising, surpassing love.

"Fin," she said, the story done. But Étienne's eyes were glassy and unblinking.

Above their beds, the sun shone through a high window, the sky more blue than blue. And as she wondered what awaited her in death, if she might travel beyond the blue, a new song entered her heart, not of vengeance or love but a promise. Her head dropped to one side, facing the shell of Étienne. "*Je te trouverai*," she sang—I will find you—and the soul inside breathed its last as Sølvi of the north.

PART TWO

NOCTURNE

EVAN
Kafkaesque

I WANT TO TELL MAYA about Mom. I want to tell her about the bird in the park, and what happened at the party last week, and I don't know what she could possibly do about any of it, but telling her things is the whole point, isn't it.

"You seem . . ." Maya tilts her head, studies my face in a way that makes me wonder what I seem. ". . . cheerful," she says.

An unexpected wrinkle.

"Do I?"

"Yes."

I shrug. "It's Tuesday."

"Ah. E.T. and Jet's?"

"We've done E.T. seven Tuesdays in a row. I'll be making a case for *Wall-E* or *Fantastic Mr. Fox*, and as far as pizza goes, obviously Jet's is the superior slice, but I need to peruse the weekly coupons. Might be a Domino's week, depending."

"Papa Johns usually has good coupons."

I do this thing where I flare my nostrils, and people everywhere know I mean business. "Sure, okay, Papa Johns. I mean, I've got this old racist bike tire in my garage. We could melt some cheese on that, save the money."

I sit in the silence that follows the thunder of a joke cracked with confidence: therein lies a strange, terrifying vulnerability.

We talk about school, inevitably, how my first week of senior year is going, obviously. I've got two classes with Ali, landed the good AP teachers (i.e., the teachers whose eyes and voices haven't run out of batteries yet), plus, a second year in Creative Writing with Mr. Hambright. All told, I should be ecstatic. I should be doing cartwheels. But talking about the final year of high school always leads to talking about what happens *after* high school, and these days, I'd rather crack jokes that don't land than talk about What a Bright Future I Have.

When it's clear my heart's not in it, a heavy hush falls over the room.

Outside, a cloud drifts in the sky; inside, shadows travel across the carpet. One slow exodus follows another.

I've never understood people who are uncomfortable with silence, but I have to think they weren't very comfortable in the first place. The absence of noise is the presence of mind, a body's place to breathe. Silence is a big part of what we do here. Some days, our sessions stretch out before us, a vast and remote wilderness where no conversation could possibly grow. Some days, I'm like, I *literally have nothing to talk about*, and we'll talk about nothing, and I still feel better than before we started. Most of the time, though, the hour starts and talk blooms, radiant and surprising, and by the end, I am half my size and full of air, in real danger of being blown away by a mild gust of wind.

That's what therapy is, I think: working toward zero gravity.

"Coming up on the one-year mark," Maya says.

"Hmm?"

"Almost a year since your dad left. How're you doing with it?"

"I don't know. Better than Mom."

"In what way?"

"At least I can talk about it. I can say out loud how much I hate him. She tries to pretend it's no big deal."

"She ignores it," says Maya.

"She belittles it."

"How so?"

When you think about it, most families boil down to the same core elements: geography (this is our house); biography (this is who we are); and philosophy (this is why we're here). More than a foundation, it's a mutual agreement. A code. So when someone you live with leaves, it's more than a departure; it's the arrival of a new code. Our family coped with this code in different ways: Will retreated into his own world; I started having storms; and Mom . . .

"She calls it their *inversary*," I say.

"She calls what what, now?"

"The one-year mark of Dad leaving. As in *inverse anniversary*."

"Ah."

Mom is a champion, I tell Maya.

She says she knows.

Dad sucks a wad of fuckballs.

She says nothing for a second and then asks if I've had any recent storms.

"Not for weeks."

"That's great, Evan. I'm really proud of you."

Through the window, I see a bird land on a branch; in one of the adjacent rooms, someone starts playing music, the same song

I'd heard in the park that night, and in Mom's bedroom the morning after.

"Evan?"

I want to tell Maya about Mom. I want to tell her about the bird in the park, but for some reason, when I think about that night, my brain becomes a feather, my thoughts become chirps, and my mouth, a useless little beak.

"What are you thinking about?" she asks.

Another aimless cloud shifts in the sky; I watch the slow exodus of shadows across the carpet, recalling that day in infuriating detail.

"The formation of the earth," I say.

When Dad told us he was leaving, I thought he meant his job. When I realized he meant *us*, I asked the only logical question: "Why?"

"It's like . . . Pangaea," he said, and I wondered if he'd always been such a bullshitter, or if this was a more recent development. "Remember? That school project I helped you with? The world is always changing, Evan. Over time, and for no real reason."

Outside, the shining sun lied about what kind of day it was.

"So you're leaving for no reason."

Dad sighed, as if I were the one who'd ignited this garbage fire of a conversation. "It's more complicated than that."

It wasn't, though. Dad had a reason, and that reason was a brunette called Stacey. According to Facebook, Stacey had a gap in her teeth, a poodle that looked like a wilted potato, and a nearly grown son called Nick. Nick had a job at Staples and a longtime girlfriend named Ruth. Ruth was an Uber driver and had a way of smiling at the camera like she was about to eat the lens. This was the family he'd traded ours for.

But I wouldn't learn any of this until later.

On that day, I listened to Dad bloviate about Pangaea, confusing his own shitty life choices for inevitabilities, while Mom hovered in the kitchen doorway, an oversize glass of wine in hand, as much a part of the conversation as she was a part of the room.

"What about Will?" I asked, hoping Dad could spot the question under the question: *What kind of monster willingly says goodbye to such a cosmic gift of a child?*

Dad's eyes darted to the top of the stairs, and for a split second, I worried Will was sitting there, that he'd overheard everything. But he wasn't. In a move I then understood to be well orchestrated, he'd been sent to a friend's house for the day. "Your brother will be okay," Dad said, and then dove back into how much he loved us, how nothing would change that, how it wasn't our fault, as if the notion that I was to blame had even crossed my mind.

As he talked, he shifted around on the couch, and I thought, *We'll have to get a new couch.* And when he sipped coffee from his favorite NASA mug, *We'll have to get new mugs,* and on the bookcase over his shoulder, I spotted the first-edition Salinger he'd given me for my sixteenth birthday, which, of course, would also have to go. And it occurred to me that a home isn't just a house or the people you live with—it's the things those people used. Things have a way of taking on the lives of those around them, so when someone in the house betrays you, it's a betrayal multiplied in perpetuity: your favorite book turns to drivel; coffee in space-related paraphernalia, undrinkable; couches, unsittable. And when the betrayer walks out the front door for the last time, you'll have to dig a tunnel under the house, or exit through the chimney, because fuck that door.

"I know it's a lot," Dad said, sitting on a couch that was dead to me. "Talk to me, Ev. What are you thinking?"

In my head, I counted to twenty. Slowly.

Mom stood in the doorway; she took a prolonged sip and then winked at me over the glass, and it was hard to know if I'd always loved her more than Dad or if our current situation had already rewritten my entire history.

We both knew how much he hated silence.

After another leisurely ten-count, I ambled over to the bookcase, pulled down the first-edition Salinger. *Catcher* was fine and all, but give me the Glass family all day, every day. I had an older copy of *Franny and Zooey* in my room upstairs, but *Raise High the Roof Beam, Carpenters* had always been my favorite, worth showcasing in our living room library. It had meant a lot when Dad gave it to me: proof that he knew what I liked and wanted to make me happy. When I'd first unwrapped it, I knew it was old—it was a used library copy, no dust jacket—but didn't know it was a first edition until he told me to check the front page. And when I thanked him, it had been the kind you offer when you feel truly seen.

Only now—

Looking back, I couldn't help wondering about a few details. Like the blue notes in Mom's voice when she'd recently read about the used bookstore that was going out of business. Or how the wrapping paper, which I'd so eagerly torn away, had been immaculately applied, even at the corners, and when I tried to think of a time when Dad had wrapped a gift, all I could come up with was him paying someone in the mall to do it for him.

Mom, however, was an expert wrapper.

"The decay of radioactive elements," I said quietly, staring at the faded cover in my hands as the knowledge of its origins washed over me. And I wondered how many other prized possessions contained two stories: one within, one without. "And leftover heat from the formation of the earth."

When I looked up, Mom was crying in the doorway, but smiling too, and words like *tectonic* and *mantle* and *core* came to mind, and I knew we'd be okay.

"I'm not sure I follow," said Dad.

I handed him the book, willing him to feel the extra weight of his story. Of history.

"Pangaea," I said. "When your whole world breaks apart, there's always a reason."

SHOSH
dispatches from frozen places

SHOSH STARED AT THE FISHGRAY sky and listened to the song it sang for her. When her mother walked in, Shosh didn't turn around. The way she saw it, knocking was a prerequisite for acknowledging entry.

"*Shosh*. My God. One of these days, you're going to fall right out the window."

Not long ago, Shosh realized that the windows in her room aligned with the height of her bed. Naturally, she'd pushed the bed right up against the wall, so now, when she opened the window, she could recline on her bed with her legs hanging outside. Some nights, she lay there, inches from the open air, watching the stars come out. A few times, she'd watched the stars disappear into light as the sun rose.

"Your dad ordered takeout. It'll be here in twenty."

"Okay," said Shosh, and she thought *gray*—fish-hued or otherwise—wasn't the right word for the color of the sky.

Was *bleak* a color?

"Sho—"

"I said okay, Mom."

Shosh sipped from a can of Diet Coke—half of which had been replaced with vodka from a large handle she kept under the bed—

and listened to the soft click of the door closing behind her, the sound of Lana Bell's sock-footed mope down the hallway.

In the days following the incident at Heather's party, her parents had mostly ignored her. They both had work, and as she'd already graduated, they really didn't know what to do with her. In another world, her room would have been packed up by now, her car full of clothes and desk lamps and various dorm room sundries. She should be crying and hugging her parents, pulling out of the driveway, heading into the bright lights of a promising future on the West Coast.

Shosh took another sip, stared at the sky. She had a sudden image from years ago, a children's Sunday school class, maybe, of angels and trumpets and clouds parting. And she wondered if that was where this music was coming from, some perverse version of the divine.

Over the last week, she'd heard no fewer than three distinctly different songs, as if the ongoing disaster of her life required a soundtrack. She couldn't deny they were the perfect accompaniment: ethereal and weepy, they seemed to follow wherever she went, an audible rain cloud. Sometimes she could make out lyrics, but more often than not, they were muted and faraway, to the point where she occasionally wondered if there was a logical explanation—music from a neighbor's house, maybe, or a glitch on her phone.

As if her phone were listening, it buzzed in her pocket. She pulled it out to find a text from Ms. Clark: Still waiting, Ms. Frost . . .

In the pie chart of Shosh's life, her biggest slice had always been acting. Music was a close second, but as some combination of the two had indirectly ruined her life, she was done with all that now. Weeks ago, when she'd told Ms. Clark as much, her teacher had said, "So what will you be making, then?"

Shosh had been half-drunk at the time, sitting on a nearby park swing. "I don't understand the question."

"It's pretty simple, Shosh. People like us make things. When we don't, we fill that part of our soul with lesser things. Vodka, for example. So what I'd like to know is—*what will you be making*? I don't require much, but I can tell you, the degree to which I have the patience for these late-night drunk-chats directly corresponds to your answer. So think carefully."

"I'm not drunk."

"Double down, then. See where that gets you."

After considering for a minute, Shosh had said a single word: "Poetry."

It wasn't acting, it wasn't music—as far as she could tell, no one could say for sure what it was. One thing she knew now and wished she'd known then: being an artist was hard; being a poet was damn near impossible.

Sipping in her window, she flipped over to Instagram and scrolled her saved "winterscape" photos. Recently, she'd seen a picture from a suggested account of a rural bungalow in Norway, and before she knew it, she'd followed that account and a dozen like it. Now her feed was full of cabins in snow, resting precariously atop craggy mountains, wedged between enormous evergreens, washed-out frosty palettes, all of which seeped the essence of a word that was both direction and place: *north*.

Alas, the remote wilderness was idyllic only so far as Instagram allowed it to be. Obviously, she couldn't pack up and move to one of these snowcapped cabins—no matter how much her Thoreauvian heart wanted to—and so why not turn them into art?

For this particular couplet, she chose a balmy orange cabin buried in snow, awash in the faint glow of dusk. The sky was something deep—not purple, exactly, but what purple was always trying to be. A mossy tree hung over the scene, its branches frosted white like the beard of a giant. "There is a place we like to go," she whispered, and even though the words sounded familiar, she typed them onto the screen, just as the second line came to her . . .

> there is a place we like to go
> where secrets hide in trees of snow

Positioning of text was key. Top-of-frame, casually off-center, just the right font. In the bottom corner, she typed **cabin couplet #6** and hit post.

There were many things in Shosh's life that she could not control. Like how many times her parents would have to pick her up from the police station, or how many bottles of vodka would mysteriously dwindle from the freezer, or how many vehicles she might drive into pools. Only time would tell. But she could find beautiful cabins in her feed, couple them with mediocre poetry, and hit post like a motherfucker. As far as habits went, it was easily her least toxic.

EVAN

storms

I SCROLL THE JET'S APP, study each coupon like it's an algebra assignment. If the eight-corner cheese is $12.99, can we swing breadsticks at $4.99, given x = taxes, and y = delivery, tip, and convenience fees?

"Convenience fees," I say to no one, to my tiny kitchen, and look: I'm a big believer in the idea that words matter. You can't just slide one word in front of another to make it mean what you want. Like a pleasant root canal or a boisterous funeral, all the positive qualifiers in the world won't make your fee convenient.

The front door opens, the familiar sound of Will's backpack hitting the floor, and in seconds, he'll round the corner in that red hoodie he wears every day, eyes bright and face flushed from the bike ride home. We'll discuss dinner plans (Jet's versus Domino's), entertainment plans (E.T. versus literally anything else), and then spread our homework on the dining room table until the glories of Bubba Night begin.

"Jet's coupons are pretty meh, bud," I call from the kitchen. "We can do breadsticks and pickup, or no breadsticks and delivery—what do you think?"

But he doesn't respond. Instead, I hear the sound of his footsteps clamoring up the stairs, his bedroom door opening and closing, the internal machinations of my brain, wheels spinning at this unprecedented turn of events.

At the bottom of the stairs, I look up toward the top landing, which is a pretty accurate sampling of the rest of the house: cramped; discolored carpet; walls in desperate need of a new coat of paint. Across from Will's room is the door to my bedroom, with a half bath wedged between the two. Whatever pieces of the house changed when Dad left, the upstairs has remained blissfully *ours*.

Bubba Night started years ago, when Will was two, and things were still things, good stuff around every corner. Dad's poker night fell on the same night as Mom's group exercise at the Y, and suddenly Tuesday nights became "Bubba Nights" (*bubba* being Will's word for *brother*). I was young, but old enough to be in charge for a couple of hours. Every Tuesday night, we'd order pizza and watch a movie and basically have the run of the house for the evening.

Things are different now. Dad turned out to be less of a "dad," *per se*, and more of a dog with his head hanging out the window of a moving car. The YMCA is a luxury of the past, and in the year since Dad left, Mom picked up a second job tending bar at Ramsey's Diner, a restaurant down the road from our house. We used to be frequent patrons of Ramsey's, but no longer. (See: luxuries of the past.) All this to say, even though Will and I have the run of the house *every* evening, the sanctity of Bubba Nights remains intact. Tuesdays have always been, and will forever remain, pizza and movies and magic.

At the top of the stairs now, I knock lightly on Will's door.

"Come in!"

My brother's room is a permanent mess of stuffed animals,

Dog Man books, LEGO sets, train tracks, scattered Minions, and Star Wars figurines. "Hey," I say, and even though I can't see him, I know exactly where he is.

In the corner, from somewhere in the depths of an oversize cardboard box, comes a muffled "Hi, Evan."

Last year we got a new refrigerator, and honestly, I'm not sure who was more ecstatic: Mom, over the automatic icemaker, or Will, over the giant box it came in. After raiding the house of every flashlight and roll of aluminum foil, and then attaching those items in strategic places on the refrigerator box, he wound up constructing a very impressive rendering of E.T.'s spaceship. Much to Mom's dismay, he then took a Sharpie to either side of his new spaceship and drew two large words right on the walls: PHONE and HOME.

The kid would live in a refrigerator box if we let him.

"Will, would you mind exiting the spacecraft for a second?"

A prolonged rustle from deep within the belly of the cardboard rocket. Eventually, his little head pops out a side window: wispy white skin, shaggy brown hair that I still can't figure out which way to part, bright blue eyes and long eyelashes that induce something akin to Love at First Sight in most everyone he meets. To look at Will is to experience firsthand that people are generally good, that life is a beautiful gift. Right away, you know he's a sweet kid, a soft, too-good-for-this-world kid, and I'm not just saying this because he's my favorite human on earth (he is), but there's a light in his face, a look that somehow feels happy and sad all at once, heavy and featherweight, like a candle burning from the bottom of a well, and he may leave a mess wherever he goes, and occasionally forget to stop talking, but I love him more than anything loves anything else.

"There you are," I say.

"Here I am."

"I missed you today, bud."

"I missed you too."

And suddenly, I notice: *No Band-Aids.*

I try to hide my surprise, pretend like the absence of Band-Aids is no big deal. "I don't know if you heard me about the coupons. I'm thinking we skip breadsticks tonight, and spring for delivery. Not really in the mood to go pick it up, you know?"

I wait for something, anything, but he just stands there, looking at me, wearing zero Band-Aids.

Time to level up.

"Plus," I say, "I'm really in the mood for E.T. tonight. Feels right, don't you think?"

Will tilts his head. "I thought you said you needed a break from E.T."

"I changed my mind."

To be clear: Will keeps Reese's Pieces in his desk, wears a red hoodie every day, and is probably the only second grader who rides his bike to school. It's only a block and half, but still, it took some convincing before Mom agreed. The straw that broke her back was when he declared, "I'm an E.T. kid, Mom. E.T. kids ride bikes."

E.T. kids ride bikes. How do you argue with that?

"What do you think?" I ask. "Should I cue up E.T.?"

He does that thing where his head sways a little, and he closes his eyes, as if everything rides on the answer to this question. "No . . ." And then, quietly: "I've already cried today."

He gives me a half smile, ducks back inside the spaceship; I just stand there, heart in my shoes.

After a few seconds of listening to him rustle around inside his giant cardboard box, I say, "Okay," and then follow that up with the only thing I've got in me: "I'll be right here."

There's this scene in E.T. where the kid, Elliott, cuts his finger on a blade. A little pinprick of blood. He holds it up and says, "Ouch," and E.T. raises his own finger, all lit up like a firefly, and heals Elliott's cut just by touching it. In the background, Elliott's mom reads Peter Pan to Elliott's little sister—Tinkerbell is dying, and the only way to save her is to clap your hands and say you believe.

A week after Dad left, Will walked out of the bathroom covered in Band-Aids. Mom and I were concerned, obviously, but he acted completely normal, as if being covered from head to toe in tiny bandages was a perfectly reasonable way of life. In the year or so since, he's only referred to them a handful of times, and never as Band-Aids, always as "ouch-shields."

I'm not afraid of big love. And maybe it's weird for a seventeen-year-old to think this way, but sometimes I worry what kind of dad I'll be. I worry because a dad should love his kid more than anyone else on the planet, and as far as I'm concerned, that position is filled. I worry because, when I hug Will, I feel the fragility of his life, and I imagine him as a tiny-boned bird in the middle of a raging storm, and I wish I could save him by clapping my hands and saying I believe, but I can't. I wish I could tell him his ouch-shields will protect him, but I can't do that either. The truth is, fragile things rarely fare well in the world; more often, they farewell to it.

Storms start in the gut.

Overwhelming dread, as tangible as they are unpredictable.

Then, slowly ascending from stomach to chest, swelling in size and scope, rooting me to the ground, stealing my breath, my motion. From there, storms explode in every direction, a sudden detonation extending through my shoulders, arms, hands, tingling and alive in nightmarish ways, and my face is hot, my heart pounding—

Breathe . . .

Just to breathe.

To feel myself existing.

What is real, what isn't.

In my own room now, I shut the door, and all around, air turns to mist; crossing the floor to my bed is an exercise in endurance, more like swimming than walking. I sit on the edge of my mattress, my heart an arrhythmic firework as images of Will come in flashes: he's in his refrigerator box; he's drawing at his art table; he's consumed in the fevered frenzy of creating something new. His haphazard drawings, the way he staples pages together to make a book, the way he loves the things that he loves, like a drowning person loves a life buoy, how he thinks lemonade is called "lemolade," and between the absence of Band-Aids, a pass on E.T., and skipping out on Tuesday rituals, something is *wrong*, something is wrong, something is *wrongwrongwrongwrongwrong*—

Breathe . . .

Feel myself existing.

Storms beget storms: having one leads to having one leads to having one leads to having one—

Breathe . . .

"Five things I can see," I say, and look around the room: dusty guitar in the corner, one; Dad's old record player, two; Grandad's older radio, three; yard-sale couch, four; sketch pad on the bedside table, five. "Four things I can feel." Bedsheets, one. Computer, two. Phone in my pocket, three. Charcoal pencil, four.

Three things I can hear . . .

Two things I can smell . . .

By the time I pull a mint out of my bedside drawer (*one thing I can taste*), the storm recedes, the fireworks end, the skies of the room begin to clear.

I stay where I am, waiting. Some storms come in waves. Some hit you hard and leave you wrecked in their wake. Too early to know which kind this one is.

When they started a year ago, I was having them all the time. Back then, Mom was on the phone constantly—with my doctor, and eventually, with Maya. It was a season of listening, of learning new terms: *grounding techniques*; *decatastrophizing*; *mindfulness*. Maya has been teaching me to speak storm, teaching me how to respond so they don't come as often or hit as hard.

One of the first things I told her was how the term *panic attack* felt wrong. "In what way?" she'd asked, and I explained how *panic* felt too feeble a word, and *attack* felt too familiar. I said, "It shouldn't be called what it is, it should be called what it *feels* like." When Maya asked what it felt like, I said the only word I could think of that came close to describing the vast uncontrollable nature of what was happening inside my body: "Storms." Maya nodded, and said, "We'll call them that, then," and that was when I started trusting her.

Exhausted, I fall backward on the bed, stare up at the slowly rotating blades of the ceiling fan. I wonder about the absence of Band-Aids and what that might mean. I wonder what in the world I'm supposed to do with my night, seeing as this is my first Tuesday alone in years. And I wonder if there is more than one kind of storm: some that look like panic attacks, and some that look like refrigerator boxes.

SHOSH

rogue amphibians

THE STORIES OF FROG AND TOAD were among Shosh's earliest memories. Unlike the countless characters, movies, and plush playthings that went from *obsession* to *attic* in the blink of an eye, Frog and Toad remained steadfast bulwarks of the sisters' relationship through the years.

"I'm totally Toad," Stevie said late one night, around Thanksgiving last year. Per family tradition, they'd spent three days gorging themselves, not just on food, but on the entire Star Wars movie collection. Now, in an effort to cleanse the palate, they were sprawled in bed, halfway through one of the earlier seasons of *Project Runway*.

"Get the fuck out," said Shosh. "No way you're Toad."

"Toad is next-level thirsty."

"Exactly. Which is why I'm clearly him."

They had the entire Lobel collection, knew every story by heart, but their favorite was called "Alone." In it, Toad arrives at Frog's house one morning to find Frog gone, and a note from Frog explaining that he wants to be alone. Distraught, Toad searches for Frog and, after finding him on a rock in the middle of a river, hustles home to pack a picnic of sandwiches and iced tea. When he gets back to the river, he orders a turtle to carry him to the rock. The turtle wisely points out that if Frog wants to be alone, perhaps Toad should leave him alone, which of course sends Toad into a tailspin, and just as he starts yelling apologies to Frog for all the annoying things he does, he falls off the turtle's back and into the river. In the end, Frog tells Toad that he woke up feeling happy, and that he just needed a minute to sit and think about how charmed his life was. The final lines of the story are, "They ate wet sandwiches without iced tea. They were two close friends sitting alone together."

"I've committed to move wherever you land for college," said Stevie. "That is some pathologically thirsty shit. Extra Toady."

They'd had some version of the same conversation for years, like a video game you never finish, just save your place, come back to later. As far as which sister was more like which anthropomorphic amphibian, it only mattered inasmuch as the tattoos they were planning to get: one sister would get Frog; the other would get Toad; each tattoo would include the words *alone together*.

"Frog is a Jedi master," said Shosh, sitting up in bed. "I'm barely Lukin' it on a good day."

"If George Lucas handed out superlatives, I'd get Most Pathetic Padawan."

"If Jar Jar had a kid with Salacious Crumb, and that kid got drunk? That's me."

"I'm as useless as Darth's cape."

"Why *does* he have a cape?"

"Why does *anyone* have a cape?"

"People in capes are phonies."

"You know who's not a phony? Arnold Lobel."

Shosh kissed two fingers, then threw them heavenward. "May he rest in peace."

"Sneaking in the quality queer content since 1970."

Onscreen, Heidi Klum had just wrapped up a three-minute soliloquy about her own boobs when Stevie paused the episode. "You ever think about the beginning of 'Alone'? Frog wakes up and decides he wants to spend time on a rock in a river. And what's the first thing he does?"

"Leaves a note," said Shosh.

"It's not like they had *plans*. But he left a note. Because he knew Toad would show up."

It often felt as though the sisters were hiding under the same blanket, living their lives in a secret world no one else could see.

A few minutes later, during one of Tim Gunn's patent teary-eyed speeches, one sister said, "Tim Gunn is totally Frog," and the other said, "The *most* Frog," and when that episode ended, they let the next one begin, and though neither of them said it, they knew it didn't matter who was Toad and who was Frog; all that mattered was their secret world under the blanket, and the certainty that even when they were alone, they were alone together.

EVAN

night devices

SEPTEMBER NOW. ONE OF THOSE end-of-summer nights when bugs break loose the gates of hell, as if they can sense the weather on the cusp, their time on earth almost up, gotta get while the getting's good.

I've always liked to draw at night. Our backyard is a half-acre hodgepodge of miniature hills and overgrown bushes, an ancient apple tree in the far corner, everything surrounded by chain-link fence. Back when Dad was still around, the four of us had picked out small but meaningful items and buried them in a time capsule under that apple tree.

Metaphor of metaphors, the tree appears to be rotting now.

I sit in the soft grass with my headphones on—connected but silent, awaiting music—sketch pad right up in my face, and it's almost like I'm not even here. Like when Will was a toddler, and we'd play peek-a-boo, and he'd close his eyes thinking if he couldn't see me, I couldn't see him. Willing invisibility.

Mom's been in bed for two days. I keep her company when I get home from school, run interference with Will. We've decided to tell him *some* things but not *all* the things. Mom doesn't want him worrying, but we also don't want to flat-out lie to the kid. She had the idea to frame the whole thing in the context of his tonsillectomy. "Remember how you felt afterward?" she'd asked him. "Spinny-head?"

"Spinny-head was fun."

"Okay, well, after the fun, you were sore for a few days, but you were fine, right? I'm having a similar procedure, but I'll be fine, just like you were."

"What kind of besieger?" he'd asked, staring right through her.

I looked at her like, *Told you.*

"The kind of besieger that's none of your business," she'd said, and then explained that she wouldn't be able to pick him up for a while, or hug him normally, and then I turned on E.T. before he had a chance to ask any more questions.

It's been a lot of me and Mom these days. In the evenings, we play Scrabble in her room. I try to convince her to drop the second gig at Ramsey's Diner. The health insurance comes from her day job as a legal secretary anyway, but she says we need the money, plus the restaurant has been really understanding—they're giving her as much time as she needs—so she's keeping both. We talk about school, but I can tell she's all up in her head, because we go from that to debating the Scrabble-validity of the word *hangry*, to the word *word*, to the difference between *word* and *Word* with a capital *W*, and now we're on her religious upbringing.

"I spent most of my twenties planting flags," she tells me. "And most of my thirties pulling them back up." She says her faith has evolved, but that doesn't make it less true or important or real. She says, "It's less about being sure, and more about finding comfort in the unsure," and I tell her that makes sense, even though it clearly doesn't, and I wonder about the ways mortality affects language, all these big ideas in small places, like a zoomed-out scene with a close-up script.

I will say this: at a whopping five points, let's hope the word of God is worth more in life than it is in Scrabble.

A breeze on my face.

The bugs do their thing.

It's been two weeks since that night in the park with the quiet bird and the sad song. The following day, I heard the same song coming from Mom's room; I've heard others like it at school, in Maya's office, in my bedroom, in the car. A couple years ago, Ali got me into an artist called Julianna Barwick, and these songs remind me of her: ethereal and multilayered, vocals like a stray grocery bag in the wind. They're acapella, mostly, though one song has a piano that sounds like it was recorded in the back of a cave, everything shimmery and out of reach.

There is no discernable pattern to their comings and goings. If storms start in the gut, working their way out, the songs are the exact opposite, starting in the ether and working their way into my soul. Intangible, invisible, infuriating, like a pouring rain from the clear blue sky. I try to remind myself that music is everywhere all the time: passing cars, open windows, phones in pockets, but just when I convince myself of some logical explanation, I hear the music again, in all its illogicality.

A few days ago, I had the idea to record the song in voice memos, but when I played it back, it was nothing but static. I've studied the faces of those around me, looked for signs that they hear it too, but nothing.

These days, sleep is a hallway with infinite doors.

And so I come outside, sit in the grass with the nightbugs, and draw. I worry about Mom in her bed, and Will in his box, and the brain in my head. And when the song eventually arrives, it rolls in steadily, breaking like a wave in slow motion, the voice of the singer rising and crashing gently, soaking me to the bone in its foamy brine.

"What is happening to me?" I ask the summer moon.

When it doesn't answer, I trade its light for the light of a more responsive device: open Apple Music; play the first loud thing; draw, disconnect, disappear.

SHOSH
morning reflections

SHOSH STOOD IN THE UPSTAIRS hallway, inches from a door that hadn't been opened in months.

It was either too late to be called night or too early to be called morning—not that it mattered. Not so long ago, love had run through this house like blood through a vein. Mornings had been nothing if not proof of this: her dad's secret waffle recipe; the way her mom rushed into every room as if summoned by the rising sun, pushing back curtains, singing made-up songs of the day's glorious possibilities. Their world hadn't been perfect, but it had the varnish of perfection, a shine reserved for those whose lives were intact, whose loved ones were healthy and happy. At the time, Shosh had pretended to be annoyed by it all, but the truth was, now, every time her alarm went off, waking her to an empty room, every time she stuck a frozen waffle in the toaster, she felt the lingering residue of her old life, a house drained of love, embalmed with an assortment of disappointing stopgaps.

But somehow—somewhere beyond this closed door—the warmth of love remained.

She reached out, ran a finger across the glass-encased vinyl. Stevie had found the record in a garage sale, and when Shosh pointed out that she didn't own a record player, she'd said, "It's *Pet Sounds*, Shosh. You don't leave that shit behind."

And yet here it was, despite her sister's best efforts, left behind.

At least once a day, Shosh stood in this spot. She never opened the door. As far as she knew, it had been closed since Stevie's death, all her things inside exactly as she'd left them. This space was all that remained, not only of a house that had once been filled with love, but of a belief that love propelled the universe. Of course, Shosh knew better now. While love had compelled the sisters to formulate a plan to be together, the universe had used that plan to keep them apart.

Staring into the framed vinyl, its green cover blurred, Shosh saw her own reflection in glass. "You forgot to leave a note," she whispered, and imagined her sister in the afterlife, sitting on a rock in a river, alone . . .

An alarm clock sounded from her parents' bedroom.

Morning, then.

Shosh raised her aluminum can in salute, drained the rest of the vodka Diet, and, for the first time in a long time, found herself itching to sing.

EVAN
the appendages of Gordon Walmsley

ON THE FIRST DAY OF junior year, Ali and I walked into the cafeteria, and she was like, "I can't with this place," and I was all, "Yeah," and she was like, "It smells like a yeast factory run by a family of sick badgers," and I said, "Okay, then," and thus, our time of lunch was reallocated to the library. Seeing as neither of us are wild about change, here we are, over a year later, eating lunch among the literati, nary a sick badger in sight.

Ali is sprawled on a couch, boots propped up like she owns the place; she eats her usual SunButter and honey while pretending to read *Swann's Way*. I can't remember whose idea it was, but early on we decided to spend our library lunches working our way through the most pretentious books we could find.

"How's your book?" I ask, knowing full well she hasn't gotten past the first page.

"Great, duh."

I have this theory that the only people who actually get Proust would never admit it. And look, I know there's no accounting for what a person likes or doesn't like, and fair enough, but I also know that it requires a very specific skill set, not to *read* Proust, but to *enjoy* Proust.

"Remind me what that one's about?"

Ali takes a giant bite, gazes at me from behind the open book. "I mean, it's not really what it's *about*, is it? Proust is above all that."

"Like plot and character and such."

"Exactly."

"Still. If you had to summarize . . ."

"It's very—*surreal*," she says, waving her SunButter sandwich around the room as if to demonstrate just how surreal. "I suppose it's about a man who has a difficult relationship with sleep. How the thought of sleep actually wakes him up."

"Interesting."

"It is," Ali says.

"That's literally the first page."

Proust collapses on her stomach. "You've *read* it?"

"I've read the first page. Which was enough to know I didn't want to read more."

If one were to stumble across the frayed rope of my friendship with Ali, and follow it to its earliest origins, that person would find themselves at a third-grade gymnastics recital, in a dimly lit backstage, during a brief intermission.

It's a thin line, the difference between kids doing gymnastics and a pack of wild macaques swinging from jungle vines, a distinction largely unnoticed by my peers. I was just a little guy, but I was starting to spot things like that, starting to question the *why* of things. Like the six-inch-high balance beam. Even at eight, I was like, *Are we really doing this?* And it wouldn't have been a big deal, except the week before, I'd constructed an immaculate Statue of Liberty out of LEGO, and nobody gave a shit. And since letter grades weren't a thing at that age, after receiving 4s in every subject ("mastered standard," whatever that meant), I'd used Google to grade my own tests.

Straight As across the board. Again. No shits given.

But five consecutive somersaults? Bingo! Gangbusters! Unbridled praise. An audience of otherwise reasonable adults lost their ever-loving minds. I remember doing the last somersault, hearing the uproarious applause, and looking down at my uniform, wondering if it was something to do with the leggings, or the satin sashes we were all forced to wear. And suddenly it occurred to me that the requisite attire seemed disproportionately essential in the pursuit of gymnastics excellence.

By the time I exited stage left, I'd seen through the bullshit.

The worst thing about seeing through bullshit isn't the bullshit itself, but the fear that you're the only one seeing through it.

All of which is to say, I was in a fairly existential frame of mind when fellow macaque-in-leggings Gordon Walmsley pulled out his shiny new pocketknife and started showing it off. "It has lots of appendages," Gordon kept saying, like he'd just learned the word *appendage* and was bursting to use it.

Before that day, the only thing I knew of Gordon Walmsley was that he had enormous teeth, and his breath smelled like Taco Bell ate itself for lunch, which is to say, I generally gave Gordon Walmsley's head a wide berth.

"Hey, Evan," said Gordon.

I could smell the chalupa on him.

"You have to see this," he said.

Bet I didn't.

"It has a toothpick, see?"

There's a level of responsibility that comes with seeing through bullshit.

"And a nail filer, just in case."

It's not that I *wanted* to punch Gordon Walmsley in the face; his face needed punching, and as I was the only self-aware macaque, it was on me to make it happen.

Gordon Walmsley pulled out one of the larger blades. "But this is my favorite appendage."

And I punched him. Right in his giant teeth.

As it turned out, those teeth required quite the bulbous head to house them, which needed a thick neck to cradle it, which necessitated a tree-trunk-like physique: Gordon Walmsley was huge, and I would have been toast were it not for this little tornado of a kid who came out of nowhere and *took his ass down.*

From then to now, Ali Pilgrim has saved me more times than I can count. She's a wartime consigliere, a force of nature, and above all, my best friend in the world.

She tosses *Swann's Way* on the end table, opens a bag of chips, and nods at the book I'm reading. "I thought you hated Melville."

"I hate *Moby-Dick.*" I flip the cover of my book around. "This is *Bartleby.*"

"What's it about?"

I set the book down, pick up my sketch pad. "I would prefer not to."

"You're impossible."

"No, I mean—that's what the book is about." As I draw, I explain the philosophy of the Bartleby character, how every time his boss asks him to do anything, Bartleby just says, "I would prefer not to."

"I would prefer not to," Ali says, trying it on for size, and it's times like these when I can't help thinking about next year. Whether I wind up at Headlands or not, who knows where Ali will land. Either way, we likely won't be in the same city, and I wonder what it will be like to miss her. The ripped jeans and lace-up boots, graphic tees and flannels; the way no one other than me really knows her, and yet, when she enters a room, everyone leans slightly in her direction.

Back in third grade, when she tackled the chalupa macaque, I felt the little-kid equivalent of *this girl is the one*. As we got older, I could tell she wasn't into me like that, and then it became clear she wasn't into boys like that, or maybe anyone like that, and that's where we are, and I love her so much. I love how she loves *The X-Files*, *Schitt's Creek*, and all things Middle-earth: unabashedly. I love how she loves celebrity gossip: unapologetically. I love how she loves Chili's: hungrily. Most of all, I love how she loves herself: unconditionally. There's a kind of ownership that comes with having a best friend like her, this little collection of understandings you keep like charms on a bracelet. *I know you. Here's the bracelet to prove it.*

I think my best thoughts when I draw, even when the drawings themselves aren't much to look at. "Here," I say, ripping the page out of the sketchbook, handing it over. "For you to remember me by."

Ali takes it and immediately smiles. The drawing is a crude rendering of us standing in a cafeteria surrounded by vomiting badgers.

"Evan."

"Ali."

"You know you can tell me anything, right?"

"Yeah?"

"Good. Because you've been compulsively tucking your hair behind your ears all afternoon."

"What?"

"It's your tell."

"It's not my tell. I always tuck."

"You rarely tuck, unless there's something on your mind."

I guess that's the thing about having someone else's bracelet—they have yours.

"I was just thinking about next year," I say. "How much I'll miss this."

"No, that's not it." The usual softness in her eyes is replaced with hunger. "Ever since that night in the park. I think my subconscious has been tracking your weirdness since then, but only now communicating the data to my brain."

"Your subconscious should check its sources."

"You've been sporadically distant since Heather's party."

"Sporadically distant?"

"Don't do that."

"Do what."

"That thing. Where you calmly repeat the last words of my sentence because you don't want to answer the—come on. Just tell me."

"Ali, look—"

"Aha!" She points to my hand, which, much to my chagrin, is midway through a hair-tuck. "We were at Heather's house," she says. "You'd had a half dozen vodka tonics—"

"*I'd had three.*"

"—Heather talked shit about your brother. You left, I followed, you threw up in the park . . ." Ali pauses, thinking. "What am I missing?"

"Ali."

"You know you're gonna tell me eventually."

First Maya, now Ali, and I don't know *why* it's so hard to talk about Mom out loud. It's like—so long as I keep the news to myself, there's a chance it's not real.

"Evan . . ."

"I hear songs," I say, like the words are trying to squeeze into an elevator before the doors close. And before my brain has a chance to analyze the ways in which I'm using the songs to deflect from Mom, I dive into that night in the park, how I heard the first song then, and have been hearing more like it everywhere I go, a whispery poet singing secrets in my ear.

"That's fucked up," Ali says.

"Thank you."

"Do you hear a song now?"

A beat, listening . . . "No."

She nods slowly, deliberately. "Well. Not that you needed extra reasons to get shit-faced, given the inappropriate collection of molecules that is Heather fucking Abernathy. But if I was hearing a song no one else could hear, I'd probably want to drown it out too."

I don't clarify Ali's misunderstanding. If the songs can take the heat for my drunken behavior, all the better.

"What are they about?" Ali asks.

"They're pretty quiet and echoey. There's one about trees in snow, I think? But I don't really know."

Ali sinks her face into her hands.

"What?"

"You're hearing songs no one can hear, and you're not even listening? Did it occur to you that you're hearing them for a reason? That the universe, or God, or some great Eye in the Cosmos, or *yourself* in another reality—"

"Myself in another reality?"

"Did it occur to you that someone might be trying to tell you something?"

I'd considered the possibility that Ali might think I'd lost my mind. I hadn't considered the possibility of a good scolding for not listening. I explain to her how, when I try to record the audio in voice memos, it just picks up static, but she stares at me, arms crossed. Luckily, the chime goes off before she can further harangue my lackluster handling of the situation.

We exit the library, step into the ocean current of hallway chatter and motion.

"You think I'm crazy?"

Ali turns to me, puts both hands on my shoulders, and suddenly it feels like we've formed our own little pod in the sea. "I think you should start keeping track of the lyrics. See what the songs have to say before you worry where they're coming from. And who knows. Maybe they'll unlock the mysteries of the universe. Nothing's impossible."

"Except for catamarangutan."

Ali sticks her finger in my face. "Just because catamarangutan hasn't happened, doesn't mean it's not possible."

"Ali."

"I mean their wingspan alone—"

"Alison Pilgrim."

"You don't think an orangutan could captain a seaworthy vesselcraft?"

"You can't hear yourself, can you."

"Say you're on vacation. Some luxury resort, and you book a catamaran for an afternoon of maritime pleasure."

"That doesn't sound like me."

"Tell me you wouldn't die if you climbed aboard to find an orangutan was captain of the ship."

"Probably, we would all die."

We turn from each other, exit our pod, face the raging current.

"Your ghost music," says Ali. "That's all there is? That's the thing you haven't told me about, right?"

I'll never understand myself. Why it's so hard to talk about important things with the people who see you. Or maybe that's why it's hard. Maybe it would be easier to tell Maya about the songs if she weren't so good at seeing me. Maybe it would be easier to tell Ali about my mom if she didn't know me so well.

"Yes," I say, wondering what it will feel like to lie to Ali. "That's the only thing I haven't told you."

All these words, like broken glass in my mouth.

SHOSH
what I'd be without you

THE PIANO WAS SMALLER THAN she remembered. Dustier, too.

Shosh sat alone in the echoey-quiet auditorium, lightly brush-ing her fingers across the black and white keys. She could pretend all she wanted, but the truth was, she missed it. All of it. From the piano, to backstage, to the chorus room—even that musky scent of fear: the smell of the stage. Closing her eyes, she could feel the nip of terror that came in the prolonged seconds before the curtains parted, and the rush of relief when they finally did.

In that moment, life made sense.

Acting had always been the only kind of hard she enjoyed. As a child, she'd constructed makeshift stages in the dining room, used cardboard boxes and quilt curtains, reimagined her favorite movies with herself as the lead. In time, this mimicry turned to ingenuity, and Shosh was performing original one-act plays, often with Ste-vie or one of her parents on piano, performing a score written by Shosh. *A natural talent*, everyone said, and so naturally, it was a talent that needed cultivating: private lessons on the weekends, books on method and the history of theater, auditions for the token Preco-cious Kid Character at the community theater, so by the time Shosh got to high school, she was a star well on its rise.

She'd always been confident, driven, single-minded. With

Ms. Clark's help, Shosh learned to channel that single-mindedness without letting it consume her. She was Cinderella in Into the Woods, Belle in Beauty and the Beast, and starred in a half dozen other musicals, until eventually, she realized something: she could sing, yes, and dance, sure, but it was the acting she loved most. The living of other lives. She did The Wolves and The Crucible. She read Stanislavski's An Actor Prepares and Hagen's Respect for Acting, and through it all, Shosh learned how to dive so far into character it no longer felt like acting, just living.

The cultivation of her talent led to an inevitable question: Which college? After countless hours of researching programs, scouring testimonials, and huddling with Ms. Clark, the University of Southern California became the clear choice. LA felt daunting, but less so with the knowledge that her sister would join her the following year. An art history major at Loyola, Stevie had taken advantage of summer sessions and was on track to graduate a year early, and then move to LA to be with Shosh.

"You're not supposed to be here," said a voice.

Shosh swiveled to find a girl in the aisle behind her, all blue hair, high-top chucks, arms crossed as fuck. The auditorium had been empty when Shosh got here, and though she hadn't heard anyone enter, she'd mostly been in her own head.

Shosh pulled out her flask, swigged, looked around. "You know—I thought it was just the piano. But this whole place is smaller."

"Than what?" asked the girl.

"Than how I remember."

The girl tilted her head, as if studying Shosh from a different angle. "How did you get in here?"

"How do you know I'm not supposed to be here? Maybe I'm a sub."

The girl's eyes drifted to the wall by the stairs leading up to the stage, where no fewer than four frames hung, each depicting photos or school clippings of the jewel of Iverton High drama, Shosh Bell herself.

"You got into USC," said the girl. "*And didn't go.*"

"That is correct."

"I mean—they *accepted* you."

"Yep."

"And you said *no thanks.*"

"Technically, I just said nothing."

The girl glanced at the exit, and it occurred to Shosh that her time was likely limited. She rolled up her coat sleeves, turned back to the piano. It may have seemed smaller, but it felt the same as it ever had.

"So . . . if you're not going to USC," said the blue-haired girl, "what are you going to do?"

Shosh rested both hands on the keys, closed her eyes. "God only knows," she said, and then, quietly, started playing the song of the same title. She knew it well, had sung it so many times with Stevie. During the first verse, her voice filled the auditorium like ink in water, slow and pure, and it felt like she'd never left this room, just continued performing one song, one play, one line after another.

Somewhere behind her, the auditorium door slammed shut, but she didn't stop singing. And when she heard the door open again—and again, and again—she only sang louder, no longer pure but full of regret and hunger and the thousand unnamed furies of loss. She belted the song into the rafters, enveloping the room in hypnotic wonder, and even though she couldn't see the crowd gathered behind her, she knew a captive audience when she had it. And so she sang this song that was both a question and an answer, this song she and her sister had loved, even as its potential terrified them. And she no longer wondered what she'd be without Stevie. She knew exactly what she'd become.

EVAN

221b

"ARE YOU SERIOUS?" ASKS SARA.

"You *can't* be serious," says Yurt.

Sara looks at Ali. "He's joking, right?" Then, to me: "You're joking."

"Little jokeroo?" says Yurt.

"No," I say. "I mean—yes, I am serious. And no, I'm not joking."

Sara leans back, folds her arms; Yurt watches closely, mimics her to a T.

Creative Writing is a notoriously difficult class to get into. Not for writing-related reasons, but because it's well known that Mr. Hambright doesn't give two shits about the Way Things Are Done. "Trust," he'd told us on the first day of class, in that mesmerizing monotone. "In this class, we'll talk about process, format, voice. I'm not here to babysit. I don't care about your test scores. I literally do not. You guys are young *adults* and I *trust* you'll do the work to the best of your abilities. And if you don't, you're fired from my class."

Every few months, rumors swirled that Mr. Hambright was on the brink of losing his job, the general consensus being, the man just made too much goddamn *sense*.

"How're the Girls today?" Hambright asks, ambling over to our little circle.

First week of junior year, the four of us—Ali, Sara, Yurt, and me—co-wrote a mash-up fanfic piece entitled *The Golden Gilmore Gossip Girls*. It received a light chuckle from Hambright (the highest of praise), as well as a nickname that stuck: we've been "the Girls" ever since.

We go around and give Hambright a quick rundown of where we are in our respective stories, intentionally using Hammy-approved verbiage (*letting the draft simmer* and *sitting with the notes*), and then, to my everlasting dismay, Sara says, "Evan's been in love with the same girl since forever, and he's too chickenshit to tell her."

I stare her down. "Real deft pivot, Sara."

"I speak the truth," she says, to which Yurt chimes, "Truth hurts, yo."

Jason Yurt is a conversational parasite, grabbing ahold of whatever healthy host sentence is within reach and latching on. He's made an art of it, though. In less capable hands, that shit would grate, but it's like his thing, to the point where the whole school loves him for it.

Plus, we're all pretty convinced he's low-key in love with Sara.

"We're supposed to be critiquing each other's writing," I say, trying to right the ship. "Not each other's love lives."

"Two sides of the same coin," says Hambright. "You wish it away now, but romantic rejection is a motivating factor behind a lot of important work. Rejection turns to isolation, and then you're in the land of Hemingway and the Brontës. Not to mention Cervantes, who was widely believed to be in prison when he first conceived of *Don Quixote*."

"Chin up," says Sara. "You've got prison to look forward to."

"Jailbird, yo."

Hands in pockets, Hambright deadpans, "May I inquire as to the unworthy recipient of Mr. Taft's aforementioned unrequited love?" At which point the circle is on the cusp of losing it.

"I'm just gonna—real quick—" I pull my hoodie over my head, tug the drawstrings tight. "There we go."

Ali dives into the story of how I fell in love with Sherlock Holmes in the fifth grade. "You were dressed as a Teletubby, if I remember correctly," she says.

"I *was Sonic the Hedgehog*," I say, and everyone loses it as memories of that fateful day wash over me, how Riley Conway came to school on Halloween dressed as Sherlock Holmes, how she really went for it, too, complete with a checked-wool suit, authentic deerstalker, and pipe. As it turned out, my preadolescent heart (among other parts) found this level of commitment to one's fictional hero wholly irresistible. In the years since, I may or may not have had a recurring dream in which heated discourse between Holmes (Riley) and Watson (Yours Truly) leads to an inevitable carnal encounter that might best be described as an urgent mélange of tawdry steampunk dream-sex.

That day in class, our fifth-grade teacher told Riley he applauded the commitment, while I could only pray she hadn't noticed the secondhand Sonic the Hedgehog costume furtively staring from behind the periodic table.

I was a lost cause, then and now.

"Cut to three weeks ago," says Sara, taking the reins of the conversation. "Cervantes here is at a party, getting cozy in the corner with Sherlock—"

"We weren't *getting cozy*," I say, but my head is ensconced in a hoodie-cocoon, and I can't be sure anyone heard me.

"—when he up and *vanishes*," says Sara. "Not just from the crush in the corner, but from the party altogether. I had *assumed*, until *now*, that the reason Evan ran was because Riley rejected his advances."

"Run, doggo, run," says Yurt.

"I take it that's not what happened," says Hambright.

"*He never asked her out*," says Sara.

"In Evan's defense," Ali chimes, "and for reasons we won't go into at the moment, he needed a way out of that party."

All hail Ali Pilgrim! Hero and national treasure!

"*However*," she says . . .

Down with Ali Pilgrim! Traitor to the nation!

"I don't think he actually likes Riley all that much."

I can actually *feel* Sara lean in. "Continue," she says, and Yurt is all, "Go on," and I shit you not, ole Hammy scrapes a chair across the floor and sits, and I've now retreated so far into the depths of my hoodie, I'm in real danger of tearing the fabric.

Ali dives into a psychological discourse about how Riley is a placeholder for some fantasy girl that doesn't exist. "She's like a perfect ghost," says Ali. "She's not real, so no one can be as good as her."

It's quiet for a second; Hambright clears his throat, lowers his voice. "I'm going to say something now."

The air changes in an instant; I emerge from my hoodie like a shy groundhog, and when I look around, I can tell I'm not the only one who's tracked it. Something is happening.

Hambright chuckles under his breath, and I could swear he

mumbles *perfect ghost* before continuing: "When you're a kid, your friends are random. Kids in your class, kids in the neighborhood, kids whose parents are friends with your parents, people who happen to be in your orbit. But then you get older. And you start looking around, noticing your friend group is a lot smaller than it used to be. It's not a bad thing, just—more intentional. Fewer people in your orbit. I'm not saying this to the whole class, because it's not true for everyone. But I think there's a good reason you guys are friends. It's not random, and that's rare at your age. Don't forget that, okay?"

Another group calls for help. Hambright stands, smiles, walks away.

"And just like that," says Ali, "as mysteriously as he arrived . . ."

We watch him cross the room, hands in pockets, calmly instructing the other group.

"What is it about him?" says Sara, and Yurt, in a surprising display of autonomy, says, "He waters the root."

Whatever awe our group had directed toward Hammy is now turned to Yurt.

"You know, you don't always make sense," Sara tells him. "But when you do, you make plenty."

Yurt, sensing a moment, decides to capitalize on it by putting both hands behind his head and leaning so far back in his chair, he falls over.

"Nice while it lasted," says Ali, and talk turns to college, plans for the future, a conversation I could recite in my sleep: Sara is shooting for DePaul; Yurt's dad's friend works in admissions at Duke, so the Yurt clan is crossing fingers and toes; Ali is quiet on the subject, and as always, we assume she'll land in the arts, maybe film or photography. When it's my turn, they ask how the application for Headlands is going, and I say it's too early (*true*), and that I'm not totally set on a gap year in Alaska anyway (*false*), and even if I was, I likely didn't have the je ne sais quoi to get into the Glacier Bay program (*fair*), "and even if I do get in, I probably won't get the requisite financial aid, so."

The group stares at me as I simmer in a stew of blistering self-assurance.

Luckily, the chime rings, saving me from further humiliation. We pack our stuff, head for the door, and as soon as we exit Hambright's class, it's clear something's up. The halls are abuzz with activity, everyone hurrying in the same direction. When Ali asks what's going on, some passing kid says, "Shosh Bell is in the auditorium," and now we're hustling down the hall with the rest of the crowd. As soon as we step inside the auditorium, the din quiets, the buzz from the hallways diminishes, all eyes face the front.

I've never met Shosh Bell, but I recognize her from the hallways, and basically every school musical. Onstage now, she plays the hell out of a piano, singing at the top of her lungs. The song is familiar, but I've never heard it sung this way: like the song cheated the singer, and now she's taking revenge.

"I'd *murder* for her hair," whispers the girl next to me. Under the circumstances, it seems an odd thing to say, but I sort of get it.

Shosh Bell looks like a controlled explosion: she wears an oversized plaid coat, boots, a T-shirt with UFOs; her hair is riotous, long and dark against pale white skin. "*Chic feral*," whispers Sara, and Yurt mutters, "No way of knowing *what* that hair is gonna do next."

On the other side of the stage, as if waiting in the wings, the drama teacher stands in the shadow of a curtain, watching with a look I can't quite make out.

We stand there for the duration of the song, mesmerized by it, until eventually it ends, and—in the echoing stillness of the auditorium—someone starts clapping. Now everyone is clapping, and when Shosh looks up, even from here, I can see her eyes: blue like polar ice, salient and sad. It's not the face of someone who just completed a virtuoso performance; it's the face of someone coming up for air.

SHOSH
the moth

"So . . ."

"Yeah," said Shosh. "That was totally normal, right?"

Ms. Clark nodded. "A hundred percent."

Together, they sat on the edge of the stage, looking out over a sea of empty seats. More than a second home, this was their sanctuary, the place they'd spent countless hours living other lives.

"Don't you have a class to teach?"

"Meh," said Ms. Clark. "The kids can fend for themselves."

"So it's your lunch break, then?"

Ms. Clark pulled an apple from her purse, cracked a giant bite.

Shosh smiled, said nothing. She wasn't going to be the one to start this party.

"What are you doing, Shosh?"

What was she doing? She'd been standing in the hallway at home, staring at the Beach Boys record on her sister's door, when she'd felt a sudden urge to sing. But rather than turn for the guitar in her room, or the piano downstairs, she'd come here.

"I don't know," said Shosh.

Ms. Clark took another bite, chewed, looked down at her apple. "We built a deck this summer. Or, you know—*had* one built. There's a fire pit and a pergola with little lights strung all over. It's peaceful, you should come see it. One night last week, Charlie noticed all these moths flying right into the lights. He's got that lisp, you know? 'Da bugth burnded theythelf, Momma.'" Ms. Clark smiled the way a parent smiles at the benign cuteness of their offspring. "Naturally, he asks why they fly straight for the light, and naturally, I have no clue. So I look it up. Phototaxis, it's called. An organism's response to light. Cockroaches are negatively phototactic—they run from it—moths are positively phototactic. No one knows why, but one theory is related to moth migration."

"Moths migrate?"

"Some do. And they use the moon for navigational cues. Their whole orientation depends on how bright the sky is relative to the ground. As the earth rotates, the moon moves across the sky, and the moths recalibrate their flight paths to match. But they can't differentiate between the light of a lamp and the light of the moon, so in those moments, the lamp becomes their moon. When they actually hit the thing, it causes complete disorientation." Ms. Clark took another bite of her apple, looked out into the darkness of the auditorium. "I remember a girl. Confident, ambitious, diligent. Lively. She didn't have many friends, but the ones she had, she was loyal to. When she cried onstage, you cried. When she laughed, you laughed. She knew what she had and knew what it cost. Knew where she was going and how to get there. This girl had an expertly calibrated flight path."

"So I'm the moth, is what you're saying. And the theater is my moon?"

Ms. Clark looked at the apple in her hand, and Shosh knew what she was going to say before she said it. "Stevie was your moon,

Shosh. And at the risk of grinding the metaphor into the ground, you're headed straight for the lamp."

Shosh felt the cold metal of the flask in her coat pocket and wondered how long before she could drain what was left. *I could leave*, she thought, *drink the day away*, but then Ms. Clark's arm was around her, and Shosh was leaning her head onto her teacher's shoulder. Tucked in the safety of the swan's wing.

"I miss this place," said Shosh. "But I wish I didn't."

"If only we could choose the things we miss."

Shosh once read that the nature of acting was transactional. The actor offered little pieces of their soul, and in return, the audience gave them the only thing that really mattered: their full attention. Maybe that was why she'd come back to this place. To see if there was anything left of herself to give.

"What's your moon, Ms. Clark?"

"Drugs, definitely. Doing drugs, selling drugs, anything with drugs, really."

In the cocktail of existential crises, laughter was a tonic.

"For real, though."

"For real?" Ms. Clark sighed. "Teaching. Never would have thought it when I was younger, but there it is."

A minute or more passed like that, the two of them onstage, and Shosh wondered how many times this place could reinvent itself: classroom, home, sanctuary, lighthouse.

"One thing about her?" said Ms. Clark.

Shosh took a breath, and one thing became seven, memories of Stevie multiplying like the evening's first stars.

EVAN
the big bang

"BETWEEN THIS AND HER STUNT at Heather's this summer, it's a fairly obvious cry for help," says Sara.

"SOS, yo."

After Shosh's impromptu performance, the whole school is asking some version of the same question: how did the girl who graduated with honors last spring—a theater rat, by all accounts, set to go to USC this fall, with fame and fortune to follow—wind up in the auditorium, possibly high, definitely drunk, belting "God Only Knows" by the Beach Boys?

"What stunt at Heather's?" asks Ali.

"Oh, come on. I know you left before it happened, but that shit was all over social." Sara goes on to tell us how Shosh drove Chris Bond's truck into Heather Abernathy's pool. She supplements the story with photographic evidence posted by a variety of partygoers who were there, and now everyone around me is taking out their phones, heading to Shosh's profile, commenting on her overall badassery. Ali says her coat looks like the one Kaley Cuoco wore in *The Flight Attendant*. Yurt doesn't know who Kaley Cuoco is, and when Sara says, "From *The Big Bang Theory*," Yurt coins a new nickname for Shosh that ultimately falls flat: Big Bang Cuoco.

These are the things that happen, though I barely clock them.

I nod and smile, but I'm not thinking of today's disruption, or the beautiful girl who disrupted it.

I'm thinking of a different performance, one that started the minute Shosh's ended.

Thus far, the mysterious singer has been content to stay in the background of my life, hushed and sparse. But that's all changed now. Beginning in the auditorium, and now all through the halls—at this very moment—she sings in my ears, making herself known in new and voluminous ways, billowing, undulating, lapping one lyric on top of another, until her song is an ocean, and I am swept up in its current.

SOMEWHERE IN THE
NORTHERN ATLANTIC

Your drowning thought is a songbird no one can hear.

You sing anyway, from the beginning.

The childhood daydreaming—

—of love and distant lands.

(So often felt the same.)

The meandering music, songs simmering under the tongue.

Studies in secret—geology, philosophy, Latin, botany.

Learning to love learning.

Not a girl's place, Father said.

Negotiations in the mirror—

Who are you?

And at church, that constant struggle.

Asking for a sign, if only symbolic.

Please, something, anything, but nothing.

And then—

A Voice in the night.

Leading you to Massachusetts, to yourself.

To Amherst, lovely Amherst.

Academia, blossoming, silly boys growing on trees.

And that day on the green, bird-watching.

Birds remind of heaven, she said.

You turn to see her, thus ending your Before.

I love birds, you said. *They can go anywhere.*

Smiles, assessments, introductions.

I'm Emily, she said.

Siobhan, you said.

Thus begins your After.

Talk of God and death, talk of art and immortality, and now—

Bird-watching with Emily.

Reading with Emily.

Singing with Emily.

Everything with Emily.

Your voice is a dream I had, Emily says of her simmering songs.

You wonder at the color of blush.

Not in her "circle of five"—so be it.

Secret is better.

You have more, you have Birds, and Birds have wings.

But Time flies too.

Amherst ends—Emily is gone.

(Birds forever ruined.)

You marry William—a decent man.

Because the world is the world—the Way It Is.

A grand bridal tour, you suggest. *Somewhere north, snow and ice.*

Maybe love would come in a distant land.

(The two still felt the same.)

Later, William says. *First, children.*

Settling in New York, waiting for *Later*.

And when no children come, you know why.

When William gets sick, you know why.

When you bury him, you know why.

Ashes to ashes, lust to lust.

Asking for a sign, if only symbolic.

Please, something, anything, but nothing.

And then—

A letter from Emily.

My dearest Shiv . . .

(Arise, arise, beautiful Birds!)

And you think back to Amherst, lovely Amherst.

Bird-watching on the green.

They remind of heaven: Emily's reason.

They can go anywhere: your reason.

Now, at fifty-four, you know the truth—

I am the Bird.

Your *Later* is here—time to fly.

New York to Liverpool on the SS *Arctic Tern*—not bridal, but grand.

Bag packed, her letters in your pocket.

I would not paint a picture, they say.

Though she could, you've seen her drawings. But no.

I'd rather be the One, she writes.

You understand because you understand her.

It makes you smile.

Bon voyage, two weeks at sea.

Ice fields in the Northern Atlantic.

So much ice.

Too much ice.

The slowness of a capsize.

People scurry like rats.

Negotiations in mirrors, *please, something, anything,* but nothing.

Ashes to ashes for all.

High in the sky, a seabird glides.

Memories of Amherst, lovely Amherst.

Her letters soaked and safe in your pocket.

Sinking in the cold, a smile, a song.

Of childhood daydreams.

Of love and distant lands.

(No longer felt the same.)

I will find you, you sing, sinking . . .

PART
THREE

FUGUE

EVAN
listen . . .

I AM A SONG COBBLER, fitting together bits of broken melodies. I am a lyric collector, sifting treasures for missing connectors, tossing duplicates. The music swells from the ground, from thin air, from nothing. I don't know when or why, but I am ready for it. Ready to hear what she's trying to tell me.

I call her *Nightbird*.

There's this place. An undeveloped plot of land not far from our house, full of trees, overgrown shrubs, a little creek slowly winding its way like some ageless artery. There are no signs indicating city or county ownership, no warnings to KEEP OUT or STAY AWAY. Lopped off on all sides in favor of subdivisions and strip malls, this little wood is a relic from another age, and while it's tempting to think of it as an old woman clinging to life, I see it for the cunning survivor it is, an ancient wild outlasting the modern world by hiding in plain sight.

Every day for the last two weeks, during the hour-long window before Will gets home, I come here to draw and to listen. Sometimes Nightbird comes; sometimes she doesn't. Preparedness is key. My phone is always at the ready, no longer open to Apple Music (my attempt to block out the songs), or voice memos (my attempt to prove the songs), but rather, my Notes app. Per Ali's suggestion, I've been keeping a lyric log; so far, I've identified pieces of three separate songs:

NIGHTBIRD SONG LYRICS

(my notes in **bold**; lyrics in *italics*)
SONG #1:
By far the one I hear most. I think I have the first and third verses in full, but only sections of the chorus and second verse. Not 100 percent sure about that final line. French??

(Breathe out)
I'm taking it all in
(Quiet now)
Drifting down Brooklyn
What started out cold is freezing all alone

_____

For every bridge I cross
(You'll never win)

_____

I can take anything so long as it's you plus me
But that math made you leave
You say being happy is _____
But all I want to do is find the one who hurt you

_____

Looking so hard in all the wrong places

_____

Just another false start

_____

_____

It will happen soon
In the lucid moon
I don't know what you said
But your song is in my head
Je t'aime, je t'aime, je t'aime

SONG #2:

**Only heard this one a few times. I think these
are from the middle portion but can't say for sure.**

There is a place we like to go
Where secrets hide in trees of snow

_____

_____

From the Seine to the sea, your voice is in me
In the madness of two, I will find you

SONG #3:

**Almost completely indecipherable. I've got
what I think are the opening lyrics but not sure.
The vocals and piano blend together to the point
you can't tell them apart.**

Please don't ask why I never try
You know as well as I
The difference between loss and love

Deciphering the voice of Nightbird isn't always easy, and
since her songs rarely start at the beginning or play to the end, I
sometimes go days hearing the same section of one song over and

over before hearing an entirely new section days later.

Hence, preparedness.

While I wait, I lean back against a tree and sketch a portrait of Will from his younger days, the phase when he mixed up the word *obsessed* with *excessed*. "I'm *excessed* with E.T.," he would say, and we would hide our smiles, not wanting to ruin the beauty of his innocence.

Not far away, a bird lands on a branch.

I look up from my sketch pad, stare at the bird long enough to question who's staring at who.

"I'm *excessed* with this place," I tell it.

It chirps. *Same.*

When it flies away, I return to my sketch pad, the folly of trying to capture pure innocence in graphite.

SHOSH
the living of other lives

MOST SOCIAL SPACES WERE SOCIAL for a reason. A nightclub, for example. If you weren't already going with friends or a date, then you were probably going in the hopes of meeting someone, of surrounding yourself with bodies dancing in the dark, the comforting anonymity of a pulsing crowd. Coffee shops were a natural gathering spot for friends, and while you might go to one alone, you would probably bring a book, or a computer, with a plan to do something in a place that wasn't your home.

Going to the movies, however, was in no way enhanced by the presence of others. For two hours, you sat in a dark room in front of a giant screen, which instructed you, right at the very beginning, to kindly shut the fuck up. Movie theaters were designed to be an immersive experience, a time to get lost in another world, another life. And nothing could pull you from the wondrous lives of others like a friend on a phone, or a dad who wouldn't quit asking what was going on, or a mom who clicked her tongue in disapproval every time a character cursed.

If going to the movies alone were a sport, Shosh would be a world-class Olympian.

"I don't understand," said the theater employee, who looked approximately twelve years old.

"I just want a ticket." Shosh held her debit card through the window.

"But you won't tell me what movie you want to see."

"It's not that I *won't* tell you, like I'm keeping my choice close to the vest. I don't *care* what movie I see."

"You don't care," said the employee.

"I literally do not."

The man-child sighed, took her card, swiped it, ripped a ticket, and handed them both back. "You're gonna hate it."

The Discount was one of those places that made no bones about the nature of itself. Some contractor had missed some zoning law, and the place was built before they realized they weren't legally allowed to, you know, *show* movies. Not new releases, anyway. So the suits put their heads together and came up with a plan to salvage the money they'd already sunk into the place. Now anyone in Iverton could see four-month-old movies for two dollars.

Aside from the stage itself, this had always been her favorite place. Birthdays, holidays, weekends—she'd spent half her childhood either at the Discount or wishing she were. At concessions, she ordered a large Diet Coke with extra ice. In the bathroom, she dumped out half the soda, pulled flask #1 from her coat pocket, and poured to the top. Back in the hallway, she handed the ticket to the ticket-taker, who pointed her in the direction of theater nine, and by the time she got there, the previews were underway.

Two hours later, Shosh left theater nine as the credits rolled, went to the same bathroom, relieved herself, emptied the remaining portion of flask #1 into the cup's icy dregs, and then calmly walked into theater thirteen.

Two hours after that, she went back to concessions, ordered a half-price refill of Diet Coke, then—back in the same bathroom— emptied half the soda into the sink, pulled flask #2 from a second pocket (the wonders of her coat never ceased!), refilled, and walked into theater three.

It was around this time that Shosh began to lose track of things. Not big things, just things like what time it was, how long she'd been here, how many movies she'd snuck into. She hated the actors in this particular movie, though it had nothing to do with the quality of acting (the ability to discern good acting from bad being another skill set she seemed to have momentarily misplaced). No, she hated these actors because they'd done it: They'd successfully gone from whatever town in which they lived to this screen in Iverton, Illinois. They'd caught the dream she'd once pursued, when dreams were a thing that made sense to pursue, and she thought, "Fuck these people," or maybe she said it out loud. Patrons in the rows ahead were turning to stare, and it occurred to her that the person who'd been making the shhhhhh sound every few minutes was perhaps shushing her. "The fuck are you shushing?" she said to the back of his head, and much like Toad sealed his fate when he climbed atop the back of a river turtle, Shosh knew she'd sealed her own when the man stood and left the theater with a look of deter- mination. Not sticking around to get kicked out, she left.

Now she stood alone in the parking lot.

It was dark out, but that couldn't be right. She'd Ubered here this morning. Surely, she hadn't been here all day.

Pulling out her phone, she dialed Ms. Clark—for a ride or just for company, she wasn't sure—but hung up before anyone answered.

She was sober enough to know she was too drunk for Ms. Clark.

"'Toad looked through the windows,'" she said, considering the Uber app on her phone. "'He looked in the garden.'" No, no more Uber. She was feeling broody, and broody Shosh liked to walk. Putting her phone away, she turned in the general direction of home, reciting the story as she walked. "'He did not see Frog.'"

At some point it began to rain, lightly at first, and then a torrent.

"'Frog and Toad stayed on the island all afternoon.'"

Still walking, drenched from head to toe, she thought of the last time she was this wet, climbing first out of a submerged truck window, and then out of the pool altogether.

"'They ate wet sandwiches without iced tea,'" and just when she was beginning to reconsider calling an Uber, she saw it. Through the pouring rain, neon lights in the window flashed, as if broadcasting a safe haven in a stormy sea: INK YOUR FACE TATTOOS.

"'They were two close friends sitting alone together,'" she said, and walked inside.

EVAN

implications of the limitless imagination

I DON'T LIKE TALKING ABOUT therapy. And look, I get it. First, I complain how hard it is to share important things, and then I say I don't want to share important things. Consider my multitudes unleashed. I don't know, maybe it's different for other people, but for me, my therapy is mine and you can't have it.

"Okay," says Maya.

"Not—I didn't mean you," but I think she knows, because she smiles, and I suddenly realize how little I know of her.

Maya is an anomaly: soft and hard, elusive and direct, the most inscrutable human to ever wear a heart on a sleeve. Her office walls are decorated with the kind of art that makes every attempt to say nothing at all: colorful swatches, calm-handed brushstrokes, not a single statement to be made. There are no framed photos. No portraits of children laughing in fields or barefoot families in bed, and I wonder if she has kids, a partner, someone to come home to. Maybe she doesn't want that. Maybe living alone, for Maya, isn't a stepping stone to not living alone.

"Was someone asking you to talk about therapy?" asks Maya.

"Hmm?"

"You just conveyed some pretty strong feelings about not wanting to talk about therapy. Which is fine. But it makes me wonder who was asking."

"It just feels like—back in the eighties, or whatever, it was totally taboo. Which sucked, obviously. But now it's like basic health care. And I know talking openly is how you destigmatize a thing, it's just—some of us would rather keep it to ourselves, is all."

When I'm in this office, my brain processes things at different speeds, like a jacked-up OS going a million miles a minute. "I have this friend," I say. "Or—we *used* to be friends. Heather. She had this party at the end of summer, and she was going on and on about her therapist this, and her therapist that, and I was just like, *That's not how this works.*"

"How what works?"

"*This.*" I wave my arms around the office. "I'm here because of the storms. Because I need help. I'm not here so I can get drunk at parties and talk about how I have a therapist too. Like it's a badge of honor."

Maya doesn't say anything, but we both know it's the kind of quiet with a short shelf life.

I lean back on the couch, look around the room, then look back at her. "What."

"I was thinking about my dad's hernia operation."

"Okay . . ."

"I was a kid. It was a minor outpatient procedure, he was back at work in no time. But that man spent the rest of his life finding ways to insert his hernia operation into every conversation he was part of. Family dinners, holidays, strangers in line at the grocery. It was impressive, actually, the ways he could contort a conversation to fit the words 'bulging intestine.' Years later, after he died, Mom mentioned in passing how scared he'd been to have surgery. He didn't sleep for days leading up to it, apparently." Wherever Maya had gone in her own head to find this story, she's back now, eyes on me. "People need therapy for all sorts of reasons. Sometimes those reasons are clear. Sometimes, less so. Some people think talking about it openly makes it small, and that's valid. But some people *need* to make it small. They find comfort in bringing it out of the shadows, giving it a name. So they talk about it. A *lot*, sometimes. You don't have to wear your therapy as a badge of honor, Evan. But I would encourage you to think twice before judging someone who does. Some people need a badge."

There's this feeling—which I've recently become familiar with—of being absolutely owned. We sit in that space for a minute: Maya waiting patiently, professionally; me feeling like a newly neutered dog. Eventually, she clears her throat, and when she says, "There's something I'd like to talk about," my stomach sinks.

In my experience, it's never a good sign when the thing you need to talk about requires an introduction.

"I debated whether to bring it up," she continues. "You haven't mentioned it, and I wanted to respect that. But I think it's important for you to know that I spoke with your mother about what's going on with her. If you'd rather not discuss it, I understand. But I thought you should know that I know."

Sometimes I hate Maya, to be totally honest. Sometimes she says something so true, it scalds the skin around my ears. Mostly this happens when we talk about Will, and how I want to take care of him, protect him from the world, and she reminds me I'm not his dad, and I'll have a sudden inclination to set her office on fire.

"She says they think they caught it early?"

I offer Maya a single nod; at the moment, it's the only tool in my belt.

To her credit, she spots my nonverbal hint like a pro and switches gears. "What about storms? Have you had any lately?"

I look out the window. "Not since that one Tuesday." Quiet, and still reeling at the thought of Mom and Maya's conversation, an image bubbles to the surface of my mind: golden crosses and maroon carpets, red hymnals in wooden boxes attached to the back of pews. "We used to go to church together. Heather's family and mine."

"This is your friend who threw the party."

"Ex-friend. And the only reason I went to her stupid party was because Ali said if I didn't get out of the house, I was going to turn into a literal hermit's asshole."

"Okay."

"The idea being, if a hermit never sees the light of day, imagine a hermit's—"

"No, I get it, thanks." A brief smile, and then: "Do you still go to church?"

"Yes. No. I mean—we stopped a few months after Dad left."

On the coffee table, a little potted plant. I don't know flowers. Gun to my head, I'd guess daisies. They're right next to the tissues; I'm not sure how I missed them before.

"Somebody fell, scraped up their knee or something," I say.

"At church?"

"At the party. We were in the basement, and somebody cut themselves."

Lilies, maybe? Irises. Whatever they are, it's a full-on bloom, white and yellow.

"Heather was helping this guy with his cut, and when she pulled out a box of Band-Aids, she started talking about this kid who used to go to her church—'some weirdo kid,' she called him, who wore Band-Aids all over his body. She said there was clearly something wrong with the kid, but no one would acknowledge it," and now I'm wondering if these flowers are even real, if something so perfect could also be a living thing.

"Did she know she was talking about your brother?"

"It was pretty crowded. I'm not sure she knew I was there."

Maya considers. "It's not the first time you've heard someone talk about Will like that."

"Are these real?" I point to the flowers on the coffee table. "They can't be, right?"

"They are."

I lean over to smell them, and yes—definitely real.

"Evan."

"I just don't understand how anyone could leave him." I touch a soft petal, half expecting it to fall off, but it holds steady.

"Leave . . . Will?"

"He's the softest kid. Sweet and quiet, and he'd live in a refrigerator box if I let him, and I just—I don't understand how anyone could leave him."

"Have you spoken with your dad recently?"

I tell her I haven't, and that if Dad wants to talk, he knows damn well where to find me, and then I scoot to the edge of the couch, lean over the coffee table, just really get my face good and buried among the petals in the flowerpot, and at some point, it occurs to me that I have to stop with the flowers.

"Evan, I'm curious—when you heard what Heather said about your brother, how did you respond?"

"I didn't. I left."

"Leaving is a response."

"You know what I mean."

"You didn't say anything to her?"

"No, but—I'd had a lot to drink."

"I didn't know you drank."

"I don't. Usually."

It's quiet for a minute, and I can tell she's waiting me out. An art form all its own: sit; stare; say nothing.

"Actually—I didn't leave right away."

Maya watches, waits, a true master of her craft.

"After that thing about Will, she started in on all the ways our bodies take care of themselves. How a cut finger heals on its own. How the heart beats, the lungs breathe, and the more she talked, the more I drank. Got so I couldn't feel my feet, and then when I finally could, I took off. Ali chased me. We made it about a block before I vomited in a park."

Do you understand, Maya? Please say you see it, that slow, angular flood of light across my bedroom floor. Please say you see the quiet bird in the tree. All my befores ending, my afters beginning. Please say . . . "You've seen the movie, right?"

She doesn't have to ask which one. "It's been a while."

"Their hearts light up. Bright red. It's part of how they communicate, E.T. and the other aliens. First time we watched it, Will said it reminded him of us. We were on the floor, backs against the couch, an open box of pizza on the coffee table. When the little alien hearts lit up, Will didn't miss a beat. 'It's like us,' he said. 'My heart glows to you. And yours glows to me.'"

If feeling things were a disease, mine would be a terminal case. I grab a tissue from the box, wipe my eyes, and when Maya says,

"It's more than a movie for you guys—it's a language," it suddenly occurs to me why I've been so preoccupied with the flowerpot on the coffee table. It reminds me of the flowerpot in the movie, the one whose petals mimic the health of E.T., wilting and blooming in tandem with his life and death.

"He stopped wearing them," I say quietly.

A beat, as Maya processes. "When?"

"Like a month ago. Left for school one morning covered in Band-Aids. Came home in the afternoon, they were gone. He won't talk about it. I don't know why I didn't tell you last time—"

"It's okay."

"I'm not going to be the one to tell him to toughen up."

"I know."

"I'm not going to do it."

"Evan—why do you think you left Heather's party?"

"We're still on that? I told you what she said about Will. If I didn't get out of there, I was going to punch her in the face."

"What she said about your brother was inexcusable. But I don't think that's why you left."

That image again: my room as light falls across the carpet.

"I couldn't breathe," I say. "I don't care what Heather says, the heart is a muscle, and if it's not glowing, it's dying—"

The moment the word is out of my mouth, I know the truth. And when I look at Maya, I see the face of someone who got there long ago, who's been waiting for me to catch up.

"Sometimes," she says—carefully, gently—"our bodies don't heal themselves. Do they?"

I grab another tissue from the box.

• • •

The night my mother told me she might have cancer I was pretending to be asleep. My eyes were closed, so I couldn't see her poke her head in the door, couldn't see the light from the landing unfold across my floor in that slow, angular flood. But I knew it was there.

The things you memorize without meaning to, impressions against eyelids.

"Ev?" she whispered. "You awake?"

Pretending to be asleep is the most childish of retaliations: wide awake in the dark, eyes closed, *this will really show her*. As if getting home late were her fault. As if she wanted to go from one job to the next.

But still, I lay in bed like a child scorned, driving home the point: *Yes, Mom, you're late. How late? Just look at me. I'm dead asleep.*

"Evan?"

It was still summer, the room sticky-hot. Exactly twenty-four hours later, Ali would be holding back my hair while I vomited in a park.

I heard the door begin to close, and I can't say what made me do it, but I opened my eyes and sat up. "Mom."

The door swung back open. "Hey. Didn't mean to wake you."

We were whispering, our eyes darting to the closed door across the landing. Ever since Dad left, our mutual love of Will had transformed into some new thing, a sibling-parental hybrid, as if there had been a "Dad" placeholder in our house, and in the absence of Actual Dad, we'd combined forces to fill the role.

In a way, Will was the constant in the variable of our family: we were never *not* thinking of him.

Mom said she wanted to talk, but then she just stood there,

unmoving in my doorway. I wasn't sure if she was waiting for permission, so I said, "Okay."

"I wanted to talk to you about—" She stopped midsentence, finally entered my room, shut the door, and switched on a floor lamp.

"Hi," she said.

"Hi."

I'd often wondered at my mother's possibilities aside from the reality in which she'd landed. Dark hair, dark eyes, the same freckled white skin she'd passed to Will and me. Unlike some of my friends' moms, she embraced age in a way that allowed age to embrace her, and if she was a little haggard these days, well, you could hardly blame her. My mother speaks like a novel, wielding beautiful words at will, specific words, perfectly suited to the topic at hand. She's the kind of smart that surprises people and smart enough to be kind to people, and maybe most of all, she's the kind of funny that comes from being smart and kind, and I love her so much. In another world, she might have done something grand, something big, something . . . else. Selfishly, I'm relieved we live in this world. But I sometimes wonder if she is.

"I found something," she whispered, leaning against the inside of my closed door.

I don't know what I expected her to say next. A misplaced necklace, maybe. A pair of socks behind a dresser.

"I found a lump," she said. Slowly, she raised her hand to her chest. "In my breast."

I had no words. I tried to say something, but all that came out was: "When?"

"Last week."

"Okay."

"I had a biopsy yesterday—"

"Mom."

"I'm fine. Sore, but—" Eyes on the floor, she shook her head, and when she looked up, I saw the same face she'd given me years ago, when I came home from school to the news that our ancient and beloved dog had gone to sleep that morning and hadn't woken up.

We said we'd wait to get another dog. Honor the memory.

We were still waiting.

"Are you okay?" I asked, a question that felt both stupid and not stupid.

"They said they'd call in a couple days. With results." She looked at her feet in the dim lighting, and then looked around the room, and I thought, *She's stalling*, and I realized how much she needed to not be alone right now.

"So, they don't know if it's . . ." Just the thought of saying the word made me want to chew it up, swallow it down, never taste it again. Quickly, before she had a chance to respond—"I could have driven you. If you needed a ride."

"A friend from work took me. Let me rest at his place afterward. Anyway, it was outpatient." Then, more to herself: "Silly term. Like I'm not a real patient just because I don't stay the night." Finally, her eyes found mine. "I'd decided to not tell you. And then I walked in the front door, and I came up the stairs . . ."

"And you told me."

She looked away again, wiped her eyes, and only then did I see the tears. My own tears would come eventually, but in that moment, I was overcome by a new revelation born in a subtle distinction of pronouns: I'd always hated Dad for leaving us; until now, it hadn't occurred to me to hate him for leaving her.

I got out of bed, crossed the room to her. "I love you, Mom."

"I love you too."

The next day I went to a party where Heather Abernathy talked shit about my brother, and about the body healing itself, and I had to leave a basement full of atrophied hearts. I ran down the road and threw up in some bushes, and my best friend proved her best friendness by holding my hair out of my face, and I started hearing songs no one else could hear, and for some reason, I can talk to my best friend about those songs, but I can't talk to her about my beautiful mother's cancer, and I can talk to my therapist about my mother's cancer, but I can't talk about the songs. And then I remember that we live in a world where very smart people once believed birds migrated to the moon, and it occurs to me that possibilities are endless when you understand nothing.

The world, like a small child pretending to be asleep.

Two nights later, that angular light rolled across my carpet again. I sat right up, no pretense of sleep. "Hey."

She didn't say a word; I knew the truth because I knew her.

In the coming weeks and months, we would learn new truths, some more welcome than others. There would be new doctors with new terminologies, and those welcome truths, each a cause for celebration—the successful removal of the lump; the lymph node biopsy that comes back clear; the news that chemo isn't necessary—

would be tempered by a different breed of truth, the sort that rises as the sun goes down:

You wonder what will happen if the worst happens.

You recalibrate your hopes, look for ways to bolster the suddenly shortened rope in your hands.

You negotiate with a God whose potential existence and potential nonexistence you find terrifying in equal measure.

You speak in the language of percentages, as if the years of a life were dollars saved and spent.

From the time you were a child, you were taught nothing lasts forever, and yet now, confronted with your mother's looming mortality, you are appalled at the notion that she isn't infinite.

Mostly, lying awake in bed long into the night, you wonder how you're ever expected to live in a world without the person who brought you into it.

SHOSH
the art of polite thievery

SHOSH SAT IN THE BACK seat of the Uber, staring at her phone—its screen illuminating her face like a downstage soliloquy—and wondered if she'd always been a fraud.

"You okay, hon?"

Looking up, she found a pair of watery-blue eyes staring at her in the rearview. The driver had a shock of curly blond hair and was roughly the same age as her, which made the whole chauffeur thing squirrelly and uncomfortable.

"You're bleeding," the girl said. She reached down, pulled a roll of paper towels out of nowhere, and handed them back.

Sure enough, a trickle of blood had seeped its way out from under the wrappings on Shosh's forearm. She'd expected the tattoo to hurt; she hadn't expected so much blood. After tending to her mess, she handed the paper towels back with thanks, then returned to her phone screen, her latest cabin couplet, the sinking realization of her fraudulent ways.

The photo featured a modern cabin in the woods. The sky was a deep oceanic blue, the color of true dusk; snow covered the ground, the cabin's roof, lacing the black branches in thin white stripes like monotone candy canes. But what made the cabin unique was its asymmetry: the entire right side was made of glass; inside, a warm light shimmered over a bed with a simple suggestion, not of lovers, but of a place where lovers had been recently; on the left, the roof continued as an awning over a little open-air porch.

To accompany the photo, Shosh had written . . .

I'm a crooked painting of unknowable place
with hands constructed to frame your face

"To be an artist is to be a skillful burglar," Ms. Clark used to say, the idea being, every room you're in, every person you meet, is fodder for the muse. It starts with a friend's accent, or a particular mannerism you find interesting; before long, everywhere you go, you're a bucket dipping from the well of everyone's everything. Drawing from the well becomes second nature. So much so that occasionally, what you create feels like it already existed, floating around in the air, ready to be plucked, written, claimed.

Staring at her latest poem, Shosh realized that's exactly what she'd done.

"Word of advice," said the driver. "You really shouldn't drink before you get a tattoo. No judgment. But I've got a few myself, and alcohol thins the blood. Just for future reference. I'm Ruth, by the way. Hamish."

Ruth had a thick Southern accent, and a way of talking that made you think she'd grown up with older brothers: fast, confident, the voice of a backyard brawl.

"I'm Shosh."

"Yeah, I know who you are. Don't worry, you wouldn't know me. I was a year ahead of you at Ivy. Plus, in the Venn diagram of social circles, we would've had like *zero* intersections. I mean, I'm hotter now than I was back then? Partly because I know myself better? But yeah, when I was in school, no way. You were like—not in another league so much as another galaxy. We'd probably be friends now, though."

Aside from Chris Bond's truck, Shosh hadn't driven since her sister's death. When she couldn't walk where she was going, she Ubered, and so she'd recently become something of an expert on ride-share amenities: the half-sized bottled waters, the mints in the console, the phone charger extension cords. She'd heard a slew of anecdotes and stories, updates on kids she would never meet, places she would never go, but it was safe to say she'd never met anyone quite like Ruth Hamish. "You light it up onstage, by the way," Ruth was saying. "I came to *The Crucible* four times to see you. Snuck out of class the third time. Fuckin' *inspired*."

Shosh wasn't sure whether to laugh or cry, and when she opened her mouth to say, *Thank you, but that was another life*, what came out was, "My sister was killed by a drunk driver."

A beat before those blue eyes met hers in the rearview again. "Shit."

Shosh leaned her head against the cold window, the city's passing lights a hypnotic salve. "I went to a party this summer. Didn't talk to anyone. Just drank. First a little, then a lot. Probably the only person who was drunker than me was this shitbag, Chris Bond. You know him?"

Ruth shook her head.

"He's the kind of guy who purposely waits at the stairs so he can follow the girl with the skirt. Every joke is sexual, or at someone's expense. He must have asked me out ten times. I'd tell him to fuck off, he'd laugh like it was a joke, then spread rumors he'd turned me down."

Part of her wondered why it was so easy to spill herself to a complete stranger. Or maybe it was easy *because* Ruth was a stranger. Nothing on the line when your confidante is a pair of eyes in the rearview.

"It got super late," Shosh said. "People started to leave. I saw him stumble out the door, twirling his keys around. And I knew what I was going to do. He'd parked his giant fucking Tahoe on the curb out front. I waited until he got the truck started, then I ran out and told him Heather had something for him back in the kitchen. Soon as he was inside, I climbed into the front seat, revved it up—jumped the curb, drove it through the yard, around the house, and steered that motherfucker right into the pool." An icy resolve seeped from her bones, filled her body like water in a balloon until she was bursting to be somewhere else, anywhere else, to start a new life with a new name in a new city. "Most days, it feels like I'm losing my mind."

"Sometimes you think you're losing your mind, when really, it's just everyone else lost theirs."

Shosh turned from the window to this apparent sage of an Uber driver. "That is some dope-ass shit, Ruth Hamish."

Ruth gave a quick eyebrow raise, as if to say, *I got game.*

"So you don't think it's crazy?" said Shosh. "Driving a truck into a pool?"

Ruth took a moment, and when she spoke, it was with the measured pace of a quote. "'*Because I could not stop for Death, he kindly stopped for me. The Carriage held but just Ourselves and Immortality.'* "

"Who's that?"

"Fuck if I know." Ruth held up a little flip calendar with today's date. "My boyfriend got me this calendar with little poems on each day. Hold up—" She looked closer at the calendar, zooming through a questionable yellow light in the process. "Emily Dickinson."

As they turned into Shosh's neighborhood, the ghost-singer faded in—singing of crooked paintings and unknowable places—and Shosh considered the words she'd plucked from the air, claimed as her own. More than the idea of accidental plagiarism, what bothered her most was how the songs had infiltrated her subconscious to the point she wasn't able to tell the difference between what she'd consumed and what she'd created.

She opened her phone, pulled up her most recent post, and hit delete.

As they pulled into her driveway, she thanked Ruth for the ride, but before she could climb out of the car, Ruth jotted her number down on a slip of paper, handed it back, told her to call anytime, day or night. "I don't think driving that ass-clown's truck into a pool makes you crazy," Ruth said. "I think you couldn't save your sister, so you tried to save someone else's."

EVAN
no muscles

WE DON'T GO OUT TO eat often. Mom's work schedule and radiation appointments make it nearly impossible. Alas, tonight the stars have aligned: in addition to a rare evening off, Mom won a Chili's gift card in some raffle at her day job, and that shit is money on the table.

Just before we left for the restaurant, she mentioned the leftovers in the fridge with that adult tone, like, *We really should*, to which I pointed out the fact that it's been three weeks since we learned the cancer hadn't spread, that she wouldn't need chemo, and we've yet to celebrate. "Seems like some tasty apps are in order," I said. "Or those little honey-chipotle chicken tenders, at the very least."

I could see her wheels turning. "They're called *crispers*," she said.

I said, "Heck yes, they are," and lo! that very hour, we're sitting in a booth at Chili's, waiting on plates of crispers *and* tasty apps.

What can I say. We're a wild ride, the Taft family, baller to the bitter end.

"Did it work?" Mom asks.

"Not yet." I'm on my phone, trying to register Mom's gift card in the Chili's app, which supposedly gets you a free appetizer.

"And you're telling me it's not a thing?"

"It just says 'Download our app, register your gift card, get an appetizer on us.'"

"*Download the app, get a free app.* How hard is that? I should have gone into marketing." Mom does her trademark huff-and-headshake. "Oh, hey, we should have invited Ali. Isn't Chili's, like, her thing?"

Chili's is, in fact, Ali's thing. But we only have one gift card, which probably won't cover all of us as it is, and I didn't want Mom to feel pressure to pay for her. I don't tell her any of this; instead, I shrug, like, *Too late.*

Across the table, head buried in an illustrated storybook adaptation of E.T., Will is singing, "*Download the app, get a free app,*" over and over to the tune of John Williams's iconic score.

"If it makes you feel better," I say, "the app sucks. This is infuriating."

"Are you mad?" asks Will, without looking up from his book.

"Not at you, bud. I'm mad at technology."

"Technology can't even walk or talk." He flips a page, calmly continues. "Technology doesn't have *muscles.* You shouldn't be mad at something with no muscles."

Mom smiles, shrugs like, *He's got a point.*

"I need to urinate soon, Mary." Will consults his watch, pushes a few buttons. "In two minutes."

My brother is the only kid I know who gives himself a bathroom countdown. In most houses, the beep of an alarm is a wake-up call. In ours, it signals the call of nature.

"You know I prefer it when you call me Mom."

"Your name is Mary," he says. "Just like Elliott's mom in E.T. Also, Evan's initials are E.T."

I look up from my phone. "Okay, that's . . . weird."

"Honey—" As if to prove her Mom-ness, she shifts into full-on Mom tone, and then says a thing I've said in my head a million times, but haven't been able to usher past my lips: "I noticed you stopped wearing your ouch-shields."

Imagine a Chili's at the bottom of the sea, dark and still, volume turned to zero, chairs and tables and silverware floating like half-filled balloons.

Will, head buried in his book, doesn't even come up for air. "Old news, Mary."

Mom shrugs, a clear attempt at the old Nonchalant Ploy. "Makes no difference to me. You do something every day for a year, and then you stop. I'm just curious, is all."

Alas, the alarm on Will's watch goes off; he sets down the book, shuts off the alarm, and looks at us across the table. "Whose turn is it to take me to the bathroom?"

SHOSH
everything happens for a reason (and other nuggets of actual bullshit)

"I KNOW IT'S BONKERS, BUT Evansville doesn't have a Chili's, and I've been craving these fajitas like I'm angry pregnant."

Shosh watched her friend shove half a stuffed tortilla into her mouth; she would have been disgusted if she weren't so relieved to be spending time with someone other than her parents or the good folks at Iverton PD.

"Are you?" Shosh asked.

"Ammawut?"

"Pregnant?"

"Hmmnoway."

A fellow stage rat from Shosh's year, Ella Tubb had texted this morning to say she was in town for a family funeral (some great-aunt she hardly knew), but could Shosh do a quick bite while she was here, her treat.

"So how is it?" Shosh asked.

"Could use more cilantro."

"I meant Evansville."

She shrugged. "It's good. Theater department is great, though none of the teachers are Ms. Clark. We're doing *The Wild Party*. I'm Kate. What else. My roommate is batshit. Her parents were, like, evangelical fundamentalists? Cabin in the mountains, end-of-the-world-type shit, so yeah. She's pretty much gone off the deep end. Keeps a chart on our wall of her sexual exploits, so that's fun."

In the months after Stevie's death, there had been a wave of online condolences. Friends had called or texted to say they were sorry, they were thinking of her, but it was the summer after graduation, and most everyone was either gearing up for college or squeezing in some decadent vacation in their final weeks of freedom. Whatever social foundation had been in place the past four years was already crumbling by the time Stevie died. Which made Ella's text this morning all the more meaningful.

Still, there was a part of her that couldn't help feeling jealous of Ella. Theater had a competitive edge, to be sure, but when you're in the lead, the competition is the stage, the dream.

She and Ella had been running the same race; now Shosh was watching from the stands.

"How are Lana and Jared?" Ella asked.

Shosh tried to find the words to describe the current state of her parents. "It's like—we're living in the same house but different countries."

Ella wiped her mouth with a napkin, slowly pushed her plate aside. "And how are you? *Really?*"

Shosh used to smile. She'd seen photos, anyway, versions of herself as a happy person. She tried to throw one on now, like the old days. "I'm dandy."

"*Sho.* Did you or did you not drive Chris Bond's Tahoe into Heather's pool?"

"He was drunk off his ass, about to drive home."

"I see. So you were sober when you climbed behind the wheel? I've heard the hero narrative, Shosh, I'm not buying it. How many times have you spent the night at my house? And how many nights did Mom wake us up at two a.m., stumbling into my bedroom, passing out in the middle of the floor? I don't doubt your good intentions. That's how addiction works. Believe me, I know."

"What do you want me to say?" Shosh picked at her burger, tried to think of a way to steer the conversation elsewhere. "I fucking miss her."

"Of course you do. But you can't just wither up. That's not what—" Ella froze, as if saying Stevie's name aloud might remind Shosh that she'd died. "She wouldn't want that for you."

"You didn't *know* her."

Like a genie from a bottle, their waiter appeared. "And how's my favorite table doing? Those fajitas come out okay?"

"We're good, thanks," said Ella.

"Actually—" Shosh grabbed the drink menu from the center of the table, pointed to an enormous frozen beverage exploding from the beach with the words *Tropical Sunrise Margarita* etched in rainbow across the sunny blue sky. "Can I get one of these?"

Thus began the dance of assessment. The first move was hers, in which she assessed the gatekeeper: their waiter appeared to be in his late forties, on the cusp of losing his hair, but with a certain leftover look of youth, as if clinging to the bottom rung. This was good. She could work with this. Having offered up her inquiry, she waited as the gatekeeper took his turn: she felt his eyes on her, trying to pin her age, could tell he was debating whether to be cool or play by the rules. In this case, as Shosh had predicted . . .

"Sure." The waiter smiled at them both. "Couple of pretty ladies like you."

"Dude," said Ella. "Gross."

The waiter's smile disappeared; he turned to Shosh. "I'll be right back with your drink."

After he left, Ella said, "Ew."

"Yeah."

"Tell me that's not a thing you do."

Shosh shrugged, went back to her burger. "I look older than I am."

"You're an incandescent fox, Sho. Of course he's bringing you a drink."

"Incandescent fox?"

"And what about that?" Ella pointed to the tattoo on Shosh's forearm, which had just peeked out from under the sleeve of her coat. "You dupe the artist, too?"

"I'm eighteen. I could get a sleeve if I wanted."

"Is that a *toad*?"

"Not *a* toad. It's *Toad*. From Frog and . . ."

"What does it say?"

Reluctantly, Shosh pushed her sleeve up to reveal the single word tattooed below the image of Toad: *alone.*

"It's not a big deal," said Shosh.

"Seems pretty fucking sad."

"It's just a—look, can we not?"

They ate in silence for a few minutes, but by the time Shosh's vat of tropical margarita arrived, Ella was back to being the concerned friend. She chirped about times to mourn and times to move on; twice, she said the words *everything happens for a reason*, and Shosh wasn't sure which had turned more saccharine: her beverage or her friend. "I need to pee," she said, suddenly done with both.

Ella nodded toward the now empty glass basin. "I should think so."

"Listen—" Shosh pulled out her phone, started a text to Ruth. "I appreciate you're trying to help. But I'm fine. Really." She finished the text and slid out of the booth. "Can I Venmo you for the food?"

"I'll take care of it. You're not driving, are you?"

"I don't drive," said Shosh.

"I can give you a ride—"

"I've got it covered." Shosh leaned over, tripped, regrouped, kissed Ella on the cheek. She thanked her for dinner, turned for the restroom, and left them both wishing Ella had just stuck to the funeral.

It seemed odd that trust was linked to time, the amount of one dependent on the amount of the other. Shosh hadn't seen the world yet. Given her limited proximity to its vastness, what made her think she'd already met those she would love most in this life? In that sense, when it came to trust, wasn't geography more important than time?

One friend she'd known for years, no longer around.

One friend she'd just met, told her to call anytime.

EVAN
strangely accurate descriptors

WHEN PEOPLE CLAIM PIGS ARE clean animals, I can only assume they mean compared to other barnyard livestock. You put a pig in your grandmother's dining room, and no one is like, "Okay, but that pig is fucking *spotless*." By the same logic, you could call the Chili's restroom clean—but it is still a public restroom.

The second we step inside, Will takes a massive sniff. "It smells juicy and exhausting in here."

A stranger chuckles from a nearby stall.

I tell Will to do his thing. He sidles up to the lower urinal while I wait by the sink, and of course here, of all places, Nightbird decides to join us. She's loud again, almost as loud as that day in the school auditorium, watching Shosh sing at the piano. It's Song #1, the one I hear most often, but she's in a section I've never heard. I pull out my phone, open Notes, excitedly add the new lyrics, my fingers trying to keep up, when—

"Looks like the kid needs a boost."

The stranger from the stall is behind me now, pointing to Will, who's also standing right there, looking up at me, arms outstretched.

"Right. Sorry." I tuck my phone away, lift Will up by the waist so he can reach the faucet. "Why didn't you say something, bud?"

"I did. You were in a galaxy far, far away."

Whatever galaxy I'm in, I'm still there when we walk out of the bathroom, and run right into someone in the hallway. "So sorry," I say, only when I look up, I see that it's not just anyone: the oversize plaid coat, the chic-feral hair, eyes so bright, they make my feet sweat.

"It's fine," Shosh says in a sort-of laugh, that amused lilt Mom occasionally gets whenever she has a third glass of wine. "Chili's restrooms are notoriously prone to collision." She steps closer, and for a second, I think she's about to kiss me. A waft of alcohol on her breath—*Unfortunate*, I think, *but not a dealbreaker*—and then, all conspiratorially, she whispers, "I'm thinking of writing a letter."

For a second, we stare at each other like that, so close I can hear her breathe. And then her eyes change, the air turns thick, and I don't know how to explain what happens next, but it feels like one of those children's books where a kid stumbles into a portal and finds themselves in a whole other world. And it's not just her eyes, but her smell, her lips, the beauty spot on her cheek—she is a world I want to explore, and yet, somehow, a world I already know.

"Evan," says Will, tugging my hand.

The moment passes; Shosh looks down, smiles at Will, and disappears into the ladies' room.

As if trailing after her, Nightbird dissipates completely.

"You know her?" Will asks.

"Sort of . . ."

"She's pretty."

"Yeah."

I'm about to lead Will back to our table when it occurs to me that this morning's wardrobe choice—my favorite Puma pants—was a crucial misstep.

Shosh had been quite close.

My Puma pants are quite thin.

"Evan."

"One sec." I pull out my phone, pretend to scroll for a solid thirty-count, and when I'm fairly confident in my ability to walk upright through a crowded room, I put the phone away, and look at Will. "Okay. Potatoes?"

"Potatoes," he says.

I pick him up, toss him over my shoulder in that way that makes him giggle, and carry him through the restaurant, back to our table, where Mom is smiling. "Delivery for Mary Taft," I say in a deep voice. "Got a sack of potatoes with your name on it." The giggling ramps up, and my mind may be split in a million directions, but my heart has a singular glow.

When I was a kid, some friend gave me a LEGO minifigure. I didn't have any LEGO, wasn't sure what to do with it, so I named it Bumpy (for the round bump on its head), put it on a shelf, and forgot about it. Then that Christmas, I got a whole box of LEGO, and suddenly, put into context, Bumpy made sense.

A gust of wind rattles my bedroom window. Outside, early vestiges of fall: a respite from heat, when old things die in beautiful ways, and the rest of us ready our bones for the impending wrath of Lake Michigan. It's late but I'm wide awake, sitting in bed, toggling from Notes to Maps to Notes again, quietly singing the new lyrics, and thinking how—plugged into the old ones—the song suddenly, put into context, makes sense:

> *(Breathe out)*
> *I'm taking it all in*
> *(Quiet now)*
> *Drifting down Brooklyn*
> *What started out cold is freezing all alone*
> *(Just quit and jump in)*
> *For every bridge I cross*
> *(You'll never win)*
> *Just tack it up as a loss*
> *I can take anything so long as it's you plus me*
> *But that math made you leave*
> *You say being happy is the trending virtue*
> *But all I want to do is find the one who hurt you*
> *All about the full stop*
> *Looking so hard in all the wrong places*
> *Saying wrong things, saving wrong faces*
> *Just another false start*
> *Get up now, get up and down Division Street*
> *As winter light ascends in victory*
> *It will happen soon*
> *In the lucid moon*

According to Maps, there are dozens of Division Streets across the country. But when you consider the rest of the lyrics . . .

I flip over to messages, text Ali: **You awake?**

Within seconds, three dots, and then . . .

Ali: For you? Always

Me: I need to go somewhere. Would your voice like to join?

Ali: Call whenever!

I climb out of bed, throw on my coat and shoes. The night suddenly feels vibrant and alive as I hurry down the stairs, deftly skipping the traitorous squeak on the second to last step, open the front door, close it behind me with a soft click, dial Ali . . .

"So where're we headed?" she answers.

"I got new lyrics at Chili's tonight—" Even as the words are coming out of my mouth, I regret them.

Dead silence on the other end, followed by a quiet "Interesting."

"Ali—"

"No, I'm fine. I mean, you know Chili's is, like, my thing, but no big deal."

"Alison? We had a gift card. It was a last-minute thing. But yes, okay, I apologize for having dinner with my family and not inviting you."

"Your sarcasm is noted. Continue."

"Thing is, I think you were right."

"Obviously." Then: "About what."

Of all the Division Streets in America, there is one in particular of special interest. Only a mile from my house, the street is familiar not because of proximity, but because of a certain residence known to all in Iverton as the Winter Lighthouse. Each year on December 1, an otherwise unremarkable house on Division transforms into the stuff of legends: the siding and roof, the windows and doors, every inch covered in twinkling bulbs; giant fake snowmen watch a giant fake Santa climb a giant fake ladder to the roof; and while all of this is certainly a draw, it isn't what compels the general public to pile into vans with hot chocolates and flannel pj's year after year. That distinction belongs to the largest luminous inflatable this side of the Mississippi, a fifty-foot baby Jesus—arms outstretched, improbably upright—crowned by a giant shooting star with the words ASCEND IN VICTORY printed on the tail.

On a clear night, rumor has it you can see the shimmering infant from the high-rises of Michigan Avenue.

Probably, you could see him from space.

Thus, the house earned its nickname: the Winter Lighthouse.

After a left on Chestnut, I tell Ali about the latest lyrics from Nightbird, focusing especially on the final lines of the chorus—

> Get up now, get up and down Division Street
> As winter light ascends in victory
> It will happen soon
> In the lucid moon

—a long sigh on the other end of the line, followed by: "No shit."

"I don't know who Nightbird is or why she chose me, but the songs are starting to feel less mystical, and more geographical."

"Like she's drawing you a map," Ali says.

"Question is, a map to where?" And even though we don't figure anything out that night (it's far too early for the resplendent Christ child and his ascending lights of victory), Ali stays with me on the phone, and we toss around theories as I walk up and down Division. And I wonder if there's ever been a more satisfying sound than the rhythm of shoes hitting pavement on a quiet night, the streets cold and empty, the evening stretched out like a blank canvas, your friend's voice in your ear.

When I get home, I tiptoe into the kitchen for some water, only to find Will's progress report on the counter with a Post-it from his teacher: *Will's math scores are below average—needs work!!* And for the second time tonight, I'm thinking of a toy called Bumpy. I'm thinking how frequently value is tied to context, and how often we try to separate the two. I'm thinking of the things we place on dusty shelves, and I wonder if maybe, under different circumstances—in an environment that better reflects the nature of their designs— perceived flaws might become revelatory attributes.

On my way out of the kitchen, I crumple the Post-it, toss it in the trash.

SHOSH
home phone

ONCE UPON A TIME, PEOPLE didn't have phones—houses did.

Shosh stood in the kitchen, staring at a spot on the wall where, years ago, the home phone had once hung. She had no memory of a home phone, but this unpainted patch—in the exact shape of that prehistoric communication device—was proof of its existence, a true eyesore of a memorial.

It was late. When she'd gotten home that night, the house was quiet, likely asleep. She'd shrugged off her coat in the living room, come to the kitchen for a snack, and even though this beige outline had always been there, it was as if she hadn't seen it until now.

How could they leave it like this? It's not like it required major construction. Just a touch-up. But then, these were the same parents who refused to enter their dead daughter's room. Avoidance was their MO.

A little voice, in the back of her mind: *They aren't the only ones who haven't gone in her room.*

Shosh took out her phone and dialed Ruth.

"Hum-hey."

"You awake?"

"Whattimeisit?"

"What was that poem you quoted. The Emily Dickinson."

Ruth cleared her throat like a bullfrog in heat. "I don't . . . know . . . anything . . ."

"I'm staring at a spot on my kitchen wall."

"Okay."

"I'm staring at a spot on my kitchen wall that's been unpainted for as long as I've been alive. In the shape of a landline telephone, if you can believe it."

A beat, then: "Imma take a leak. Hang on."

When Ruth got back on the line, Shosh asked about the statute of limitations on paint touch-ups. "I'm thinking ten months, right? Longer than that, and you're just a lazy son of a bitch."

"Lazy is one possibility," said Ruth.

"You've got another?"

"Well. If you're not too lazy to do a touch-up, you're trying to prove something to somebody. So you leave it. To make a point."

Shosh thanked Ruth, hung up, then retrieved a brush and half-empty bucket of paint from the garage. And when the kitchen was done, she went upstairs to take care of the other thing, only instead of opening the door to her sister's bedroom—not to clean the room, not to change anything, just to be in it—she walked right past it, shut herself in her own room, googled "Emily Dickinson immortality," and read poems until the sun came up.

EVAN
phone home

"I WISH YOU'D LET ME come with you."

Mom slips her cereal bowl into the crowded top rack, a spot perfectly allocated for a bowl of its size. In the same motion, she pulls a soap pod out from under the sink, drops it into the dishwasher without looking, shuts the door, and presses start.

If there were some sort of dishwashing Olympics, there would be no contest.

"Mom—"

"I don't know what you want me to say, Evan. The appointments are seriously not a big deal."

"Great. So I'll come with. No big deal."

She studies the calendar on the kitchen wall. "I was thinking taco casserole for Bubba Night this week? I feel awful you guys are always stuck with pizza."

"We love pizza."

"I could make a double batch. That would cover Tuesday and Wednesday."

Without even knowing it, she starts scratching the spot on her chest again. Yesterday, when I asked her about it, she said it was "just a radiation burn," which, *what the hell*. Only after I pushed did she explain that she'd started to get a little sunburn in the square shape of the radiation beam, and that she'd gotten some creams for it, but because the treatments were five times a week for ten weeks, there was really nothing to do but wait for the ten weeks to end. That was when I told her I was coming with her today, and she got all sarcastic about me thinking I could protect her from a sunburn, and I said that's not what this was about, and here we are.

"Assuming you guys could limit yourselves to not eating thirds," she says, still staring at the calendar, scratching away. "I don't know what it is about taco casserole that turns my boys into a warren of feral foxes."

"Earth."

"What?"

"A group of foxes is called an *earth*."

"Really?"

"Mom."

"Wait, how do you know that?"

"I'm coming with you."

She turns from the calendar, and I can see in her eyes that she's clocked my tone: we are now speaking as adults. "No, Evan. You're not."

"You said some people bring family with them. I don't like the thought of you being there alone."

"Too bad."

"Mom—"

"Goddamn it, Evan, I need to make it ordinary!" She turns away; I freeze, the blood rushing to my face, and when she turns back, she's smiling through tears. "Do you know how many texts I get from women who—they're looking for support, someone to share the experience with, and maybe one day I'll need that too. But right now, I need it to be ordinary. I go by myself. Like any old appointment. Yeah?"

I swallow my own tears down. "Yeah."

"Okay." She brushes her eyes with the backs of her hands, turns to face the calendar again. "I'm going with taco casserole."

When Mom had the lumpectomy back in August, it crossed my mind that someone should tell Dad. I thought about calling him, but then his name came up in my Instagram feed as a "suggested follow," and because I couldn't *believe* Dad was on Instagram, I clicked over to his account, where I found a trove of photos that induced a waking nightmare, followed by one of my more memorable storms. There were photos of Stacey on the beach. Photos of them on walks with that wilted potato of a poodle, or with Stacey's son and his girlfriend, and through it all, Dad's happiness was on display for all to see. And so began a new mentality as it related to my father: "Fuck him," I said that day, tossing my phone on the bed.

But on this day, as Mom drives to her radiation appointment alone, I decide to call him. Yes, it involves reaching out, but given my aforementioned mentality, the call is less an olive branch, more a nightstick.

I make the call from my room.

"Hello?" answers a voice I don't recognize.

"Um—hi?"

"Oh, hey. Is this Evan?"

And here I was, all ready to rumble; I can feel the nightstick slipping away. "I'm sorry—who are you?"

"I'm Ruth. Your dad's girlfriend's son's girlfriend."

Even as part of me feels my spirit exit my body, the other part of me acknowledges the absurdity of the moment. I almost ask after the wilted potato of a dog.

"Guess this is kind of weird, huh," says Ruth, a comment that requires no further action on my part. "Greg says you're headed to Alaska next year? Good on you, man. I've never been, not sure I could handle the cold, you know?"

I am not having this conversation with my dad's girlfriend's son's girlfriend, with whom, apparently, he is on a first-name basis.

"Is *Greg* around?" I ask.

By the time Dad answers, I almost forget why I called.

"Hey, kiddo."

"Hey, Greg."

Silence, and then: "Okay."

"Did your cell phone transform into a landline?" I ask. (Zing!)

"What? Oh—sorry, no. I was . . . preoccupied."

A quick mental tally of that particular word uttered in that particular way leads to the conclusion that Dad's preoccupation had occurred in either the bedroom or the bathroom, and either way, gross, moving on.

"Mom has cancer." Like that. Make it hurt.

Nothing on the other end of the line. Just breathing.

"We don't want anything from you," I say. "I just thought maybe you'd like to know the woman you spent—" *Shit.* How long were they together? I try to calculate on the fly, but before I get there—

"Twenty-one years, bud."

"The woman you spent twenty-one years with has breast

cancer, and I thought you'd maybe want to know."

Somehow, in the ensuing moments of silence, the truth washes over me in a cold wave of reality.

"Evan . . ."

"You already know."

"Just because I'm not there doesn't mean your mom and I don't talk," and now he's off to the races, ever the bullshitter, about the variety of ways people can be present. He tells me he's proud of me, tells me Mom is in good hands, and I want to say, *Yes, but my hands aren't the ones who held hers at an altar and promised to be with her in sickness* . . .

"You're just like him," I say quietly.

"Like who?"

One of the more brilliant moves in E.T. is that you never see the dad. You feel him in the absent spaces: when Elliott and Michael find one of his old shirts in the garage and remember the way he smells; or early on, when Elliott makes his mom cry by simply mentioning how their dad went to Mexico; and later, when Elliott and Michael miss curfew and their mom has to go out looking for them, we hear her mutter the word *Mexico* under her breath, and we realize she's not mad at her kids for not coming home—she's mad at her husband for leaving.

Dee Wallace is the actress who plays the mom. I looked it up. "*Mexico*," she says, backing out of the driveway to go look for her kids.

Sometimes, it just takes one word to communicate a world of emotion.

"Fuck you, Dad."

Sometimes, it takes three.

UNST, SHETLAND ISLES

UNCLE ARRAN CURSED THE DAY Ewan's mother died. Not because of any extraordinary love lost for the woman, but because of the paints she'd left in young Ewan's keep. He'd often scowl at Ewan, mumble something about a waste of time, and Ewan would shrug, as if to demonstrate how little the paints meant to him.

A lie. He loved painting more than anything.

Ewan spent his days in the sixareen with his uncle, fishing for herring or cod off the northern shores. It was tiresome work; in the evenings, Uncle Arran would collapse in the croft and declare in a great heaving sigh, "Hit's göd ta lay you doon in your ain calf grund." Ewan would pretend to agree, but the truth was, he *wasn't* comfortable—not in his own home, not in his own skin. Each week, he counted down the days to his one day off, when he could finally carry his paints to the coastal shore and let himself be himself.

To be born and raised in a place is to mistake its peculiarity for normality: Ewan was always lonely, he just never knew it.

Though to be sure, less lonely when his mother was alive. Back then, they would stand at the edge of the sea together, gazing across the distant horizon—Norway, just three hundred kilometers away—and imagine Vikings in ships, the terror of looming invasions and ensuing battles, and Ewan would smell the fish, echoes of his ancient past all mixed up with his present, here, on this island tucked in the Northern Atlantic. He supposed it was beautiful—sandy beaches and coastal cliffs, rolling grasslands and grazing sheep—but at fourteen years of age, it was a fine line between beauty and boredom. Ewan longed for more, though more of *what*, he couldn't say, only that he felt closest to achieving it while painting.

He kept to small rocks on the beach, painting miniature tableaus so as not to waste too much stock at once. However, on occasion, the unnamed desire burned too bright for small rocks, and when this happened, Ewan retreated to a section of beach where the cliff wall was flat and north-facing, veiled from the prying eyes of his uncle.

Here, in this hidden alcove, Ewan painted her.

He had no name for the girl. Any attempt to give her one felt overreaching, and because she did not exist anywhere aside from the swimmy-sea of his mind, Ewan was content to paint her against cold rock many times over. The girl had freckles and flowy hair held back by a headband. The band itself was distinctive for its wings, one on either side of her head, as if the girl was about to take flight. Befitting, given the fact that Unst was rife with seabirds. They often joined Ewan in the secret alcove, gathering and flapping, wailing and diving as he worked. In their chaos, Ewan found calm, and a certain inspiration when it came to the finer qualities of the girl's face: like a seabird, she was bound by neither land nor water.

Only when he finished a portrait, stepping back to admire her face, was Ewan able to agree with his uncle. "Aye," he would say. "Hit's göd ta lay you doon in your ain calf grund."

• • •

Everything tells a story. Some stories are born in the wrong place, at the wrong time. Some need to be painted into their proper place. That's what Ewan was thinking one bright spring morning when Uncle Arran told him to pack a bag. "Gyaan ta da sound," was all his uncle said, and Ewan felt a stirring of the spirit.

At least twice a year, Uncle Arran disappeared to the nearest town with supplies of wool and salted herring, only to return days later with empty hands and black eyes, flooding the croft with the vinegar-stench of drink. This was the first time Ewan had been invited to accompany his uncle to town, and while part of him wondered at the change of heart, he suspected the answer was found in Arran's ever-worsening cough. His uncle was not a young man, nor healthy, nor particularly warm; but neither was he cruel. If he was to leave this earth, he would not leave his nephew stranded in the north winds.

It was a daylong journey. As they traveled, Ewan listened to his uncle sing songs in Norn, of boats and strong gales. "*Starka virna vestalie, obadeea, obadeea*," sang Arran, and Ewan wondered at the life of his uncle, who he was now, who he might once have been.

Entering town, Ewan saw things he'd only imagined: buildings of stone, alleys and shops, a dock with ships and rolling casks. The hills were still there, the coast and the grasslands, traces of the past mixed with the present. A world he knew beneath a world anew.

"Dunna staand dere laek a midderless foal," said Uncle Arran, and Ewan hurried behind him, down one street, then another. Eventually, Arran pointed to a stoop, told Ewan to wait, and then disappeared inside a building.

Ewan sat and waited. He tried to let his senses acclimate to the buzz of town.

Minutes passed when, from the din, a song began to emerge, a high lilting melody like nothing he'd heard. The song arose from a small cluster of tents down the street, vendors selling wares. Ewan stared at the tents as the scales of his mind tipped one way, then the other: the potential reprimand of his uncle weighed against his own curiosity. In the end, it was no contest.

He stood, hurried down the street; among the vendors were crofters, carpenters, fishermen. But when he finally pinpointed the location of the song, he could barely believe what he was seeing—a tent full of paintings. He entered this tent as if entering a church: reverent, fearful, endlessly aware of his own shortcomings. Canvas paintings were everywhere, stacked on tables, packed in crates. Temporarily distracted by the abundance of color, he forgot about the song, instead riffling through the nearest box to find paintings of cobbled streets, of ships sailing on the ocean. There were birds and musical instruments and a curious depiction of a woman sinking under waves, a small smile on her face. Just as he was about to stand and leave (surely Uncle Arran would discover his malfeasance any minute now), Ewan froze, felt his heart in his boots—

He stared at the painting, wondered how it could be. He was shocked, of course, mystified, but there was no doubt. The hair, the eyes, the nose with that point he always hated—

It was all there. He was all there.

It was him in the painting. Like staring in a mirror.

"Fine day a wadder," said the quiet voice of the vendor behind him, and when Ewan turned, he found himself face-to-face with a girl his own age, freckles scattered across her nose and cheeks, hair held back by a band with wings. "I found du," said the girl, and for a moment, they stared at each other, two souls painted into the proper place, and Ewan's heart lifted from his boots to his chest to his throat, flew right out of his head and into the sky, bound by neither land nor water.

PART FOUR

SONATA

EVAN

that ghost is not your daughter

I'M STILL GETTING DRESSED WHEN the doorbell rings. Downstairs, I hear Will let her in, and now the sound of mumbled discussion, the Grand Inquisition of which I can scarcely imagine, and by the time I finish getting Michael's iconic "knife-through-head" hat in place and clamber down the stairs, Will is all-out grilling Ali.

"I don't get it," he says.

Ali eyes me like, *Help.*

I shrug like, *Told you.*

She looks back at Will. "You've read *The Lord of the Rings*, right?"

"I'm seven."

"Right. Okay. Well. There's this hobbit named Frodo Baggins."

"You're Frodo?"

"Even better. I'm Frodo's wayward cousin, *Alfredo* Baggins."

After a solid eight-count of Will just staring at Ali, I hand her the E.T. mask and large white sheet, which she accepts with tired resignation.

"I really thought this would be the year," she says, dutifully donning the mask.

"Alfredo Baggins?"

"I thought it was funny."

Ali throws the sheet over her entire costume, E.T. mask and

all. I pat her on the back, tell her there's always next year, knowing full well that she'll be E.T. every year until Will no longer expects it, at which point, Ali's Halloween costume will be the least of my concerns.

Mom comes out of the bedroom dressed like Michael and Elliott's mom in the movie, and to her credit, she absolutely owns the leopard-print, cat-masked ensemble. Will, of course, is dressed just like Elliott—or really, he always is, but right now he's dressed like trick-or-treat Elliott, swapping out the red hoodie for a gray one and adding gray face paint and a cape.

"Okay, guys," says Mom, holding up the Polaroid camera, even quoting the movie before taking our photo: "'Ahh, you look great!'"

A couple shots in, Will turns to Ali with all the stoicism of a bored cat. From under the thin white sheet, Ali meets his gaze until finally giving in and crouching low to the ground in her best physical mimicry of E.T.'s stature. After a few more photos, we head out for an evening of fan-fic dream-cast trick-or-treating.

Some two hours later, returning as heroes, we dump the candy on the living room floor, reporting the high points of horror and hilarity to Mom, and together we turn to the TV, our spirits filled with ghoulish goodwill, ready to experience the true meaning of Halloween: the annual E.T. viewing.

Yes, Will and I have seen it roughly fifty times since last Halloween, but Mom and Ali haven't seen it since, and even if they had, you don't mess with the Taft/Pilgrim Halloween traditions. Eventually, we arrive at the spot in the movie where the characters are trick-or-treating, and as our cosplay was so exquisite, it almost feels like the actors in the movie are cosplaying us. In the scene, the kids are trying to get E.T. out of the house without their mom realizing, so they put a sheet over his head and pretend he's their little sister, and their mom is all, *Oh, Gertie, you're such a cute ghost*, and if I have one gripe with the film, it's this plot point.

"So wait," says Ali.

"Don't do it," I say.

"I'm just trying to clarify."

"It's not worth it."

Ali points to the screen. "I get the woman has a lot on her plate, but . . . does she really think E.T. is her daughter?"

"I'm with Ali." Mom unwraps a single-serving Twizzlers, lets it hang from her mouth as she talks. "I've never been super clear about what's going on here."

Will picks up the remote, pauses the movie, and proceeds to explain in detail *exactly* what is happening and why. I love it when he gets this way, like we're patients in a waiting room, and he's all, "Hi, I'm Will Taft, ETMD, and I'm afraid you have a severe case of Acute Boring Normalness."

Needless to say, when he's done, he pushes play, and no one asks another question for the rest of the movie. And in the final scene, hyped up on sugar and feelings, all four of us weep openly, and I don't know—some families golf together, some bake pies, some garden or go to the beach. As for us, we cry together at heart-warming cinema.

"Okay, Will. Time for bed." Mom slaps her knees, makes an ungodly amount of noise getting off the couch, and I can't help but worry. Then she catches my eye, smiles, and I worry about *that*. Is she smiling because she's okay, or is she smiling to keep me from worrying because she's not okay?

"What do you say to Evan and Ali for another special Hallow-een?" she says.

Will stumbles to Ali, throws both arms around her neck. "You're a pretty okay E.T.," he says, and Ali hugs him back, all, "Thanks, Will," in love-laced sarcasm.

And now he's in front of me, those little arms wide open, head tilted off to the side, and it occurs to me that for the rest of my life—from now until the day I die—every embrace will be measured against this.

"My heart glows to you," he says in my ear.

"I'll be right here," I say.

And I consider the physics of love, wonder how it's possible to fit the whole world in a hug.

SHOSH
last times

IT WAS THE KIND OF fall night when the stars felt like rain, the sky an umbrella tilting to shield her. Shosh sat in the open window of her bedroom, legs dangling, her attention split between the symphony above and the cacophony below. The neighborhood was full of costumed children, scattering and gathering like ants to a found crumb. Parents followed the younger ones, while older ones wore bloodier, sexier costumes, and running under it all, the ghost-singer sang of loss and love and trees in snow.

This was her life now: a film with its own original score.

She drained the last of the can, went downstairs, grabbed another from the fridge; back upstairs, on the floor of her room, she pulled a handle of vodka from under her bed. From the open window, she emptied half the Diet Coke onto the dying rosebushes two stories down, then refilled the can from the handle.

Across the street, a unicorn laughed with a Jack Skellington.

A group of superheroes, Marvel and DC alike, cut through a yard together.

A family of children in both Cubs and White Sox uniforms.

How harmonious was the world on Halloween night.

Her phone buzzed; she pulled it out to find an incoming Face-Time call from Ms. Clark, but when she swiped to open, a different face peered back at her.

"Well, hello, Baby Yoda," she said, smiling.

In possibly the cutest voice of all time—dead serious, and with a slight lisp—Charlie responded, "My name ith Grogu."

"Right," nodded Shosh. "Grogu, sorry."

Charlie craned his neck, as if trying to poke his head through the phone. "What are you thuppoth to be?"

"I am"—Shosh made a scary face and turned one hand into a claw—"*a creature of the night*," she said in a raspy voice. Charlie smile-screamed, dropped the phone, and ran away.

For a second, Shosh was left staring at the Clarks' living room ceiling, until Ms. Clark picked up the phone. "Hey, sorry. He insisted on calling to show you his costume."

"I'm glad he did. Big night for the little man."

"You have no idea. We got halfway through trick-or-treating when he suddenly needed to pee. Which, I won't bore you with the details of potty training, but let's just say is a big win right now. How are you?"

"Oh, you know. Sitting here, watching the neighborhood lose its mind."

"Please tell me you're not in that window again."

"I'm not in the window again?"

She saw it in her eyes first—the transition from jovial to sour—and Shosh knew she was sunk.

"Can I ask you a question?" said Ms. Clark.

"Okay."

"Why do you think you drink?"

The topic had been alluded to, danced around, but never directly approached. Shosh could easily list a hundred little reasons—and one reason so big it threatened to consume her from the inside out—but all she said was, "Why not? It's not like I drive."

Ms. Clark flinched, looked away—likely toward the bathroom, where little Charlie was taking care of business. "I don't have time for this right now," she said, sighing, then looking back at Shosh. "I'm glad you don't drive, Shosh. That tells me you're considering the safety and well-being of others. I only wish you'd give yourself the same consideration."

When the call ended, Shosh realized Ms. Clark had left off her usual request for Shosh to tell her one thing about Stevie. It was a small thing, and obviously Ms. Clark had her own shit tonight to worry about, but it left Shosh feeling undone. "One thing about her," she said to the bustling neighborhood below, "was that she loved trick-or-treating."

Down below, a little kid in a ghost costume was yelling at a Darth Vader for leaving him behind, and Shosh had a sudden memory: She was twelve, Stevie fourteen. They'd always gone trick-or-treating together, only that year, Stevie had brought a new friend. Shosh couldn't remember her name, but the girl had shown up at their house without a costume, and kept her head in her phone all night, and Shosh had been so mad at Stevie for bringing this girl along. The year after that, Stevie said she felt too old to go out, which made the year with her stupid friend their last time trick-or-treating together.

Her phone buzzed with texts from Ms. Clark:

> Let's talk soon, OK? I'm here.
> And do me a favor?
> Get out of the goddamn window, pls and thx

Pushing herself backward into bed, Shosh considered the wording of Ms. Clark's initial question: Not *Why do you drink*, but *Why do you think you drink?* The inclusion of those two words—*you think*—implied Ms. Clark had her own opinion on the subject. If you're going to ask an imposing question, worded in such a way as to make it clear you've got your own answer, you should be forced to weigh in, thought Shosh, irritated, flipping back to their thread.

> Shosh: Out of the window, happy now?

Ms. Clark: Very, thank you

> Shosh: So . . .
> Why do *you* think I drink?

Ms. Clark: You're the only one who can answer that

> Shosh: She's gone. And she's never coming back

Ms. Clark: I know
And I don't doubt that reason
But I think sometimes . . .
. . .
. . .
It's possible to lose something so big that it overshadows other losses.

Shosh was pissed. Stevie had been her moon; Ms. Clark knew this was true, but apparently, losing one's moon wasn't enough of a reason to want to numb the pain. She tossed her phone to the floor, stared at the ceiling, listened to the distant sounds of kids begging for candy.

Her mom, as a teacher herself, had always had a soft spot for Ms. Clark. "The best ones don't educate, so much as lead students to the pond of education," she liked to say. Which fit Ms. Clark to a tee. Getting straight answers had always been a challenge; rather than answer your question, she'd calmly take you by the hand and lead you to water.

It's possible to lose something so big that it overshadows other losses.

Shosh closed her eyes and tried to remember the last time she'd been onstage—properly onstage, not some haphazard, drunken haze—but she couldn't. For years, theater had consumed her, but like a final year of trick-or-treating, you don't always know your last time is coming until it's gone.

EVAN

impossible migrations

"I WOULDN'T SAY I THINK about skunks *every* day."

"Very sensible of you."

"I do wonder about their pee, though."

"You're only human."

Ali and I are on the floor in my bedroom, half watching *The Nightmare Before Christmas* on my laptop, holding tight the spirit of Halloween. I've got my sketch pad, drawing Jack and Sally as vampires; across the hall, Mom still hasn't come out of Will's room. Ten-to-one, she fell asleep in his bed. She's always doing that.

"So like—the stuff they spray to ward off predators," says Ali. "Is that skunk piss?"

"Did you know there are hundreds of new ocean species discovered each year?"

"Are they so evolved they've learned to weaponize their own urine?"

"Makes a man wonder what kind of seafood he *could* be eating, is all I'm saying."

"I had this dream once where I was being chased by a fish with feet," says Ali.

"Did it catch you?"

"I ducked inside a Five Guys at the last second."

"Well, now I want Five Guys."

"What do you think it means?"

"I think burger cravings are pretty straightforward."

"My dream, Ev."

"Well, there's the obvious," I say.

"What obvious?"

"Didn't you catch like four buckets of fish with your uncle last summer? Makes sense they'd wanna hop out and catch you."

A light knock on the door and Mom pops her head in. "Hey, guys."

"Hey," I say. "Thought you'd fallen asleep in there."

A massive yawn. "I did, actually. That kid has the softest bed in the house."

"How'd he do?"

"Sweet buddy is sweet." She points to my computer on the floor in front of us. "Jack in Christmas Land?"

"Christmas Town, Mom."

Ali sucks in a breath. "Good thing Will's not here; he'd flip a lid."

Mom is all, "Well, actually," and then explains how even though the place is technically called "Christmas Town," later, in the town hall scene, Jack refers to it as "Christmas Land" via song. Having set us straight, she watches the movie for a second, hums a few bars of "What's This?" before yawning again. "Okay, kids. I'm off to bed."

I hop off the floor, cross the room, and hug her.

"Tonight was good," she says.

"Tonight was great."

A quick goodbye to Ali, and then Mom leaves, and Ali says, "Your mom's my hero."

"Same."

"You said she got a second job?"

"Yeah. Why?"

"Nothing. She's just gone more than usual. And seems tired."

I don't know how much longer I can keep Mom's cancer a secret from Ali. I have no idea why it's so hard for me to tell her, but the leading theory is that my brain has its own brain, which has a mind of its own, and I mean, that shit's out of my hands.

Ali picks up my half-finished sketch of Sally sucking blood from Jack's neck. "I swear to God, Evan. If you wind up going to college, and you don't go to art school, I will hunt you down. This is brilliant."

"It's just a doodle." I grab it back.

Ali shakes her head, all, "Evan, Evan, Evan."

"Stop it."

"Evan, Evan, Evan, Evan."

We've had some version of this conversation ever since her birthday a few years ago when I gave her a framed sketch of Mulder and Scully at a bowling alley with David and Alexis Rose. Thing is, I know my drawings aren't *bad*. But I also know how good you have to be to be good. And I'm nowhere close.

"What's the latest from Nightbird?" asks Ali.

"Nothing new since our trek to the Winter Lighthouse."

"Lemme see the lyrics again?"

I open my Notes app, hand her my phone. On my laptop, Jack corrals everyone in Halloween Town to band together and steal Christmas. "Will says the songs in this movie were written before the screenplay. Can you imagine? I mean, the sheer coordination it would take—"

"'Drifting down Brooklyn.'" Ali drops my phone, pulls out her own.

"What?"

Typing, scrolling, she says, "You don't drift down a city. You drift through a city, or maybe in one. You know what you drift down?"

She smiles, hands the phone to me. It's open to Maps, zoomed in on my neighborhood.

"Brooklyn Way," I read. "It's a street."

"And look." She points to a spot on the phone where Brooklyn intersects with Division. "This is it, right? The Winter Lighthouse?"

"Alfredo Magellan Baggins."

"Everybody goes with Magellan."

"Alfredo Ernest Shackleton Baggins."

We hop up, slip on our shoes, coats, hats.

"Which one is he again?" asks Ali.

"Antarctica, I think."

We're halfway down the street before it occurs to either of us that we left Jack and Sally to fend for themselves.

"Plenty of people love Hamilton, but only one family has a back patio named Lin-Manuel Veranda."

"To be fair," says Ali, "I'm guessing you're the only family whose back patio has a name at all."

She blows into her hands, her nose beet red, and even though it's late on Halloween night, our little neighborhood is tucked away, the streets quiet and cold, the moon a neon apple, big and ripe. It's the kind of night that gets you itching to make trouble (as if), like egging a house (right) or tossing a roll of toilet paper into a tree (can you even). Ali and me, we'd never do that sort of thing, but it's this feeling of possibility that brings the night alive, makes it buzz like a hive on the verge.

We walk down the middle of the street like it's named after us.

"Evan?"

"Yes."

"I asked about the Headlands application like two blocks back."

"Right."

"And you sort of derailed."

"No, I asked if you'd seen *Moana*, which led to the Miranda tangent. I was working my way to an answer."

"Okay."

"So have you seen it?"

"You mean the epic tale of Moana of Motunui, presumptive heir to the throne, who risks it all to find the demigod Maui in order to save her people from certain doom? Yes, I've seen it. I'm not a complete barbarian."

From Chestnut to Ash, we cut over to the first of the compass streets: Southview, Westlawn, Eastbrook. I tell Ali about one of the Headlands essays, which asked me to consider a favorite book or movie and break down why it affected me so much.

"Are you not doing E.T.?"

"I thought about it. And then immediately spun out, trying to think of where to start. Anyway, I'm sure this comes as a shock, but *Moana* makes me cry."

"*Sacrebleu!*"

"Right, but see, I cry in weird places. Like the scene where she's little and first meets the water? Feels the call of the ocean? I always cry at that. And Will never says a word, just crawls into my lap," and I wonder at the magical properties of walking with a friend at night, the ways it loosens the lips and soul. Eventually, we cross into a newer section of the neighborhood where city planners were less concerned with the compass, more concerned with first name alliteration: Rhodes Road; Sage Street; Daphne Drive. After a left on Adalynn Avenue, nearing Division, the air changes, and a few minutes later, we're at the intersection with Brooklyn, standing at the foot of the Winter Lighthouse.

"You still haven't answered my question," says Ali.

"The application deadline is November thirtieth."

Ali bounces in the cold, staring up at the house. "I know Headlands is the ocean to your Moana, Ev. What I don't understand is this new undercurrent whenever you talk about it. Like you know it's not happening."

We stand there, our breath coming and going in little wispy flowers, blossoming and dying in front of our eyes. Nothing proves your own mortality like breathing on a cold night.

"Mom has breast cancer."

Ali's wisps disappear. Then, one long wisp: "Shit."

"Or I guess—she *had* it? I don't really know how to . . ."

"Is she okay?"

"She had a lumpectomy at the end of August."

"Shit, Ev."

"Oncologist says we got lucky. Caught it early, so it hadn't spread. She doesn't need chemo."

"That's great. I mean—that's great, right?"

"Yeah."

"So . . ."

"She's in the middle of radiation treatments now."

"I always thought—for some reason, radiation and chemo—"

"There's a million ways it can go. Sometimes radiation and chemo go together, sometimes not. In Mom's case, they removed the lump during surgery, but also some lymph nodes to see if it had spread, which it hadn't. Radiation makes sure there aren't any lingering cancer cells. And then hormone treatment for like—five years, I think."

"Does your dad know?"

"Yes, he does, fuck him very much. Hasn't come to visit once, but I guess they talk, which was news to me."

Ali asks if there's anything she can do, and I tell her it's probably best she doesn't mention it to anyone, not even Mom, who's been really private about the whole thing. "Other cancer survivors have been calling, texting. Friends of friends, mostly, people she barely knows, looking for someone to share the experience with. Mom is nice, of course, but she wants no part of it."

"Wait—the lumpectomy was end of August, you said."

"Yeah."

"So when did she tell you?"

"The night before Heather's party."

A beat, the revelation in Ali's eyes, the same one I had with Maya, about why I left that night. Do you understand, Ali? All things bend toward atrophy. If the body is a machine, its end result is unavoidable: broken and abandoned, a rusted car on the side of the road. Please tell me you understand now why I can't leave.

"That's the undercurrent," Ali says, all these wisps, tiny proofs of life. "You're not worried you won't get accepted to Headlands. You're worried you will."

And it hits me. Why I resisted telling Ali. I know her well enough to know it won't be enough. She'll push me to go anyway, and I'll have to build my case, give her my list of reasons why Headlands won't work, show her all the ways it could go wrong.

Maya calls it *catastrophizing*. Cognitive distortion. Playing out every situation to its utmost disaster.

I call it planning ahead.

It goes like this: What will happen to Will? Dad is gone, Mom is sick, and even if she gets better, what if . . .

It comes back. Cancer does that. And even if it doesn't, what if . . .

She gets in a car accident. Or passes out and hits her head on the sidewalk? What if . . .

Dad never comes back, and Will grows up without a father or an older brother? Or what if . . .

Dad *does* come back? What if he wants to *stay*, and Mom is weak from being sick, and Will is weak from being seven, and no one's voice is strong enough to tell Dad he had his chance, and what if . . .

There's a tornado, or a flood, or pieces of an exploded airplane fall through the roof, or . . .

Nuclear fallout and I'm not here to protect them from the scavengers of a scorched Earth, or airborne disease and I'm not here to shield them, or things I've never considered, events I've never anticipated, what if I'm not here to meet all possible unnamed threats?

"Learn to investigate your own thoughts, and you can self-correct," Maya always says. "It's called *decatastrophizing*."

I try. Really, I do. I know my fears aren't logical or probable. Trouble is, logic and probability rarely factor into catastrophe. If plane crashes were probable, no one would ever fly. If collapsed bridges were logical, we'd all go the long way around. Improbable illogicality is exactly what makes the catastrophe so catastrophic. So while I would love to live in a world where the pursuit of my own dream isn't potentially detrimental to the ones I love most, I'm too busy living in a world full of possibilities.

People call it that like it's a good thing.

Just like the song says, Ali and I drift down Brooklyn. Before long, a stretch of houses dead-ends abruptly at Willow Seed Park, this little minimalist playground full of shady trees, with an old swing set, a slide, a merry-go-round. Mom and I used to come here back in the pre-Will days.

All the houses are dark, the street abandoned, Willow Seed Park empty.

"What's the lyric again?" Ali asks.

Roaming streets we don't own, naming fears we do, our lives reincarnated in one cold breath after another—it seems right that I should recite lyrics neither of us can fully comprehend.

When I'm done, Ali is bouncing on her feet again, trying to get the blood flowing. "So I'm thinking I'll go for premed," she says. "Focus on oncology."

"Really?"

"What—you don't think I'd be a good doctor?"

Whenever talk of the future comes up, Ali's is the most casual air in the group, her artistic sensibility making it easy to fill in the blanks on our own: the Bushwick loft with exposed brick, all slapdash canvases and paint in the hair; the set of some indie film, director or cinematographer; some ancient village in the Himalayas, captured in her award-winning photography.

"Outside of *The X-Files*, I didn't know you were into science."

Ali smiles. "I love you for conflating science with science fiction. And maybe on a subconscious level, Scully was an early inspiration. But I started thinking about being a doctor two summers ago."

"What happened two summers ago?"

"The bike ramp happened two summers ago."

I flash on Ali soaring through the air, having taken the jump at too high a speed, hitting at an awkward angle, and landing a solid twelve feet from the ramp. "Dr. Flomenhoft was badass," she says. "Got to the point where I didn't *hate* going to my appointments. And then there was this tech in charge of the cast, and *she* was badass, and I just thought—maybe this is my thing."

I've often imagined Ali as a plant in the corner that only gets watered every few days, so it's alive, yes, but nothing close to what it could be under the right conditions. Not that her parents and friends aren't supportive, but sometimes, when a person is so at ease in their own skin, you take them for granted. I've known her longer than anyone, and her future has always been a mystery. I think my real hope was that wherever she landed, it would be with people who knew how to water her properly.

"You know what I think?" I say.

"What."

"I think you'd make an excellent doctor. Probably the best ever."

"Thanks."

In the beam of a single streetlight, we stand at the literal end of the road, feeling the weight of the metaphor.

"You know what I think?" Ali says.

"What."

"I think preemptively shutting something down because you're afraid it won't work out is natural, but that doesn't make it right." She turns, looks at me. "I think you should let your brother's love make you better, not lesser. I think you should write that essay."

And like that, my list of reasons disintegrates.

We both look up at the giant moon, as if it might explain what we're doing here, what the songs mean, what I should do about Headlands, any of it.

"How many ocean species did you say?" she asks.

"Hundreds of new ones are discovered each year."

"And people thought birds migrated to the moon . . . ?"

"They sure did."

Eventually, we turn for home, and when I think of all the things through history that people have believed that ultimately proved untrue, it seems silly to think we know anything for sure now. But maybe that's the human condition: we'll believe in anything if it means believing in something.

SHOSH
missed connections

IVY KIDS ART NIGHT WAS a perennial program the week before Thanksgiving wherein Iverton Elementary students exhibited their artistic skills in one of three categories: a visual art show presented throughout the hallways of the school; a reading of an original piece presented in the library; or a theatrical performance presented onstage in the gym.

It was tradition for Shosh to help out with her mom's class; in years past, she'd bring a friend from school, and they'd help corral the kids onstage, teaching them cues, and quietly chuckling at the variety of first-grade shenanigans that passed for performance art.

Whose charmed life was that, she wondered now, watching from the wings as a group of small children squirmed in the moments before the opening number, a scene from *The Wizard of Oz*.

"You miss it, don't you?"

Shosh turned to find her mother beside her, eyes on the children.

"Miss what."

As she watched her students, Lana Bell's mouth curled up at each end, and while no one in their right minds could have called it a smile, it was as close as she'd gotten in months. "I know you think I came back to work too early. But I needed something that wasn't . . . to do with her. I needed an anchor, Shosh. We all do." She turned from her students to her child. "You miss it, right? Being onstage?"

She felt it in her shoulders mostly, her neck and arms too, as if she'd been thrusting a boulder up a hill for weeks. As if the mental strength required to push back against something that came so naturally had taken a physical toll. It was hard to say what irked her more: that she missed acting so much it hurt or that her mother saw it.

For just a second, Shosh imagined grabbing her mom around the waist, burying her head, crying, but instead, she said, "I need to pee."

"You'll miss the opening number."

But Shosh was gone, hopping offstage, crossing the gym for the doors. As soon as her feet hit the hallway, the voice of the ghost-singer materialized. It was the same song she'd accidentally plagiarized, about secrets hiding in trees of snow, and she was about to scream in frustration—over the music, over the stage, over her inability to outrun either—when a familiar face emerged from one of the bathroom doors.

"Oh. Hey." His eyes were a dusky blue, his hair long and half-tied back, and she knew she'd seen him before, but couldn't remember . . . "Chili's bathroom," he said.

The song was still there, though slightly diminished now.

"Right," she said. "With the little kid."

He smiled at his shoes, tucked a loose strand behind his ear. "That's my brother. Will. I'm Evan."

"Shosh."

"I know. We were in school together. I mean—I'm still in school. I'm a year younger."

Evan was cute in the way some big dogs were spineless: he had no idea what he was dealing with. Suddenly, Shosh found herself wishing she'd spent more than approximately zero-point-zero seconds in the mirror before leaving the house. Though considering he'd likely witnessed (or heard about) her drunken spectacle in the high school auditorium, and probably knew of her drunken spectacle at Heather Abernathy's party, her current appearance was the least of her concerns.

"Weird, huh?" He pointed to the bathroom door. "First Chili's, now here. I guess this is like our thing. Meeting at bathrooms."

She was about to joke that it was perfect fodder for a rom-com when the ghost-singer's song swelled, and she couldn't explain what happened next, but she could swear a flicker of recognition crossed Evan's eyes. Thinking back, she remembered a similar feeling that day at Chili's, a sense that she and Evan had once shared something—time, understanding, a place in the world. But the moment passed and they were two people alone in a hallway.

"Just so you know," he said, and when he looked at her, he spoke with resolve, confirming her suspicion that her reputation preceded her, while offering some consolation that it wasn't a reputation universally ridiculed. "Chris Bond's a primo squirrel turd. Everyone thinks so."

That night, and every night for a week, Shosh had trouble sleeping. She chalked it up to missing Stevie, to hangover headaches, to the ghost-singer's incessant songs. But on the eighth night of tossing and turning, she sat up in bed, squeezed a pillow to her chest, and reluctantly accepted the truth: Her insomnia had a name. It had dusky blue eyes and long hair half-tied back and carried itself with unassuming cuteness. "You've got to be fucking kidding me," she said to her empty bedroom. And though empty bedrooms rarely respond, on that night, she found hers to be particularly smug.

EVAN
mic drop

I GUESS THIS IS LIKE our thing. Meeting at bathrooms.

I am a lost cause.

My cause wandered into the woods alone and hasn't been seen for days.

"Hey—" Mom taps me on the shoulder.

"What?"

"I asked if everything came out okay."

She mimics a wide-mouthed emoji smile, to which I mimic a wide-eyed emoji stare. "Question. Could you possibly be a bigger nerd?"

It's not like I've never had a crush before. And in a lot of ways, this feels like that. When I see Shosh, my entire body turns into one of those lightning lamps—the nimblest of touches could set me off.

But there's something else, too, something I can't put my finger on.

"Do you know which book he chose?" Mom asks, and like the focus on a lens, I adjust from Shosh World to Real World.

"I'm guessing *E.T. Phones Home*. Maybe *E.T. Phones Home Alone?* Though he hates starting with a sequel."

In an effort to secure good seats, we got to the library early, but we should have known better. Iverton Elementary parents are no joke; as it turns out, our "early" was quite late, and we wound up standing at the rear of the crowded room, craning our necks for a view of the back of Will's head.

A teacher stands, welcomes us all to Ivy Kids Art Night, and a knot forms in my stomach. The hype in our house, building to this moment, cannot be overstated. We're still not sure which original comic Will is going to read, but suffice it to say, he's been approaching the evening with all the measured sobriety of a concert pianist. All the kids are in the front row (seemingly miles away), and while most of them are swiveling in their seats to wave at parents and friends, the back of Will's head remains statuesque, forward-facing, utterly dialed-in.

After the teacher explains how things will work—each student, in alphabetical order, will read one original story at the podium— she says, "And so, without further ado, let's give a big round of applause for our first student of the evening, Jeffrey Abrams, who will be reading his book entitled"—the teacher consults her clipboard, pauses, and then looks up with an apologetic air—"*Zombie Monster Blood Squad*," she says through a forced smile.

Mom whispers, "Bloody hell, Jeff," and as the lights dim, a kid probably twice the size of Will saunters to the podium, where he reads a rhyming story about an apocalyptic bloodbath. When it's over, the room claps while Mom and I blink.

Maggie Boone reads a story about building an armory in *Minecraft*.

Juliette Diallo reads a story about Avengers versus Ninja Turtles versus Godzilla.

Cade Hunter reads a story about the origin of football players' muscles.

Naomi Oliver reads a story about a unicorn-shark who eats people in midair.

Right around this point in the alphabet, Mom's eyes start darting around the room, and I get it, because here's the thing: When you have a Will in your life, you're on constant alert for Will breakers. Sometimes it's the obvious bully with mean eyes; sometimes, it's the one you least expect, hiding behind a grin. Our worry doesn't come from a place of shame or embarrassment, it comes from a place of protection: *This kid is ours and he's amazing and if you break his spirit, I will break your body.* Whenever this comes up with Maya, she reminds me that Will may be hypersensitive, but he's not helpless. These conversations always end with some version of me saying, "He's not like other kids," and Maya saying, "I know. But in lots of ways, he is. And you need to let him be."

After Abby Shafer finishes her story about a medieval knight in a jousting match gone awry (spoiler: he gets decapitated), the teacher introduces Will. We clap, and Mom whistles, and we try hard not to lose our shit—not just out of love, but out of fear.

Will breakers are everywhere.

"My book is called *Will's Question*," he says, standing at the podium in that red hoodie, a look of fierce determination on his face, and God, I love him so much.

He clears his throat, opens his book, and reads, "'First published in the United States of America, Taft Publishing. Copyright Will Taft.'" He pauses, leans in close to the mic. "That's me."

Someone chuckles.

I will track them down and make them pay.

"'Other books by Will Taft,'" he reads, turning a page. "'*Octopus Wins the Day. Minions Eating Pizza.* The E.T. Phones Home Trilogy.' Those are pretty good. '*The Great Snake Escape. Jack & Sally Go to the Moon. Burning Cities.*' I was having a bad day that day. '*Poomba Box Weenie. Up Fellas Up.*' Okay, I'll start reading this one now." He turns another page. "It's a picture book. So I'll describe the pictures as I read. Okay."

Another throat clear, and we're off to the races.

"'*Sometimes I ask myself,* Who am I?' This is a picture of me, standing on the edge of a cliff, screaming."

Mom's hand is suddenly squeezing mine—hard.

Will turns a page. "'*The question never gets out of my head.*' This is a picture of me looking at the reader, arms out, like this." He looks up—puts his arms out in a shrugging, *who knows* gesture—and then turns the page. "'*Just thinking about it is tiring.*' This is a picture of me sweating buckets, pulling my own hair." Another page. "'*Oh well!*' This is a picture of me trying to cheer up." And another page. "'*Hope I find out tomorrow!*' This is the last page. It's a picture of me, walking away. Sometimes I like to take really high steps—like this." Will proceeds to show the entire library how he likes to take really high steps.

There is more chuckling.

My kill list grows.

"The end," Will says into the mic, and we clap and cheer, and most of the other adults in the room clap, but you can tell they're not sure what just happened. "Sorry, wait, wait," Will says into the microphone. "I forgot to read the dedication."

The room goes quiet; Mom's grip on my hand is viselike.

"I dedicate this book to Steven Spielberg for making the great-est movie ever. And to my brother, Evan, who agrees with me about that. And to my mom"—Will leans right into the microphone and ends his reading with the loudest words of the night—"who's dying of cancer."

I know a Dairy Queen soft serve isn't literally the most delicious thing in the world, but try telling me that while I'm eating one. I have to turn on the radio just to drown out the sounds of our eager devouring. Like a pack of sweet-toothed wolves.

My phone buzzes with a text from Ali. I swipe it open to find a photo of two college applications: one to Georgetown, one to Baylor. Pretty good premed programs, she texts. Who knows if I'll get in, but I'm going for it.

I heart the photo *and* the text.

> Evan: If I could put my actual heart into this thread, I would

Ali: You kinda need that where it is tho

> Evan: ILY so much
> With fam now. BIG STUFF
> HAPPENING. More soon.

As we eat, NPR reports lewd conduct from some low-level politician, and before Mom can switch it off, Will asks, "What did he *do?*"

"Terrible things, honey." I can see the dilemma in her eyes: while she's not one to take a pass, we have enough to talk about, given what happened tonight, without the added tonnage of Men Behaving Badly.

"He said he was sorry." Will points to the radio. "I heard him."

Mom swivels in her seat to face him. "Remember that dinner at the Rays' house? When all the kids got a pack of fruit snacks for dessert? You ate yours, and then you ate Hannah's while her head was turned. And then, when your dad asked what you'd done, you said—"

"I took her fruit snacks and put them in my mouth."

Part of what makes a family is the collective sharing of stories, memories that act as shorthand: *remember when*, you say, and everyone is transported to that place, that time, that feeling. For a second, the three of us smile at this memory. But it's a joy turned sour by the absence of Dad.

"The man did say he was sorry," says Mom, eyes drifting, and I wonder who she's really talking about. "But it was the kind of apology you gave Hannah. You only said it because you got caught."

I have the sudden image of Dad squirming on the couch while Mom drinks wine in the doorway. I know about the gap in Stacey's teeth. I know about her wilted potato of a poodle and her grown son called Nick, and I've even talked with Ruth on the phone. And yet suddenly I'm wondering if I know the whole story.

"It's called a revelation of character, sweetie. And sometimes a person's character isn't what you thought." Mom reaches a hand back, rests it on Will's knee. "Will, I'd like to talk about what you said tonight."

"Can I have another ice cream?"

"No."

"I wanted water."

"Will—"

"That night, I wanted water." It's quiet for a second before Will continues: "So I got out of bed to go to the bathroom sink. And I heard you talking in Evan's room. You said you found a bump in your breast. And then you had your besieger, like my spinny-head tonsilation, but it's not the same, because Siri says bumps in breasts are cancer."

Mom looks at me like I'd betrayed her. "He didn't use my phone," I say, and before she can prod, Will says he used an iPad at school. "Siri said cancer was a disease of add-normal sale growth. And when I asked if people die of it, she said yes, a million-thousand every year. And there's no shield against it."

At first, I'm confused by his choice of words—and then it hits me. "That's why you stopped wearing them. The ouch-shields."

He tells us how, after that night, he snuck a few Band-Aids onto Mom while she was asleep, hoping they might protect her. "But they didn't work. Did they?"

Mom is crying now, gently patting Will's knee. He does this thing where he shrugs like an adult, all casual, *no big deal*, and something about such tiny shoulders performing this uniquely mundane gesture makes me want to bottle him up and keep him safe forever. "I thought maybe Band-Aids were magic," he says, looking out the window into the darkness of the Dairy Queen parking lot. "But magic's not really real. I only want to believe in really real things from now on."

It's like I can see the innocence seeping from his pores, gathering in a little cloud over his head before dissolving altogether.

Mom unbuckles her seat belt, climbs out of the car, and when I see what she's doing, I do the same. Together, we climb into the back seat with Will, a hug-mosaic of arms around necks, cheeks pressed together, and if ever a family shared all the languages of love, it's ours. "I love you," says one of us, as another says, "I love you," and the third says the same. Not a collective chorus, but an entangled cacophony.

We are a perfect mess of I love yous.

"Plus, you were in bed for months," says Will.

"It was less than a week, honey."

Will turns to Mom with a look of intense curiosity. "Are you dying?"

Mom looks back at him with equal intensity. "Here's the deal. I didn't tell you about it because I didn't want you to worry. I don't know if that was right or not, but now you know, so—cards on the table?"

"Cards on the table."

"Siri was right that lots of people die from cancer. But the thing you need to know about your old mama bear is, she's basically the luckiest person in the world."

"Really?"

"Really," says Mom. "In fact, here's a list of reasons why I'm the luckiest. First, they found the cancer early, which means it was all in one place. When it's all in one place, it's easier to get. Second, I have doctors who are basically superheroes, okay? And I'm serious about this, they should be wearing capes, flying around, rescuing cats out of trees, that sort of thing."

"That's pretty good."

"Sure is. See, they cut the cancer out first, and then they burn it. Not messing around, these folks. Which leads to the third reason I'm lucky, which is a thing called health care, which we won't get into right now, but a lot of people don't have the same options I do. Some people don't have access to doctors."

"Superheroes."

"Right, some people don't have access to superheroes. And some people could maybe see a superhero but wouldn't have any way to pay for it. So I'm lucky there, too. Now I go in five times a week for more treatment, and when that's done, I'll take a pill for the next five years or so."

"Five years?" Will counts on his fingers. "I'll be twelve."

"Yes, you will, sweetie. And that's the main reason I'm so lucky. No one else in the world has you two for their family. My Will." She kisses Will's head. "And my Evan."

When she kisses my head, her arms tighten around my neck, and I smell the lavender soap she uses—the smell of Mom—and she holds me a beat longer.

"So what do you think? Pretty lucky, huh?"

"Yup."

Will sighs in dramatically adult tones, turns toward the window, and I wonder if he's looking through it or into it, at the reflection of our love mosaic inside the car. "By the way," he says, those tiny gaseous particles seeping from his pores, gathering in a cloud, disappearing forever. "It's *William* now."

SHOSH
cornucopia dystopia

SHOSH HATED THE MALL: THE facilitated quaintness, the junk-stuffs of vendors; she hated the way it smelled, a nasal assault at every turn; she hated the teams of kiosk employees who made her feel guilty for passing on their offers to "show her something," when all she was trying to do was walk down the fucking hall. Shopping at the mall made her feel like a consumer bot looking for shiny new toys, never once stopping to wonder at the urge.

"God, Shosh. Tell us how you really feel."

She and her cousin—whose actual name was Karen, and who took to heart the responsibilities incumbent upon Karens the world over—had never seen eye to eye on anything.

"I'm not saying *you* should hate the mall," said Shosh.

"Thanks for clarifying," said Karen. "Us consumer bots, we're not so much with the words."

"*Girls.*" Shosh's mom glared down the table as she passed a giant bowl of mashed potatoes.

"*She* started it," Karen said, jabbing her fork in Shosh's direction. "With her judgmental bullshit."

"*Hey,*" said Aunt Helen. "None of that, now."

Thanksgiving had always been Shosh's least favorite holiday. Every year, they'd wake at the break of dawn, climb into the car for the hour-ish drive to Elgin, where Shosh's grandparents lived. Outside of Stevie, Nona and Pop-pop were Shosh's favorite people on earth, which said a lot about how awful her cousin's family was, that she hated the day so much. Her mother's sister, Aunt Helen, was a woe-unto-me type, the kind of woman who'd never met a conversation she couldn't bend into some story of how she'd been wronged. Uncle Bobby rarely said much of anything that wasn't mildly offensive, and ended almost every sentence with "just saying," as if he hadn't just said it.

"In my day, we didn't have malls." Pop-pop, who'd been working on the same slice of turkey for a half hour, went on to describe the strange world of his youth, where, if you wanted shoes, you went to the shoe store, and if you wanted shirts, you went to the shirt store. "Took a person all day, just getting one place to the next."

"You're slouching, Herman." Nona patted his shoulder, and he sat up dutifully, before returning to his everlasting slice of turkey. "Say what you will about the mall," Nona went on, "we get our early-morning steps there, and I'm grateful for it. Especially during the cold months."

Pop-pop chewed, nodded. "Too true, my love."

This was the way of things with Nona and Pop-pop: she was forever telling him to quit slouching, and he was forever agreeing with her asides, and the gentleness with which they loved each other made Shosh wonder if marriage was something the world had simply outgrown. Even before the shadow of Stevie's death, her own mom and dad had never been especially caring toward one another. Occasionally, they'd say I love you, and maybe they did, but if so, it was the kind of love that didn't seem to require like.

"You see that new *international* restaurant in the food court?" asked Uncle Bobby.

Shosh put her fork on her plate, fake-smiled at her uncle. "House of Pancakes?"

Before Bobby could respond, Shosh's mom jumped in. "If you're talking about the new Thai place, I've heard only good things."

Uncle Bobby shrugged, waved his turkey leg around like a scepter. "Getting so a man can't find a burger anymore."

"Isn't it wedged between Wendy's and Burger King?" said Shosh.

Karen glared at her. "Thought you hated the mall."

"Oh, I do. But see, I'm concerned about the dwindling number of places in town where men can find burgers."

"Shosh," said her dad.

"I keep a map on my wall at home. Little thumbtacks indicating establishments that provide men with burgers, and I'm sorry to say there's only a shit-ton of places left."

"That's enough, Shosh."

"Down from a fuck-ton last year."

The table was primed to erupt when Pop-pop, seemingly out of the blue, said, "Sure have come a long way with tattoos."

That close to the precipice of an explosion, the silence felt weightier somehow.

"Dad?" Shosh's mom put down her utensils, eyes on her father.

"You're talking nonsense, Herman," said Nona.

Pop-pop continued, oblivious. "In my day, they were for sailors or floozies. You wanted a tattoo, you had to know somebody. Of course, things change. Generation before mine, they were for criminals or royalty. Bet it hurts the same, though." And then, finishing off the unfinishable turkey slice, he turned a twinkling eye on Shosh. "Am I right?"

All eyes turned to Shosh.

"What is he talking about?" asked her mom.

Shosh had known this day would come; even so, now that it was here, she rued its arrival. Scooting back from the table, she lifted her sleeve, and stuck out the underside of her forearm.

"You got a *tattoo*?" said Jared Bell.

"When did this happen?" asked Lana Bell.

"Like—six weeks ago."

"I can't believe you got a tattoo."

"Why a frog?"

"It's Toad."

Uncle Bobby chuckled, gnawed.

"Sailors and floozies, I tell you."

"You're slouching, Herman."

"You remember that frog pond in our backyard, Lana?"

"I can't believe you."

"The racket those frogs used to make."

"When you tattoo a damn frog on your arm, you at least tell your mother."

"I never did get a good night's sleep."

"*It's Toad.*"

"I'll tell you one thing," said Uncle Bobby through the din. "If Karen went and defaced her body like that, I don't care how old she is, I'd put her over my knee. Just saying."

"I'm sitting right here, Bob. I'll parent my kid how I see fit."

As the table finally erupted, Shosh's tattoo long forgotten, time slowed, and space bent with it, and Shosh sat in her black hole of a family, knowing full well its gravitational origin. On some level, they all knew. It was the same pull that had turned her parents into shadows, that compelled her, even now, to carry a flask in her coat pocket. It was the same pull that had them in its orbit, sucking them into its murky core. Shosh sat in it, saying nothing. And when she looked up, she found the eyes of her grandmother, sweet Nona, fount of wisdom and love, the only other person at the table who seemed aware of the black hole. Nona smiled gently, and then nodded, and Shosh saw it for what it was: a prod of encouragement.

"She was going to get one too."

Slowly, the table quieted. Aside from Nona, all eyes avoided Shosh as she spoke.

"I always pictured us getting them together. Our chairs next to each other, so we could see the progress." Shosh looked down at her tattoo. "'They were two close friends sitting alone together.' Our favorite line from our favorite story. Those two words—'*alone together*'—they were supposed to go here."

Lightly, she brushed the single word on her forearm, and though it was half their original plan, its meaning was altered in full.

Lana Bell began to sob.

The rest of the family sank backward in their chairs, blank-faced.

The black hole at work.

And just then, as if waiting for a window of opportunity, the voice of the ghost-singer swelled through the room. Her song was familiar, the one Shosh had come to think of as "Lost Causes and

Concerns," but whereas before her voice had been hushed and echoey, most of the lyrics impossible to make out, they were now quite audible. And even though the song itself was dreamlike, listening to it felt like emerging from a dream, as if the edges of Shosh's life had been blurred for a very long time and, only now, were coming into focus . . .

> Please don't ask why I never try
> You know as well as I
> The difference between loss and love
> Look close to find the beauty behind
> All good things come in time
> The shit they say
> It's getting late
> Come, sit and drink with me
> Oh God, don't talk, just be
> Be quiet, be cold, be heart and soul
> O love, that distant land
> You'd do it all again
> In willow seed
> Where trees sing
> All thirteen
> May I ask why you never try
> When you know as well as I
> The difference between loss and love

And right there at her Nona and Pop-pop's dining room table, Shosh understood that the song contained more than lyrics—it contained instructions.

EVAN
I'll be right here

WILL—SORRY, *WILLIAM*—WANTS ME to tuck him in. He gets clingy after sharing big feelings, and I don't know if it's because he's been especially vulnerable with Mom tonight, but he asks for me, and I am 100 percent here for it.

In the kitchen, Mom gets down on one knee, wraps her arms around him, and they trade whispered I *love yous, good nights,* and *sleep wells,* and when they're done, I pick Will up, toss him over my shoulder. "Ma'am, did you order this sack of potatoes?" And like a champ, she's all, "No, sir, those are special-order potatoes for the upstairs warehouse."

I tip a fake hat. "Much obliged, ma'am."

Will giggles the whole way up the stairs; he's still giggling when I dump him into bed, and by the time I turn on the little moon lamp, I am wholly unprepared for what's waiting.

The refrigerator box is still here, but it's no longer E.T.'s spaceship. Instead, it's been repurposed into some kind of Seussical contraption: an old calculator and computer keyboard are hooked up to one end of the box in what appears to be a "motherboard" situation; kitchen pots and pans are attached via pipe cleaners wound through haphazard holes punched at random intervals; a bunch of Will's old toys—everything from a small rocking horse to alphabet blocks to his long-forgotten remote-control Lamborghini—are glued, taped, or otherwise connected to the whimsical cardboard mechanism.

"I changed it," he says.

"I see that."

The walls are different too. Whereas before, the words PHONE and HOME had been written in Sharpie, more words have been added, so the walls now read E.T. PHONED HOME. E.T. WENT HOME. NOW ELLIOTT IS ALL ALONE.

I swallow hard. Try to keep the storm at bay.

Feel myself in this place, in this space.

"I know E.T.'s not real," Will says. "But maybe there's aliens like him, with healing powers. So I built a comm-cation device. Like in the movie." He points to the cardboard creation on the floor. "If it works, maybe they can use their glowy fingers to make Mom better."

I often wonder if I'm the emotionally erratic mess of a person I think I am, or if my brother's love induces emotional erraticism.

After we get his socks and shoes off, set out his clothes for tomorrow, we read a Frog and Toad story about a kite that won't fly until Toad really gives it his all, and when it's done, I tuck him in like he likes, starting at his feet, working my way up to his neck. "A little Will burrito," I say, sitting on the edge of his bed.

"William, please."

I sigh. "I'll be honest, bud. That might take a while."

I run my hand lightly across his forehead, watch him close his eyes, and just as I'm about to start for the door, he says, "Do you think she's going to die?"

"I don't think so."

"How do you know?"

I keep rubbing his forehead, just this small sign of stability: *I am here. This won't change.*

"I don't know," I say. "But you asked what I think. And I think she's going to be okay."

He leans over, opens the drawer of his bedside table, and pulls out a homemade comic. "I made this for her. For Christmas. Don't tell."

I hold the stapled-together pages the same way I would hold a sacred text. Across the cover, in glorious rainbow lettering, the word GLOW is written in all caps. Below that: *an original comic by William Taft.* The story is short, maybe ten pages. In it, three characters—"Mom," "Kid," and "Gentle Alien"—live together in a house. They go to the park, the zoo, and Jet's Pizza. With each turn of the page, and each new adventure, the Mom character gets shorter, more frail looking; her hair goes wiry, her eyes turn dark, until near the end, when all three characters are exploring a museum, and the Mom is just a bent-over stick figure. In the final panel of the page, Gentle Alien's heart lights up (denoted by short colorful lines, like the rays of a crayon sun), and the alien looks up at the Mom and says, "My heart glows to you, Mary." On the final page, the Mom is upright, her hair full again, bright eyes and a smile from one ear to the other.

"Do you like it?"

"It's the best thing I've ever seen, William."

He climbs up on his knees, leans his mouth to my ear, and whispers, "You can call me Will. But just you."

I slide the precious comic back into the drawer, tuck Will in a second time, and turn out the moon lamp. At his door, I whisper the only thing that really matters, the thing that makes us us: "I'll be right here, Will."

Later tonight, I'll lie awake in bed, staring into the ceiling shadows, thinking of the two words Will is about to say. And I'll wonder how something so complex could masquerade as something so simple, or if he knew what he was saying when he said it, but of course, he couldn't have, not really. He doesn't know how exhausting it is doing the same math over and over again, hoping for a different solve; he doesn't know about the rotating reel in my head, the 24/7 battle of *I have to go, I can't leave him, I have to go, I can't leave him,* nor could he have known that his two-word response planted a flag on one side of that battle. These are the things that will keep me up later tonight, not replaying my words to him—"I'll be right here"—but his response, the simplest, most complex words in any language.

"I know."

SHOSH

four

"WE NEED TO TALK, SHO."

"What is it?" Shosh asked, slipping on her boots by the front door.

Her mom turned, called up the stairs. "Jared!"

This couldn't be good. Shosh grabbed her hat off the coatrack, tried to remember the last time her parents felt the need for conversational reinforcements. Just as she was pulling on her gloves, her father rumbled down the stairs, and from their body language alone, she could tell they'd rehearsed whatever was coming.

"We have some questions," her mom said.

"Okay."

"For starters, we'd like to know where you go every night."

The answer to this was both simple and not. Every night for two weeks—ever since hearing the song lyrics loud and clear at the Thanksgiving table—Shosh had walked to Willow Seed Park. She'd bundle up and trek through dropping temps, the wind chill growing stronger with each outing. Not far from her house, the park was lit by a single streetlamp and was always empty. She'd linger by the frozen creek, the snow-covered slide and merry-go-round; she'd rock on the swing set, chains creaking back and forth. Most nights, she'd lie on her back under the trees, arms spread out in the snow, and stare up at the cold stars, considering the countless possible versions of her life, ones where things had gone the way they were supposed to go.

Her nights in Willow Seed were always accompanied by the ghost-singer. At this point, she knew the songs by heart, sang along in the empty park, and while it definitely felt like she was waiting on something, she couldn't say what.

"I go to the park," she said, offering the simple version.

"You go to the park."

"Willow Seed. I like it there. It's . . . calming."

"It's *freezing*," said her dad.

"Do you meet someone there?" her mom asked.

"Like who?"

"A friend?"

"Ha. Right. Okay."

"Well, I don't know."

"Was there anything else?" Shosh reached for the knob, desperate to be out of the house.

Her parents cleared their throats and fumbled for words, and when her dad said, "We're not keeping alcohol in the house anymore," Shosh felt her mind leave her body, exit the house, float out into the night. "We know we haven't been there for you," said her mom, and Shosh was no longer human, but a big, glorious snowbird, soaring through the Iverton sky, thick snowflakes falling in the silent stillness.

"We're really sorry."

Like dead weight, she tumbled back to Earth. "You're what?"

"I know it doesn't solve anything," said her dad. His ears were red, his blinks prolonged, and Shosh realized just how close to the verge he was in this moment. "But we're sorry. We haven't been . . . what we need to be. When I think about her, seeing us like this . . ." He stopped short, his eyes watery; beside him, Lana Bell wept openly, gently.

Shosh stood there, looking at her parents, and for the first time since Stevie's death, she caught a glimpse of their old selves peeking out from behind the shroud. "You guys have been ghosts for months. And now you decide to show up?"

"Sho—"

"This is bullshit. You can't just pop in and out of my life whenever it's convenient for you. And for the record, Mom, I know *we all lost her*. The difference is, I lost a sister *and* both of my parents. So excuse me for thinking *this?*"—Shosh waved her hand in a circle— "Is *asinine.*"

Later, she would wonder why she didn't walk out in that moment. She meant to. Maybe even tried to. But something stopped her, some part of her brain that knew who she was really mad at, and by the time the rest of her caught up, it was too late to make good on the stormy exit.

Through tears, her parents told her they loved her, they were so sorry, and Shosh pushed them away, but now she was crying too, and without meaning to, or understanding how it happened, the three of them fell into a hug, an embrace both gentle and furious, knowing they would never be four again, wondering if they could ever be whole.

EVAN
Willow Seed

"DID YOU KNOW THERE'S A Stonehenge at the bottom of Lake Michigan?"

Maya squints. "Get out."

"This kid in my writing class was talking about it. I looked it up. Little mastodon carved into one of the rocks, right there at the bottom of the lake." I trail off, look through the window; outside, the snow is falling in sheets. "A person did that. Carved a mastodon into a rock. Maybe it was near their house, maybe it was in a field, maybe they were just traveling through. But they saw this big circle of rocks, or else they constructed it, and they thought, *I know what I'll do.* And now I'm sitting on a couch, ten thousand years later, sad as shit, talking about how there's a carving of a mastodon at the bottom of a lake."

"I didn't know you were sad."

"That doesn't make you sad?"

"So you're sad because of the mastodon."

It's been gray skies and a light flurry all week. Part of me is pleased to see the sky making good on its promise.

"I found this place," I say quietly, and I'm not sure why, but I want Maya to know about the undeveloped plot of woods near my house, with its ancient trees and arterial creek. And so I tell her about it, and how it's the perfect place to listen. My little wood, my relic from another age.

"You find any carvings of prehistoric creatures?" she asks.

I think for a second, and then: "Maybe that's how it works, though."

"How what works."

"Maybe carving a mastodon into a rock is like—the same instinct that compels a person to write I *was here* on a bathroom stall. We want to mean something, whether it's now or ten thousand years from now. It's not about immortality, just—a durable tombstone."

On some level, I know my anxiety is rooted in the ultimate FOMO: I love my life, and I don't want to miss it. I feel too much, probably think too much, and when you do that, things aren't always easy. When you prefer your own company to others', you turn in on yourself, get so lost in your own head, it feels like you'll never find your way out.

I don't know.

Sometimes I exist so hard, it's hard to exist.

I look up to find Maya just sitting there, watching.

"You think I'm being morbid," I say.

"You have a poet's heart. Which I would imagine is often a burden."

After a few beats of silence, she asks how things are going with Will, and I tell her about the bombshell at Ivy Kids Art Night, and how he's known about Mom's cancer ever since she told me this past summer. "It's why he stopped wearing the Band-Aids. I guess he snuck one on her ankle while she was asleep, and when it didn't heal her . . . I mean, he's known for as long as I have. Only I've had you to talk to about it. And Ali. And Mom, for that matter. Will hasn't had anyone. Not to mention, he's *seven*, but yeah, you're probably right. Nothing to be sad about."

"I never said there was nothing to be sad about."

. . .

. . .

Maya joins me in my studious observations of the snow pounding the window.

. . .

. . .

"How is your mom?"

"Good. She finishes radiation next week."

"That's great." I can almost hear her smile across the room. "So . . . things to be happy about too."

"Hey, she gets to do five years of pills instead of shots, so that's great. Plus, she won't let me come to any appointments, or tell me jackshit about what's going on, so that's awesome too. Let's see, what else. Oh! Tamoxifen has some pretty neat side effects. Hot flashes, mood swings, depression, increased bone pain—"

"How do you know all this?"

"What?"

"You said your mom won't tell you anything."

"I found the prescription in her purse."

Years ago, Dad took me to a Minor League Baseball game. There were maybe a dozen people in the stands, so every time the announcer got on the loudspeaker to introduce a batter, his booming voice echoed through the empty stadium, magnified by the utter silence of the place.

The echoes of my last sentence linger in Maya's office and will likely hover somewhere over the building for the duration of winter.

"I wasn't snooping."

"Seems like maybe you were," says Maya.

"That's not the point."

"It's *a* point."

"How am I supposed to help her if I don't know anything?"

"Did she ask for your help?"

"Better snooping in her purse than wandering the wilds of Google, I'll tell you that. Drowning in blogs describing experiences in *detail*—hey, did you know that some doctors, when talking to breast cancer patients, frame everything in terms of the likelihood of death in five to ten years? I just—"

. . .

. . .

"—am I not allowed to be angry? While also acknowledging how lucky we got?"

. . .

"Of course you are."

. . .

. . .

"Okay, then."

. . .

. . .

. . .

"Listen for what?" asks Maya.

"What?"

"The little wooded area you've been going to. You said it's the

197

perfect place to listen. What are you listening for?"

As if answering a summons, Nightbird arrives in that moment. Her song swells, rises and crashes, the piano waiflike and echoey, and it's not the loudest I've heard her voice, but it is the clearest, as if she's singing directly into my ear.

Maya's mouth is moving; I think she says my name, but she's buried under the song with everything else. And in a new turn of phrase, a part of the chorus I've never heard before, the song comes into focus.

And I know exactly where I need to go.

Driving down Chestnut, turning onto Ash, my pulse in my shoes. Part of me wishes Ali were here, but a deeper part of me knows that whatever is ahead, it's better I'm alone. I round the corner onto Division, see the crowds ahead, the lights, the towering and luminous Baby Jesus. The street is basically a parade of minivans with Rudolph noses and antlers; there are so many kids, I have to slow to a crawl until I finally reach the turn onto Brooklyn. As the Christmas clamor diminishes in the rearview, snow on the road ahead turns fresh and unspoiled, streetlights like torches lining my way.

A slow roll at the dead end—I park, climb out of the car, and stand on the curb in front of Willow Seed Park.

"*In willow seed, where trees sing. All thirteen.*" The words turn to wisps, tiny proofs of life as I count the trees, just to be sure.

Thirteen exactly.

I roam around the park for a few minutes, aimless, awash in childhood memories. The little creek is frozen, and I wonder if it's the same ancient artery that runs through my patch of hidden woods, snaking its way down storm drains, under roads, behind houses, providing lifeblood to the whole neighborhood. Drenched in moonlight, a small pavilion sits on a hill; there's a slide covered in snow and an iced-over merry-go-round, and it feels like a place of peace.

At the swing set, I brush away the snow and sit on the frozen bench. Slowly, back and forth, the chains creak under my weight.

Back, *creak.*

Forth, *creak.*

Mom used to bring me here before Will was born. We came a few times when he was little, but he's not so much with the outdoors.

Back, *creak.*

Forth, *creak.*

Being here now feels like pulling an old teddy bear out of the attic, holding some long-forgotten token of love.

Back, *creak.*

Forth, *creak.*

"Hey."

I stop.

Climb out of the swing.

Turn around.

"Hey," I say.

Her coat is covered in snow, her hair in the winter winds more feral than chic. And I'm not sure how I know, but I know.

"You hear her too," I say.

She looks around, quietly hums a now-familiar song . . .

TOKYO

· 1953 ·

THE MORNING BEFORE SHIZUKO LEFT for university, she found a boy on her doorstep. He was alone, maybe ten or eleven, skinny, but with a look of sturdiness about him. As if his feet had been planted in the ground, taken firm root. "Ojama shite sumimasen," mumbled the boy, bowing slightly.

Shizuko wondered if perhaps he was lost, but before she could ask, he raised his head, and for a split second, she could swear she knew him.

The boy reached up with both hands, held out a tightly folded piece of paper.

She hesitated—then took the paper.

The boy turned and ran away.

Music is Shizuko's earliest memory. The little house in Nikko, her obachan plucking the o-koto, as young Shizuko sat in seiza, quietly humming along. And when Shizuko's father was conscripted into the war effort, her obachan had come too, and so the music followed. After the war, when her father began teaching at the university, their trips to visit were burned in Shizuko's memory. She loved him dearly, yes, but the trips were most memorable for the university's piano, and her obachan's face the first time she saw it: a look of utter solemnity and delight, as if she was trying to rein in her love lest she break the thing in half. Even now, years later, Shizuko can still feel those fleshy hands guiding hers across the keys like a boat at sea, rowing the gentle waves of scales and chords, showing her the world.

In 1955, still a student at Tokyo National University of Fine Arts and Music, Shizuko makes her stage debut performing Mozart with the Tokyo Symphony Orchestra. Two years later, she wins first prize at the World Chopin Competition in Warsaw and continues her work as a pianist and composer. In 1963, at the age of twenty-eight, she moves to Oslo to join the faculty at the Norwegian Academy of Music. From the little house in Nikko—to Tokyo to Warsaw to Oslo—music takes her by the hand, rows the gentle waves, shows her the world.

Shizuko plays piano because she loves piano; its mastery, however, she pursues in the name of the one who'd taught her to love it.

Like a mirage, Shizuko saw the boy's face in every crowd: children she passed on the street, in shops, on trains, in the market. In time, the mirage faded, though her memory of his face did not; his folded-up sketch faded too, though her safekeeping of the sketch did not. If he was the creator of the sketch, he was an artist of significant talent.

The boy was the best kind of mystery: not altogether vanished, peeking around every corner.

Winter 1966. Shizuko is invited by the Oslo Symphony Orchestra to perform Rachmaninov's Second Piano Concerto at Oslo's historic Nordraak Konserthus. Constructed in 1903, the building is a charming landmark, said to be haunted by the ghosts of countless musicians who've performed in its magnificent hall. Unfortunately, the walls of that hall are full of other things too: namely, rot. Had last month's building inspector been sober, the concert would have been relocated, and hundreds of lives would have been saved.

Alas, the inspector is a hopeless lush.

Ritual was key. In the minutes before stepping onstage, Shizuko would find a quiet corner, or sometimes lock herself in the bathroom, and pull the pulpy slip of paper from her pocket. It wasn't superstition; it was meditation. Visualizing herself as the woman in the drawing, willing a similar level of focus. She'd long ago resigned herself to the fact of the boy's anonymity: she would never know who he was, why he'd shown up at her door that day, why he'd given her this drawing, or if he'd even drawn it. But something in the drawing centered her, compelled her to be her best, and so she kept it in her pocket.

The sketch itself was simple but powerfully rendered: a woman onstage played piano; in the middle of a spotlight, a large bird perched on the edge of the piano, broad wings spread as if about to take flight; it was drawn from the audience's point of view, set on the far-left aisle, just a few rows back.

Everything tells a story. Our lives like unconnected threads dangling in an open doorway, and just when we tie one to the other, a new thread appears. Some stories remain untethered at the bottom, and so we forget the truth: they all originate in the same place.

On her last evening on earth, Shizuko sits at the piano in the packed hall, the ghost of her obachan guiding her fingers across the keys, when she hears a yell from the crowd. She continues playing, willing the focus of the woman in the sketch, and then another yell, and she doesn't stop playing, not even when the enormous bird lands right on the piano. She can feel the presence of the bird, see it in her periphery, but her focus remains on the keys, on the music. There is no more yelling, only a silent awe of the spectacle onstage. Somewhere in the rafters, the spotlight shifts to the bird, and Shizuko feels her heart racing as she plays, plays with the passion of her life's pursuit, the love of the one who taught her to love. As she plays, Shizuko begins to hum along with the song, her mind on that little house in Nikko, and she can't say why, but it's then— still playing, always playing—that she raises her head. Her eyes rove the far-left aisle, continuing a search that never stopped, not really; a few rows back now, she looks for a face that never vanished, as all the threads of her life connect.

There—

PART FIVE

MINUET

SHOSH
the spinning night

"I NAMED HER NIGHTBIRD."

"Mine was 'ghost-singer.' But I like your thing better."

Evan and Shosh lay on their backs on the merry-go-round, slowly pushing the earth with their feet, looking up at the stars as they spun. It was late, they were freezing, but Shosh didn't mind. Talking with Evan felt more like a show, less like a rehearsal.

Plus, she liked the sound of his voice.

"Even with friends," he was saying, "the songs were like—suspicious aches in my body. So long as I kept them to myself, no one could diagnose me."

She wasn't surprised he heard the songs too, even as some part of her knew she should be. Neither was she surprised when, after a fluttery whisper from a nearby tree, a bird took flight, and she recalled a Dickinson poem she'd recently read—*I hope you love birds too.* This whole evening felt surreal, as if her life had been temporarily relocated to the inside of a kaleidoscope. Or like every step she'd taken tonight, every word, every wisp of a breeze had been determined hundreds of years ago, and she was simply seeing it through to the end.

"I get that," she said. "Though I don't really talk much to anyone about anything, so."

"You can talk to me if you want," he said, and so they traded stories about when and how the songs had come to each of them, which led to conjecture and half-baked theories about what the songs meant, why no one else could hear them. When it became clear nothing would be solved tonight, Shosh found she wasn't ready to leave. Deep down, she knew what had happened earlier with her parents was a necessary thing, but new lines in the sand were never simple, and she wasn't sure what it meant yet.

Home felt complicated; whatever this was felt the opposite.

"When I was a kid," she said, staring at the stars, "I was obsessed with space. Read every book I could get my hands on. Fiction, nonfiction, astronaut memoirs, all of it. There was this one story about NASA in the sixties. I can't remember where I read it, or if it's even true, but these astronauts were in space, just going about their astro-business, when all of a sudden, they hear this old-timey music. Like, 'You Are My Sunshine' kind of Dust Bowl radio type shit. Obviously, that far from Earth, anything that makes them feel closer to home, they're all about. So the song ends, and one of the astronauts radios NASA to thank them for the transmission, only NASA is like, *We have no idea what you're talking about.* Turns out, no one sent a transmission. So the astronauts are all looking at each other, like, *You heard it too, right?* And then NASA looks into it, and they find no record of that particular song being broadcast from anywhere on Earth."

"So what did they hear?"

"Not what. *When.* The last time that music had been broadcast was the 1930s."

"Whoa."

"Yeah. I should google it. See if it's true."

Beside her, Evan took a deep breath, let it out in one long cloudy exhale. "There's truth in every story, I think. Even the made-up ones."

Halfway home, Shosh pulled out her phone. It was late, but Ms. Clark was a notorious night owl. Sure enough, two rings in—"Hey," Ms. Clark answered. She was sitting in bed, glasses on, hair up, clearly reading. "What are you smiling about?"

"I'm not smiling," said Shosh.

"I know it's been a while, sweetie, and you maybe forgot what it felt like, but that's a smile."

Shosh felt suddenly silly. "I made a friend."

Now it was Ms. Clark's turn to smile. "Who?"

"No one. A boy in a park. Shut up."

In what could only be described as a fundamentally tragic dance move, Ms. Clark started bobbing her head up and down, making that "bow-chick-a-bow-wow" noise adults always associated with sex.

"You're such a nerd."

"And does Park Boy have a name?"

"Evan. He's at Ivy, but I don't think he's in drama."

"I question the lad's moral fiber."

"You question the moral fiber of anyone who's not an actor."

Ms. Clark yawned a massive yawn, and Shosh figured it was now or never.

"Listen," she said. "Did you, like—call my parents? Or something?"

"Did I call your parents . . . ?"

"We had a talk tonight, and I don't know. They alluded to some . . . habits. It made me wonder if you guys had been talking."

Ms. Clark nodded, and Shosh thought she saw a small smile on her teacher's face. "I can't say the thought hasn't crossed my mind. Certainly, if you were still my student, there would have been phone calls."

"So . . . that's a no."

"Maybe I should have. But no, I haven't."

"Okay, I was just—"

"I know your parents are dealing right now, same as you. But I'm guessing they didn't need me pointing out your *habits*, Shosh. You're maybe not as subtle as you think. And they're definitely not as clueless. Now, before I crash for the night . . ." Another wide yawn, and then: "One thing about her."

Something about the bird, maybe, but she suddenly had an image of Stevie sitting on the edge of her bed, some how-to book opened in front of her as she strummed a sad little chord.

"She was learning to play the ukulele."

EVAN
alone together

I GOT HER NUMBER.

The number to her cellular telephonic device.

She gave it to me, which is why I have it.

We were at the park, I mentioned how we should keep in touch, seeing as we're the only people on earth hearing these songs (so far as we know), and she pulled out her phone, said, "What's your number," like that, no biggie, so I gave it to her. And then she texted, This is Shosh, and then we left the park, Shosh with my number, me with hers.

Shosh Bell's phone number.

Which is a thing I have.

I don't walk home so much as drift.

But there's something else, too. I can't explain it, but I'm certain tonight was no accident. The way she appeared in the park, as if she'd grown from the ground like a tree. The way she hummed the song, the way we talked like we'd known each other forever. It felt planned, by design, all of which only made the night more magical, so by the time I open the front door, float upstairs to my room, I'm primed to crash when, thing of things, my phone buzzes . . .

> Shosh: Just so you know, I don't make a habit
> of handing out my number to boys in parks
> It was like a one-time thing

Evan: I'm honored 😃
Hey, also
My friend Ali is having a party this
weekend. This kitschy holiday thing
we do every year
You should totally come

Shosh: You know, I'd love to
But you may have heard, my recent track
record at parties 😕

Evan: Fair, but
A) Squirrel turds aren't invited
B) There is no pool
C) It's less a party, more a "kickback"

Shosh: I do love a kickback

Evan: It's my favorite kind of kick

Shosh: Let me think about it

Evan: Of course

Shosh: Hey thanks, btw

Evan: ??

Shosh: This is gonna sound thirsty as hell
But I can't remember the last time I hung
out with someone I didn't want to dropkick

Evan: And see, that's my *least*
favorite kind of kick

Shosh: 😆😆😆

> **Evan: For real though, I'm glad you were there tonight**

Shosh: Same. It's nice not being alone in this

> **Evan: I always prefer being alone together**

Shosh: . . .
    . . .
    . . .
    . . .
    . . .

An hour later, all bug-eyed, I lie awake analyzing every sentence in the thread for possible clues as to what might have sent Shosh into the Ellipses Vortex. Ultimately, like the thread itself, I fall into a deep and disquieting sleep.

Next morning, instead of coffee or a shower, I experience the rejuvenating effects of a text from a new crush: If that kickback invite was real, I'm in.

Play it cool, Taft.

I spend five minutes composing what I hope is an exercise in nonchalance, just letting her know the invite was real, that I'm happy she'll be joining, and I'll text the details soon. I then text Ali: I'm inviting a friend to the holiday kickback—ok?

Ali: Evan Frodo Taft

> **Evan: Please don't**

Ali: Evan Merriweather Lewis Taft

Evan: OK, the only reason I'm telling you is so you can tell the others not to make a thing out of it

Ali: Wait
WHO IS IT
?????????

Evan: *whispers* Shosh Bell *runs away*

Ali: GTFO
EVAN
DETAILS

Evan: Only if you promise to tell everyone to be chill

Ali: Fine

Evan: The last thing I need is Yurt being Yurt, calling her Big Bang Cuoco or some shit

Ali: Fine

Evan: And it needs to be a separate thread without me, or they'll all just make fun

Ali: Fine

Evan: And I want screenshots as proof

Ali: Tell me, did you woo Shosh with these same chill-as-fuck vibes?

SHOSH
Ali's holiday kickback

ALI PILGRIM WAS THE KIND of person to make you believe in a higher power. That's how Evan talked about her, anyway. Goodness, originality, the notion that she was who she was, and seeing as that was good enough for her, it damn well should be good enough for everyone else too. Shosh had seen her around school, but until ten minutes ago, they'd never met. Now, standing in the Pilgrim kitchen as Ali prepped a tray of snacks, Shosh was starting to get it. The girl just radiated a certain sunlike energy; you wanted to be in her orbit.

It was a small crew. In addition to Ali and Evan, there was a chatty girl called Sara, white with big freckles and dark wavy hair held back by a blue bandanna; a Black girl named Mavie who carried a tote full of board games; and Mavie's girlfriend, introduced only as Balding, whose volcanic eruption of red curls cascaded down her pale face like lava down a snowy mountain.

"Okay, crew. Let's review the rules, shall we?" Given the resemblance, the adult who'd just entered the kitchen was clearly Ali's dad; there was a gleam in his eye, like a TV attorney cross-examining a defendant, always three steps ahead. "As it pertains to the rules, I am appallingly resolute. It will appall you, my resolution."

"Okay, Dad."

"Number one," he went on. "If you drink tonight, you do not drive tonight. Number two. If you drink tonight, you do not drive tonight. Lastly, and most importantly—"

Before he could finish, the room chanted together, "*If we drink tonight, we do not drive tonight.*"

He nodded, his eyes meeting each of theirs in turn. "Uber, Lyft, call your mom, call your uncle, hell, call *me*. I just started that Tina Fey memoir with the giant hands on the cover? Yeah. I'll be up."

Shosh couldn't help wondering if this display was for her benefit. Iverton talked; what happened to Stevie was no secret. For that matter, Mr. Pilgrim may have heard about Shosh's little poolside episode at the Abernathy house, in which case, this was less a show of support, more a warning.

"I can drive too," Mavie said. Then, to Mr. Pilgrim: "I don't drink."

Ali's dad nodded. "So. Plenty of options. Capeesh?"

A staunch chorus of *yes, sirs* echoed through the kitchen, and Ali said, "We are sufficiently appalled, Dad," and Shosh watched as Mr. Pilgrim pulled his daughter into an effortless hug, and for the briefest moment, she wondered how different their hug would look if Ali had a dead sibling too. Shosh hated herself in these moments, wanted to drink, wanted to sleep, anything to wipe clean the residue of grief, but there was nothing for it.

Life in a black hole was bad enough without the sun boasting its brilliance.

The Pilgrims' basement redefined Christmas cheer: there was an electric fireplace, for starters, the mantel decked with stockings and glittery pine trees; an automatic train set rolled around the room, weaving between occasional mounds of fake snow, old-fashioned general stores, little groups of carolers, and snowmen galore; in one corner, an ancient wood-paneled television aired *Home Alone* on VHS; in another, blinking in time to "Jingle Bell Rock," a Christmas tree sagged under the weight of whimsy, as if every holiday aisle at every Target the world over had exploded, miraculously reshaping in the form of this tree in this basement.

"Red Drink?" Evan held out a cup of something borderline fluorescent.

"What is it?"

"Vodka, Hawaiian Punch, and like a million other things."

Shosh took the cup with no small amount of relief. It was good, if a little fruity for her taste, but after a few gulps, the uneasiness in her gut receded a little.

"Be warned, though." He took a sip, then shivered as it went down. "Last year, I had two cups, and couldn't feel my toes for three days."

From across the room, dialing up the electric fire, Ali yelled, "Is he talking shit about his toes?"

"Evan's a notorious featherweight," Sara said, serving herself a full cup from an incandescent bowl.

"I am not."

"Is Yurt coming?" Mavie asked, to which Balding rolled her eyes, all, "Fucking Yurt," to which Sara stared her down.

"Who's Yurt?" Shosh asked.

"He's more of a *what*," said Balding, smiling, sipping.

"He's a *sweet guy*, thank you very much." Sara plopped on the couch, and as everyone gathered by the fire, she explained that Yurt was a character, and like all characters, you just had to get to know him. "He has a family thing, but he'll be here. Said we should start without him."

Ali slid a cardboard box out from under the coffee table, while someone turned off the overhead lights. Between the electric fire and the sheer amount of twinkling Christmas lights, the room was still well lit, but with the added element of drama now.

"Behold!" Ali said. "As we begin this night of nights, I hereby declare the aforementioned commencement of our good and faithful Holiday Kickback, version the fourth—"

"Third, isn't it?"

"—version the third, in which we the people, henceforth and forevermore—"

"Forevermore?"

"—in which we the people, for the next *few hours*, engage in corny gamery, lively discussion—"

"I'm not sure you can say *gamery*."

"—and, most importantly"—from the box, Ali produced a truly horrific sweater portraying Santa as a muscly meathead lifting weights—"ugly sweaters. Who's got Steroid Santa this year?" Balding raised a hand; Ali tossed her the sweater, and then pulled out a green cardigan with two golden bells under an incredibly erect tree. "Jingle Balls goes to Evan, obviously—"

"Why is that obvious?" mumbled Evan, accepting the sweater like a prison sentence.

Mavie got the fluffiest sweater (all eight reindeer with furry red cotton ball noses), Ali got the grossest (Randy Quaid in a bathrobe, emptying shit into a gutter), and Sara got the sexiest (Marilyn Monroe in a Santa hat).

"And for our Holiday Kickback first-timer—" Ali held up a sweater with a dozen elves lined up, each with the photoshopped head of Elvis Presley. Across the top, in bold lettering: ELVES PRESLEY.

And so it was, half-drunk on a luminous beverage, surrounded by an abundance of cheer, wearing the worst pun of her life, Shosh raised her cup with the rest of the group, collectively toasting the night.

And then . . .

"Yo, yo, yo!" came a voice from the top of the stairs, and a thunderous rumble as the person descended, turned, and locked eyes with Shosh. "Oh, hell yes. Big Bang Cuoco, you showed."

Sara buried her face in her hands; Evan stood from the couch but seemed unclear where to go from there. Balding drained the last of her cup, smacked her lips, and said the only two words any of them could manage: "Fucking Yurt."

EVAN
Elves Presley

WHEN I EXIT THE BATHROOM, Ali is right there, leaning against the wall. "I like her," she says.

"Of course you do. She's awesome. Too bad you won't be seeing much of her. Between Yurt acting a fool and the shocking efficiency with which I shut down our text conversation last night, I'm surprised she's still here."

The basement bathroom is tucked in a little alcove beyond the stairwell. Together, Ali and I peer around the corner as Mavie and Balding act out the current scene from *Home Alone* wherein Harry and Marv get rammed by paint cans. Shosh is on the couch beside Yurt, the two of them laughing.

"Ahh, the curative properties of Red Drink," whispers Ali. "I should bottle that shit and make my fortune."

Sara rounds the corner just then, silent-claps in my direction, all smiles. "Well done, Cervantes."

"Stop."

"Honestly, I'm just happy to see you fall for someone outside the Sherlock-verse. Baker Street's a tough beat, man."

"Get me some of that bottled cocktail coin," says Ali, staring off into the distance.

Sara leans in close to me. "What's with her?"

"The usual. Plotting her future as a Red Drink tycoon." I run my hands through my hair, but keep them there, dig them in deep, let my hair fall where it may, then scratch like an animal.

Sara leans toward Ali. "What's with him?"

"The usual. He was a shit texter last night, and then Yurt pulled a Yurt tonight, and here we are."

"Ah." Sara looks back at me. "Well, she's here, isn't she? Against all odds, you've brought a hot girl to a party. And she hasn't left. I'd say that's a win, Watson."

"This is the reddest possible red." Balding stares into her cup as if contemplating the abyss.

"When I was in eighth grade," says Yurt, "I ordered the book *Sphere*."

"There is nothing redder on Earth."

"But the store forgot to ship the book. Or else, shipped it to the wrong place."

It's late, the room a cozy quilt of festive lighting, and we sit in the sleepy contentment that comes in the wee hours of the morning, tucked in ugly sweaters, surrounded by friends. We've finished Holiday Charades, Elf Toss, Candy Cane Drinking Game. We've finished *Home Alone* and *Elf* and are now halfway through *It's a Wonderful Life*, only half paying attention, half of us half-drunk.

As for me, I'm still slowly sipping my first cup, intent on leaving every shrub in the neighborhood unsullied. Not to mention, as Sara so kindly pointed out, Shosh is still here. I'd like to keep my wits about me.

"Hey—" Sara turns to Ali. "I heard you applied to Baylor?"

"Yeah. Georgetown, too, which might be my preference. I missed early action on both, so—won't know for a while."

"Baylor is a bear," says Sara. "What's Georgetown?"

"Hoya."

"Hooya?"

"*Hoya.*"

"By the time the book showed up on my doorstep, I'd forgotten I was even *waiting* on a book."

"I think it's burning my retinas."

Sara turns to me, and I can feel the Headlands question coming. Before she can ask, I point to the screen. "So George Bailey goes to the bridge to jump," I say. "But the angel jumps in first, the idea being, get George to save him. So the angel's plan to keep George from jumping is to get him to jump? It makes no sense."

"I've never seen *The Big Bang Theory*," says Shosh.

Whereas before, the room felt like an orchestra hall in the moments before a concert, when each player runs their own part separately, it now feels like the conductor has raised the baton . . .

"Me neither," says Balding, almost in a whisper.

Mavie smiles. "I haven't seen it."

One by one, it's confirmed: none of us has seen an entire episode of *The Big Bang Theory.*

"Maybe no one has," says Sara, and Yurt is all, "*Big Bang* Conspiracy *Theory*, yo."

"Why do I *feel* like I've seen it?" asks Balding.

"Between clips, GIFs, and memes," says Ali, "we've formed a composite. Like a police sketch of a suspect."

"If it's any consolation"—Sara turns to Shosh—"I get the sense that Cuoco's character kind of keeps the ship afloat."

"But people think I look like her?"

Sara shrugs. "Different hair, obviously."

"Plus," I say, "you're way prettier."

There are moments when our mouths betray us, when our brains act entirely on their own. More often than not, these moments come during times of distraction—say, while trying to account for gaping plot holes in all-time classic films, while listening to your friends ramble about mishap book deliveries and the extent to which their drink is red.

"Thanks," Shosh says quietly.

In the festive lighting, hers is the only face not smiling at me.

SHOSH
alternate routes

THE BACK SEAT OF MAVIE'S CRV really wasn't built for four, but in an attempt to avoid anyone sitting on anyone else's lap, Sara, Yurt, Evan, and Shosh sat scrunched together, making it work. Up front, Balding DJ'd, flipping through a nineties rap playlist while Mavie navigated the winding roads behind Iverton's suburbs.

Back at Ali's, when Mavie offered to drive everyone home, Shosh had asked, "You okay to drive?" It was force of habit, more than anything. In response, Mavie pulled a necklace out from under her shirt, held up a token in the half-light: "Six months sober."

It was not lost on Shosh that the very thing that took her sister's life was the thing she now relied on in her sister's absence. On a practical level, she knew there were people who didn't drink, people who couldn't or shouldn't drink. But there'd always been a clear delineation between the Phil Lessings and Chris Bonds of the world—weak people with weak minds—and people like Shosh. Maybe she drank like them, but there was a *reason* she'd stopped driving altogether.

Reasoning: that was what made her different—what made her *better*—than the Lessings and Bonds.

This was what she'd always told herself.

But now, here was Mavie. There was nothing showy about her

sobriety. When she'd pulled out her chip, her smile had been full of quiet pride, but her eyes maintained a steady spark of . . . what . . . fear? Respect? Humility? Whatever it was, it felt big, it felt pure, and in its afterglow, Shosh recognized a crack in the foundation of her logic: all this time, she'd mistaken negotiation for reason.

She liked Mavie. It was hard not to. But the fact of Mavie's existence proved Shosh's weakness, tipped the scales of her world closer to the world of Phil Lessing and Chris Bond, and for this reason, Shosh could not wait to get out of this car.

"So what do you think?" As if sensing Shosh's thoughts, Mavie was smiling at her in the rearview. "Your first Holiday Kickback."

"It was . . . really fun, actually," Shosh said.

"You sound surprised."

"It's just been a while since I've experienced fun. Was starting to forget what it felt like." And maybe in an effort to combat her earlier feelings of resentment, she felt the need to add, "Ali is great."

"You think that now," said Sara. "Wait till she talks your ear off about catamarangutan. You'll be singing a different tune then."

Yurt nodded, all, "A whole other song, yo," at which point Balding cranked the volume.

"Don't listen to them," said Evan. "I mean, yes, she will talk your ear off about catamarangutan, but Ali's the best."

Anyone else, and she wouldn't have been able to hear over the music in the car. As it was, Evan was inches away and went on to tell a story about some kid in third grade who tried to beat him up. "But Ali wasn't having it. She took him down and that was that. Best friends ever since."

A sudden image on a soccer field, a bigger kid standing over her, and Stevie coming out of nowhere . . .

. "It's good to have someone like that in your life," Shosh said.

She watched the unfamiliar roads the rest of the way home, passing trees in the night.

EVAN
good night

WHEN WE PULL INTO SHOSH'S driveway, I hop out too and tell Mavie I'll walk from here.

"You sure?" she asks.

"Yeah, it's not that far. Thanks for the ride."

Shosh thanks her too, and as the CRV disappears down the road, we turn for her house.

"It's pretty cold," says Shosh, and I suddenly feel silly for thinking this was a good idea.

"I like the cold," I say.

My theory is, if I put my foot in my mouth enough, maybe I'll acquire a taste for it.

We're on her porch now, and she turns to me, and I imagine a version of myself that grabs her by the hand, spins her around, dips her so low she thinks we're going to fall, but we don't because I'm such a badass dancer (plus, *muscles so toned*), and then I kiss her on the lips, and . . .

"Ali's my best friend," I say, so thoroughly this version of myself, it kills me.

"I know."

"Right. It's just—earlier. When I was talking about how great she is. I didn't want you to get the wrong idea. I mean, we love each other, but it's not that kind of love."

God, please, someone put me out of my misery.

"Okay," says Shosh.

For a second, we just stand there, and I consider again a world where I'd have the balls to lean in, to go for it, but alas—this is not that world. Instead, in what I can only describe as an out-of-body experience, I watch in horror as my right arm ascends, and my hand extends, palm to the side, thumb pointed skyward, and I would give anything to take it back, but the only thing worse than offering a handshake to a girl you'd rather kiss is offering a handshake and then rescinding it.

And so, I do the only thing I can: I own that shit.

Hand out, eyes locked on hers. "Thank you for a lovely evening, Shosh Bell."

A beat of silence, a beat of heart.

Glory of glories: a smile.

She steps closer.

Takes my hand, gentle, soft, warm.

Holds it, and then: up and down, slowly.

Opens her mouth, and I can smell her breath: tangy, botanic, sweetfruit.

"Good night, Evan Taft."

I can't see the future. But if we have a story, this will be right at the top. First kiss? Bush league. Our night was so baller, we shook on it.

I'm halfway home when I get a text from Shosh. Given the magic of the night, I have to read it a few times before I realize what she's talking about.

Shosh: I didn't hear her tonight

Evan: Me neither

Shosh: I haven't heard her in a while

Evan: Me neither

Shosh: I wonder why

Me too.

SHOSH
past, present, future

THE BELL FAMILY ALWAYS SPENT a week in Elgin during the holidays. Luckily for all involved, Uncle Bobby, Aunt Helen, and Cousin Karen spent Christmases in Florida (because of course they did), so it was just Shosh and her parents and her beloved Nona and Pop-pop.

The week could be summed up in one word: pajamas. Mornings were for sleeping in, waffles, Nona's famous sausage balls; afternoons by the fire with a book, grazing on an everlasting charcuterie. In the evening, they ate more, read more, watched movies, and considering the amount of snow, the amount of food, and the lack of needing to be anywhere or do anything, this week should have flown by like a dream. And most years, it did.

At first, Shosh pinned this year's restlessness on the obvious: their first Christmas without Stevie, you could hardly expect them to pretend like everything was merry and bright. The day they arrived, she walked into the bathroom to find her father crying over the sink; at least twice, after shaking cinnamon on a plate of waffles (the only way Stevie ever ate them), Nona called Stevie's name through the house, the ringing silence that followed a reminder of her absence.

It was complicated for all of them. This was to be expected.

But a few days in, Shosh couldn't ignore the extra layer of complication, one that only applied to her: I miss him, she thought.

She couldn't believe it, but there it was.

Before she'd left, they'd made plans to go to the Discount for a movie in the New Year. Suddenly, that felt like forever away, and Shosh was alternately giddy at the notion of seeing him and utterly baffled at the vigor of her affection. She found herself looking for excuses to text him. For example, the meme she'd stumbled across with a quote commonly attributed to Nietzsche, which said "*And those who were seen dancing were thought insane by those who could not hear the music.*" Obviously, this applied to their situation with Nightbird, and obviously, it was something Evan must be informed of posthaste.

Have you seen this? she texted, along with the Nietzsche quote.

Evan: Whoa. It's like he knows about us.

Shosh: Right???

Evan: That's neat

Shosh: No, that's Nietzsche 😃

Evan: NICE

Shosh: And that's not even close

Then, with more than a little thought, she sent this: **Anyway, I saw the quote, and it made me think of us.**

EVAN

US

Two letters, one syllable, all-consuming.

SHOSH
in the quiet shine

SHE WAS A MESS. NO two ways around it. But no amount of pining can speed up time, and so she looked for ways to keep her mind busy.

Ever since the realization that she'd accidentally stolen lines from Nightbird, she'd been hesitant to revisit the cabin couplet project. But staring at the latest post from the Norway account—a tiny white house in the middle of a vast snowy wood, the sun rising on the horizon—she thought how long it had been since she'd even heard the songs and figured, *what the hell.*

Her bed at Nona and Pop-pop's wasn't flush with the window, but there was a comfy chair beside it, which would serve as her poetic base of operations. She plopped down, started typing, and before long, had this:

> she went to bed convinced the night would never end
> and woke to find the sun had proved her wrong again

When Ms. Clark had first given her the ultimatum—make something or quit calling—Shosh had chosen poetry for the simple fact that it seemed entirely foreign. But the more she wrote, the more familiar it felt, until she realized why: poems were songs in hiding.

She posted "**cabin couplet #8**," then made her way downstairs to the kitchen, where a twelve-pack of Diet Coke stared at her from the fridge. She cracked one open, took a sip. She'd almost forgotten what it tasted like straight. "Okay, then," she said, grabbing three more cans and heading back to her room.

Dusk.

Snowy woods.

A log cabin beside a rushing river.

the call of sleep, I hear it now, loud as the day is long
and the river rushing, that soft rumble, my favorite
wintersong

Gray skies looming.

A black cabin by the sea.

Green grass growing right on the roof.

keep your shingles, tiles, and corrugated plastic
i put my yard on my roof, it looks freaking fantastic

A little lake full of candlelit lamps.

Center of frame, a yellow cabin.

Snowy mountain behind it.

Neon swirls above, the northern lights gone wild.

with a shivery hope, in the quiet shine
we raise a glass to auld lang syne

• • •

The next morning, Shosh woke late.

Four empty cans of Diet Coke on the floor.

Head clear, soul full.

Four texts on her phone.

The first, from Ruth Hamish: My girl *killing* it on Insta! Modern day Dickinson, you love to see it

That was sweet and all, but it was the next three that left her floating through the day.

> Evan: Hey. Wow. So. You're a writer. Good
> to know.
> Also, this may be out of line, and if it is, I
> truly apologize, but I can't not say it
> I miss you

Quicker than she'd ever typed anything, uninterested in playing it coy or cool, she responded: I miss you too.

EVAN

anything is possible and
everything is perfect

AND LO! THE DAY OF days having finally arrived—the day I'm supposed to meet Shosh at the Discount after not having seen her
for two weeks—Mom tells me she picked up an extra shift at the
restaurant.

"For tonight?"

"Neil isn't feeling great." She shrugs as if her decision isn't
ruining my life. "Figured I could use the hours."

It's still holiday break; the three of us are eating cereal in the
den, watching one of Will's latest favorites, an animated gem called
Octonauts about these anthropomorphic animals who dwell in a
delightfully cozy undersea headquarters and set out on various
aquatic adventures.

"Who's Neil?" I ask.

"Oh. Just a friend from work."

A friend from work. She'd used this same phrase when discuss-
ing her biopsy, how a "friend from work" had given her a ride,
and then let her rest at his place afterward. Most sons probably
don't want to think about their moms dating—and it's not like
I'm in love with the idea, but no one in the world deserves happiness more than my mother. If she's got a Neil or two on the side,

I'm great with that, so long as they don't get sick at inopportune moments and ruin everything.

"Shellington's my favorite," says Will, entirely enthralled by the episode.

"Is he the one with the Scottish accent?" asks Mom.

Will nods. "Plus, he knows everything. See?"

In the episode, Shellington is explaining that a certain sea creature is actually two *separate* creatures: a crab with a sea urchin stuck to its back.

"So you need me here with Will," I say.

"If that's okay." Mom points to the screen. "What's his name again?"

"That's Captain Barnacles," says Will. "He's the boss."

"Mom?"

"See, I like Barnacles," Mom says. "That other one, Kwazii, he's too big for his britches."

"Mom."

She looks at me. "What?"

"I can't."

"Can't what."

"Be here tonight. I have a—"

Sensing what I'm about to say, she smiles, tilts her head, and I know I'm done for.

"Never mind," I say.

"You have a what—an appointment?"

"It's nothing."

"A presentation?"

"Will, can you turn this part up?" I ask.

Mom leans in. "I'm sorry. I should have checked with you first."

"It's fine."

"You can have her over? Or him?" She's searching. "Or them! Whoever. Whoever it is, they're more than welcome to come here tonight."

"Thank you, Mother. We'll just reschedule. It's seriously no big deal."

In the episode, the crab and the sea urchin try to go their own ways, but as it turns out, the crab needs the urchin for protection, and the urchin needs the crab for food. "It's called *symbiosis*," says Will. Then, with his mouth full: "They can't survive apart."

I'll say.

. . .

Evan: Hey. So.
Apparently my mom picked up a
shift at work tonight and didn't tell
me
I have to stay home with Will.
I'm so sorry to reschedule last minute. We can do it tomorrow?

Shosh: WUT
UR DEAD TO ME
Kidding
No problem. I mean—bummed—but I
get it!

Evan: Thanks 🖤

Shosh: So what're you guys doing tonight?

Evan: Most likely watching E.T. for
the billionth time
FML
(But not really)

Shosh: Cool!
That's one of those classics I completely
missed

Evan: What?

Shosh: E.T.

Evan: Sorry, I thought you said
you've never seen E.T.

Shosh: I haven't

Evan: Sorry, I thought you said you
haven't

Shosh: You have no idea my capacity for
this
I will outlast you

Evan: Fair
So how about you just come over
instead?

Shosh: Depends

Evan: On?

Shosh: Is there popcorn?

• • •

The minute Shosh steps in the door, Will is turned all the way up.

He insists on giving her a tour of the place, as if our house is Downton, and he's Carson, offering a formal introduction to each and every room. After the tour, he's all, "Watch this," and then does a very basic somersault in the living room, followed by (what must be, surely to God, only an *attempt* at) some new dance move. It's all entirely underwhelming, and I can't help wondering if most kids are compelled to display their most mundane skills, or if it's just Will.

"This is for you," he says, handing Shosh a decorative New Year's hat.

"Thank you, kind sir," and Shosh puts it on, all freaking smiles, then turns to me. "How do I look?"

Truthfully, she looks *fantastic*, even with the silly hat, but I take a beat, play it cool, rest my chin in my hand and nod slowly, like a designer appraising a runway model. "In a word?" I throw both hands in the air. "Fabulous."

Will leads us to his art station in the living room, where he gives us one of his favorite assignments: do the thing you do best. "All you have to do," he says, "is think of what you're best at making. Make it. And then we all show each other what we made. If you're going to draw, though, you should know that Evan's the *bestest* drawer."

Shosh smiles at me, and I mumble something like, "Hardly," trying to hide how pleased I am.

"Okay then, Taft boys—" Shosh grabs a pen, a piece of paper, and turns for the corner. "It's on."

For the next half hour, we work on our projects in secret.

Throughout, Will continues his display of the mundane, cracking made-up fart jokes and telling stories that go nowhere. My instinct is to tell him to chill, but Shosh eats it up. Even from the corner, hard at work on her "best thing," her smiles are like a lamp in the room, and her laugh has turned into a simmering, low-key chuckle that only grows with each bad joke.

I didn't think it was possible to crush any harder on this girl, but seeing her with Will—more to the point, seeing him with her, how comfortable he is around her—is turning me into a living, breathing heart-eyes emoji.

When we're finished, Will reads this ridiculous (but admittedly, hilarious) story he wrote called *Barry's Big Burp* about a kid whose burp becomes self-aware. When he's done, we clap and cheer, and he takes a deep bow, and then it's my turn.

"So this is a robot called Q2-EV, which is basically like C-3PO's evil cousin who specializes in unnecessary destruction."

Shosh grabs the paper out of my hand for a closer look. "Holy shamoley."

"Told you," says Will.

"Evan. How did I not know you could draw like this?"

I feel my face getting hot. "It's nothing."

"This is like, *Pixar* good. I'm embarrassed to show mine now."

"Okay—" I snatch the paper back. "Come on."

"Seriously, I can't follow that."

"You have to," says Will. "Those are the rules."

Shosh looks at the paper in her hands. "Fine. But I have to turn around. I don't want you guys looking at me."

"Seriously?" I smile at her. "Don't you perform in front of like hundreds of people?"

"Believe me. That was *way* easier than this."

She turns around, clears her throat, and I don't know what I was expecting, but when she starts singing, at first, I think Nightbird has landed in the room. The song is new, unfamiliar, but her voice has a similar ethereal quality, rising and falling like waves in slow motion. Will and I look at each other, then at the back of her head as she sings.

Her voice is the kind of good that makes you reevaluate what humans are capable of: If we can sing like this, what *can't* we do?

When the shock subsides, I recognize some of the lyrics from her cabin couplet posts. It feels like an inevitable transformation, as if the poems were meant to be songs all along. She sings of rivers rushing and shivery hopes, and I find myself feeling something new, something more than a crush, different than love: I'm grateful to know her.

"That was *wayyyyy* . . . wow," says Will when she turns back around. "I didn't know you could *do* that."

I feel myself staring at her, while also not caring that I'm staring. "You're incredible," I say, and she smiles, eyes down, as I realize what I just said. "I mean—*that* was incredible."

"Thanks," she says, and the room feels suddenly lighter, abuzz, full of kinetic energy, as if anything is possible and everything is perfect. And then Will reaches toward her wrist, puts a finger on her tattoo, and effectively kills that energy with a single, innocent question: "Is he lonely without Frog?"

SHOSH
movie night at the Taft House

TONIGHT WAS PROBABLY THE RECORD for most consecutive minutes without thinking of her sister. This house, this family—she felt like herself. And it was hard to know which was more shocking: being pulled back into the stark reality of Stevie's death, or being pulled there by a child.

Not that he'd meant to.

She splashed water on her face, looked at herself in the bathroom mirror.

Will was the first person on earth to correctly identify her tattoo, not as *a* toad, but as *Toad*.

Is he lonely without Frog?

"Yes," she whispered to her reflection.

Back in the living room, Evan and Will were waiting with popcorn, lights turned down, E.T. cued up onscreen. Will sat in a beanbag on the floor, staring at his feet. "I'm sorry I hurt your feelings. About Frog and Toad."

Evan sat on the couch with a nervous smile; it was clear they'd been talking in her absence. She crossed the room, plopped down on the floor beside Will, pulled her knees up to her chin. "The thing is, my sister and I loved Frog and Toad."

"Me too," said Will.

"They're the best, right? What's your favorite story?"

"Mmm, 'The Kite.'"

"That's a good one. He sure showed those birds, didn't he?"

"They couldn't fly as high as his kite."

"Not even close. Our favorite was 'Alone.'"

Will nodded. "That one makes Evan cry."

On the couch, Evan cleared his throat. "I mean, not like—daily."

Shosh smiled, currently holding back tears. "All the Frog and Toad stories make me cry. Especially recently."

"How come recently?"

The heater kicked on, little dust particles from a nearby vent thrust into the air, illumined in the blue glow of the television, and Shosh had a sudden image of her mother bursting into her room in the morning, pulling back curtains with a flourish, launching dust everywhere. She could see them now the way she saw them then, a sort of zero gravity dance, all lit up in the morning sun—and she tried to remember the last time her mother woke her up like that.

"When we were little, whenever one of us couldn't sleep, my sister and I would recite 'Alone' over and over again. We did it together, out loud, until one of us finally fell asleep. But it was always me falling asleep first, leaving her to recite 'Alone' alone. I don't know why that never occurred to me . . ." She swallowed, looked right at Will. "She died, my sister. So I cry a lot now."

Will shifted in the beanbag until he was close enough to rest his head on her shoulder. "'They ate wet sandwiches without iced tea,'" he said.

Shosh wiped her eyes and smiled, leaned her head against Will's. "'They were two close friends sitting alone together.'"

• • •

To watch E.T. with Will and Evan was to confirm magic existed in the universe. There was a clear shorthand between them, and even though they were careful not to interrupt—there was no reciting of lines, no texting, no ridiculous exclamations of *Ooh, this is the good part*—it was impossible to hide how close they were to the movie. It was baked into their smiles as they watched, the way their reactions ever so slightly anticipated each moment, the looks they gave each other during an especially meaningful scene. Shosh knew better than anyone the shared intimacy of story, when all participants are vulnerable and willing.

She only dared interrupt once, and then, only to mention how E.T. was in one of the Star Wars prequel movies, at which point Evan chuckled, and Will pretended she'd said nothing at all. "I'm serious," she said.

Will paused the movie. "What are you talking about?"

Shosh pulled up YouTube on her phone, and when she found what she was looking for—a very brief scene in *The Phantom Menace*—she turned the screen around, and as Will's face turned from suspicion to joy, she explained her family's Thanksgiving tradition of watching all the Star Wars movies, how ingrained every scene was in her brain, and only then did it occur to her that they'd skipped the tradition this year.

For all the trauma associated with loss, no one talked about the long-term reality: grief was death by paper cuts. A 10.0 earthquake, followed by a lifetime of little jolts.

"I can't believe we didn't know about this," Will said, looking duly impressed at her display of cinematic trivia.

Evan smiled at her. "You do realize this catapults you into legendary status, right?"

"The honor of my life," she said, and when they returned to the movie, Shosh couldn't help noticing she was closer to Evan on the couch, though whether she was the one who'd sat closer to him, or the other way around, she couldn't say. Not that it mattered. The lights were off, and they were close enough she could feel the heat coming off his body. In the dark, their hands became both compass and destination: the thing they were trying to get to, and the way to get there. Though they didn't reach for each other, so much as grow like wild weeds, and when they finally did touch, it felt inevitable, a continuation of their handshake from the night of the kickback, as if her hand had imprinted itself on the memory of Evan's. His was a little sweaty, or maybe it was hers, and with Will so close, it was a hands-only party, which, okay, great—but it did make Shosh want to extend the invitation to other parts of the body.

When the movie ended, they detached, sat up, nothing to see here.

"So?" asked Will. "What did you think?"

"Amazing," said Shosh.

"Yeah?"

"A true masterpiece. I do have one question, though."

"Oh no," said Evan.

Shosh kicked his foot. "It's not a criticism. Just an honest question."

"Okay," Will said, as if daring her.

"So like—okay, great, they got E.T. home. But now Elliott has no one. So, I guess my question is, what about Elliott?"

A pregnant pause, and then Will turned to his brother with the intensity of a prowling lioness. "Evan, you should marry her."

"Okay, then." Evan stood abruptly, clapped his hands together. "Say good night to our guest, it's time for bed."

Will hugged Shosh; his whispered words took her off guard. That night, and in the days to come, she wondered at all the ways she didn't deserve those words, all the ways she'd fallen short of them, and all the ways she might yet live up to them.

"My heart glows to you," Will said.

And up the stairs they went, one boy she was falling for, one she was determined to rise for.

EVAN

she's a Tarantino

"SOMETHING'S CHANGED," MAYA SAYS, AND I wonder what she sees.

Elation, obviously. On my best day, I couldn't keep Shosh a secret.

Resolution, probably. Last night, after learning the significance of Frog and Toad, I went back and checked our early text thread, the one I'd so efficiently shut down: *It's nice not being alone in this,* she'd texted. And I'd responded with I *always prefer being alone together,* unwittingly quoting the most loaded of inside jokes she'd had with her sister.

Frustration, definitely. After finally getting Will to fall asleep, I'd descended the stairs to find my mother home from work, talking Shosh's ear off. Of course, Mom was all, "Don't mind me, I'm not even here," and then pretended to sneak into her bedroom, as if to prove just how *not there* she was, but oh, she was there, she was very much there, just so entirely *there.*

"What's different?" Maya pushes.

"Nothing. I'm . . . nothing."

"Evan."

"I met a girl," I say, and before I know it, I'm in, telling Maya all about Shosh, how we met in the park (I omit the songs, of course), who she is, how I feel when I'm with her. "It's like I'm more *me* with her. Like I'm my *most* me."

"More so than with Ali?"

"No, that was always—I've always felt that with Ali, but it's different. I don't know. With Ali, it's hard to explain, but easy to live, you know? With Shosh, it's easy to explain . . ."

"You have a crush."

"I've said a lot of things in here, right? All sorts of things I *think* I mean, or things I think I *want* to mean, but I'm not sure what I mean, or I'm unsure if I *should* mean something different—"

"You can be honest, Evan."

"She's *too fucking cool* for me."

"Shosh is."

"She's a Tarantino film. I'm Judd Apatow on a good day. So okay, not nothing, but not, you know, an *auteur*."

"I like Judd Apatow."

"Thing is, she doesn't *act* too cool for me, which only makes her even *more* too cool for me. And let's not even talk about how pretty she is, okay?"

"Okay."

"Don't even go there."

"I won't."

"Whatever outdated, misogynistic bullshit scale people use to describe beauty, Shosh blows it up."

"Okay."

"She's what *Vogue* wants to be. She's a platinum, fucking, whatever, in a world of brushed-brass shit. And I'm not just talking looks. Her *person* is astounding, which I know sounds corny, but it's true. Also, she can sing, did you know that?"

Maya, amused, shakes her head.

"Well, she can. And it's the voice of an angel. Plus, she loves Will, and guess what?"

"Will loves her?"

"Will loves her! And so does Ali, and my mom, and . . ." I sigh like a deflating blimp.

. . .

. . .

"It's okay, Evan."

"I don't want to say it, yet."

"That's okay too."

. . .

. . .

"We can revisit this conversation whenever you like," says Maya.

"Okay."

. . .

. . .

"Evan?"

"What."

"What's happening with Headlands?"

When I consider the seventeenth-century theory that birds migrated to the moon, I think less about the scientist who conceived the idea and more about the people who believed him: the miners and fishermen, the blacksmiths and farmers, people going about their days with all sorts of considerations beyond where birds might go in the winter. Is it any wonder then that what little time they could devote to the subject, they gave not to the most *probable* explanation, but to the most *interesting*? Is it any wonder that a life spent among the ordinary will bend over backward to taste even a little extraordinary?

"I missed the deadline."

Maya's the first one I've told. I thought it would be best, breaking the news to her first, before Mom or Ali.

"It lapsed," I say, shrugging, as if to prove that shit—*see how I care?* "So that's that."

I am the miner, the fisherman, the blacksmith and farmer.

I am the ordinary life. Shosh is my improbable explanation.

"Well, then—" Maya stands, puts her hands in her pockets. "Time's up."

"What?" I look at the clock. "We're twenty minutes in."

She shrugs—*see how I care?* "That's that, as they say."

"Okay, I see what you're doing. You're trying to *Good Will Hunting* me."

"You've mentioned the concept of atrophy in here, Evan. What do you think that is?"

"I'm not taking the bait."

"Everything everywhere is trying to fall apart. There's nothing you can do about it."

"You want to go to Alaska so bad, you should go yourself."

"So you don't *want* to go anymore," she says. "You don't want to go to Alaska. You don't want to be part of that program, and *that's* why you let the deadline lapse?"

"You still don't get it. I *can't* go."

"If you choose to spend the rest of your life waiting for bad things to happen, guess what? That's exactly what you'll do."

SHOSH

her favorite view

IN SOME WAYS, THE PHOTO was like many before it: a mountaintop view, miles of endless white forest spread out ahead; a scattering of cabins in the foreground, all of them covered in snow; on the horizon, the sun, either setting or rising, a majestic display of beauty.

In one way, it was quite different from the other photos she'd used: there was a person, wrapped in a blanket, staring out across the landscape. And for all the majestic beauty in front of them, the person was the clear focal point of the photo.

in cosmos vast (and still expanding)
my favorite view is you, just standing

In the bottom corner, she typed **cabin couplet #22** and hit post.

Then, stomach aflutter, she DM'd the post to Evan, along with a message: **Wrote one for you.**

EVAN
the horniness encroaches

IT TAKES ALI APPROXIMATELY FIFTEEN seconds to respond to the screenshot I sent her. Her first dozen texts are nothing but eggplant emojis, followed by hand-clapping, followed by fire, followed by more eggplants, and then . . .

Ali: She wants you

Evan: How is that possible?

Ali: The universe is vast, or haven't you heard?
When do you see her next?

Evan: Tonight. We're meeting at the Discount

Ali: CLASSY

Evan: HER IDEA

Ali: So
you gonna
you know

Evan: I mean

Ali: Right

Evan: I would very much like to

Ali: Well sure

Evan: It sort of feels like

Ali: It does feel that way

Evan: But this couplet . . .
Raises the stakes

Ali: Among other things
(see: eggplant emojis)

Evan: I really like her

Ali: So look. She's obviously out of your
league

Evan: Obvs

Ali: Having said that, three points of note . . .
1—You don't give yourself enough credit.
You're funny in a nerdy way, which is, at
times, not un-cute
2—You're smart and you have good hair
and you should remember these things
3—Because I know you, I know there will
be a moment when you convince yourself
there is no possible way she likes you. In
that moment, remember . . .
She wrote you poetry
Nobody does this for someone whose dirt-
ies they don't want to pounce

Evan: You've written me poetry

Ali: That was different
Reading this, you can feel the horniness
encroaching

Evan: I do feel that

Ali: Just remember what I said, you'll be fine

Evan: Right. I have good hair.

Ali: Plus the nerdy smart thing

• • •

Shosh tells me she's "arranged a car" for our ride to the Discount, and that I should be in front of my house at six p.m. I tell her I can drive, but she won't hear of it, and sure enough, right at six, a car pulls in the driveway, and Shosh climbs out of the back.

"Hey, you."

"Hey."

This kid at school wears the same Bowie shirt every day, and while Shosh isn't quite to that level, she does wear the same coat and boots, her hair the same beautiful mess as always. She's stunning, is the thing, and I am already proving Ali's third point correct: there is no possible way this girl is into me.

And yet, when she hugs me, her hand lingers on mine.

"Will made this for you," I say, handing her a flower cut from yellow paper, a green pipe cleaner for a stem, and she smiles like a rising sun, sticks the paper flower behind her ear, and I'm dead.

As we head toward the car, I ask if she got an Uber, and she says, "Sort of," and then, climbing into the back seat: "Evan, this is my friend—"

"Ruth?"

SHOSH
hands

IT WAS HARD TO KNOW if the movie actually sucked, or if the circumstances injected it with suckage.

It wasn't a packed house, but people were spread everywhere; Shosh and Evan had to sit in the middle of a row, and while their hands made the most of things, she was ready for more than hands.

On the way out, she texted Ruth, who said she'd be there in a flash.

"So, do you pay her?" Evan asked as they waited out front.

"Oh, for sure. I mean, she tells me not to, but we're only friends because of the job, so—" Shosh checked her phone, put it away, pushed her hair out of her face only to have the wind blow it back. "I still can't believe you guys know each other."

"Meh. We don't, really."

"Your loss, then. That girl is a bright shining star."

Evan looked unsure, but changed the subject. "Will is super jealous I get to hang with you tonight."

"Dude," she said. "That kid."

"I know."

"He's like—"

"I know."

"—the actual best."

More wind, more hair in her face; she gave up, blew into her hands to keep them warm, looked at Evan as he looked away.

Felt his eyes on her as she looked away.

People were everywhere, walking into and out of the theater, and in the middle of it all, Shosh and Evan looked at each other at the same time.

Wind. Hair.

Smiles at first.

Then, no smiles.

This, she thought, stepping closer, a sudden urgency.

Did he feel it? She hoped so, she really did.

She grabbed his hand, leaned in to tell him, only when she opened her mouth, it suddenly felt like that moment between sleep and wake. And she wondered what it was she'd meant to say.

NEW YORK CITY

· 1988 ·

THE MORNING AFTER SIGGY FIRST heard the Voice, he convinced himself it was a dream. *What I get for those late-night Skor bars*, he thought, dumping the rest of the chocolate in the trash. It was December, a bitter chill in the air; last night, he'd fallen asleep wrapped in quilts, so by the time the Voice jolted him awake, he'd sweat straight through his pj's.

Two years out of college, and nearing the end of his grant money, Siggy was working on an original musical in a one-bedroom walk-up in Brooklyn Heights. And while he was generally open to the idea of a higher power (he'd never seen a baby and not thought *miracle*), willingness to believe was not itself belief. Perhaps some would attribute the Voice to God, but Siggy remained, as ever, skeptical.

Everett's roommates called him "the Believer," a badge he wore with honor. Every Sunday, he could be found at St. Augustine's Episcopal Church; the most common book by his bed was The Book of Common Prayer, and while he couldn't prove his faith, it had never occurred to him to try. In his final year at NYU, Everett studied art history and lived in a residence hall in the East Village. When he wasn't busy with church or school, he liked to finish his days toiling in a quiet passion: jigsaw puzzles.

Recently, he'd acquired a series of thousand-piece US bridges. After completing the Golden Gate and the Mackinac, he'd moved on to his beloved Brooklyn Bridge. Painting would always be his first love, but puzzling offered something art could not: a decisive end point. On average, it took him ten days to complete a thousand-piecer, but he was heading into his third straight week working on the Brooklyn Bridge with no end in sight. The problem was, the entire palette was a washed-out gray. Sky, road, water—other than the city lights, and a tiny bird in the corner, Everett could hardly tell the pieces apart.

"You're going out in this?" his roommate asked one night, as Everett put on a coat and hat. It was after midnight, the winter wind howling through the alley behind their building.

"This puzzle's got me cross-eyed," said Everett. "I need to walk."

Six blocks later, when he realized where his feet were taking him, he couldn't help but smile.

It wasn't the chocolate.

The Voice had visited Siggy every night for two weeks and always with the same command: "GET UP." Determined to uncover the source of the Voice, he'd tried staying awake, but when it came, there was nothing to see, only a bird fluttering on the window-sill. His days were filled with headaches and involuntary naps; his music suffered, he barely ate, and under it all, an anxious dread as the clock ticked toward bedtime.

One night, in a desperate attempt to escape, he left his apartment and wandered the streets of Brooklyn, carefully sticking to familiar routes, and eventually wound up in the middle of the Brooklyn Bridge, staring across the East River.

"Hey."

Siggy wasn't a native New Yorker; born and raised in Tromsø, if someone talked to you, you at least acknowledged their existence. But by the time he'd finished his first year of college here, he understood the unspoken agreement of New Yorkers everywhere: at all costs, eyes dead ahead.

"You okay, man?"

The rules were clear and unwavering, which meant this guy was either an assailant or, worse, a tourist. But when Siggy turned to tell him off, all that came out was, "Oh."

The night took a pleasant turn, and before Siggy knew it, they were talking about the musical he was writing. "It's a nineteenth-century Parisian love story," he said, blushing.

"Romantic," said Ev.

"With cholera."

"Ah. So . . . a tragic romance."

"Is there any other kind?"

Everett smiled. "I think so, yes."

Seven years later, in 1995, Siggy and Everett will recount this story at their joint bachelor party. Siggy will say it was love at first sight, a storybook meet-cute for the ages. Everett will shake his head—"You should get a doctorate in revisionist history," he'll say, and then tell a version that's less of a meet-cute and more of an intervention. "You had that look in your eyes, Sig. I was scared for you." And while their memories of the night will differ in subtle ways, there is one exchange they remember perfectly:

"I haven't slept through the night in weeks," Siggy said that first night, eyes on the East River.

When Everett asked why, Siggy said he'd never believe him.

"Guess what my roommates call me?" said Everett.

At their joint funeral in 2006, Everett's mother will tell the story through tears, how her son met the love of his life because he couldn't finish a puzzle. Siggy's sister will say how lucky it was her brother couldn't sleep, how some people are destined to find each other. And in the front row of St. Augustine's Episcopal Church, a six-year-old girl called Birdie will stare at the two caskets, knowing Papa and Daddy are inside, that they'd had an accident on a cold mountain in the country where Daddy was born.

Sitting there, she will try to get her head around the scope of time: the seconds it takes to die; the forever of being dead.

Their story was known by all who knew them. But the only people who knew about the Voice were Everett and Siggy.

"I hear a Voice," Siggy told him that first night on the bridge. "It says the same two words over and over again."

"What does it say?" asked Everett.

Eighteen years later, right in the middle of her aunt's eulogy, Birdie will stand and scream, "*GET UP!*"

PART
SIX

OPUS

EVAN
blue

SHOSH'S BEDROOM IS AN INSTITUTIONAL mess: it's been a mess so long, it no longer feels messy.

"I like that you have long hair," she says, gently pulling a few strands of my hair to their fullest length.

"My friends are obsessed with yours," I say.

"Really? It's always such a wreck."

When we first came upstairs, she showed me how her bed lined up with her window, and said she often sat half in, half out. It's too cold to open the window tonight, but that didn't keep us from the bed. I'm not sure how we wound up like this—Shosh sort of lying down, with my head in her lap—but I am here for it.

"Have you heard Nightbird lately?" she asks.

"No. You?"

"Not since that night in the park. It's funny, but when I think about the songs now, it's like they were shapes in a cloud no one else noticed. Out in the open, but only if you knew where to look."

"You sound like her, you know. When you sing."

She doesn't say anything for a minute, just slowly runs her hands through my hair; when she finally does speak, her voice is thin, and I can tell she's working up to something. "Stevie used to say music is the thing you come back to. You might leave it for a while. You might think it's forgotten you, but when you're ready, it's ready." Silence for a second, and then: "I miss it."

"Music?"

"Music. Acting. All of it. The only thing more exhausting than quitting is pretending I don't miss it."

"So don't quit."

"You sound like Ms. Clark."

"The drama teacher?"

Shosh nods. "But we're only nine years apart. Plus, we spent every waking moment together the last four years, so she's basically family. She was a huge help with the application process at USC and keeps trying to convince me to reapply, but—that part of my life is over."

If my time with Maya has taught me anything, it's the depths to which a person can believe something is true when it isn't. Every storm I've ever had, I was convinced I was dying. Half the things I've said in Maya's office have proved false, but when I said them, I believed them unequivocally. I hear those depths now in Shosh's voice. She's not being dramatic or looking for pity or understanding. She's stating what for her is a very simple truth.

"When Stevie left for college, that first year was devastating. We were so close, it was just a matter of time before I joined her at Loyola. Then the acting took on a life of its own, and everybody was like, New York or LA, but I was always fine with Chicago. Loyola is a solid program. One night on the phone, she got real quiet. Said it didn't make any sense, just because she was older and got to choose first, that I should follow her. And that was that. From then on, wherever I landed for college, she was coming with me.

At some point it occurred to us she'd have to transfer during senior year unless she graduated early—but you know what you have to do to graduate early?"

I don't say anything; it's not really a question.

"She was on her way to summer sessions when the truck hit her," Shosh says. "She was on that road at that moment because of me. My dream, my ambition."

I want to tell her it's not her fault. And I almost do, but then I think of all the times I heard those words when Dad left, and how empty they rang. And I think of all the times Maya could have responded with some rote solution but, instead, chose to meet me where I was.

I want my words to count. I want to meet Shosh where she is.

And so I tell her about Mom's cancer, and about Headlands, and how even though it was my only dream, I didn't even apply because it would mean leaving Mom and Will behind. "It's not the same, I know. But I get having a dream you can't chase."

When I'm done, Shosh waits a minute; I can tell she wants her words to count too.

"Sorry about your mom," she says.

"I think she's okay. But it comes back, you know? And if that happens, I just—can't see not being here."

Gently, Shosh moves my head, pulls a laptop out of a pile of pillows. "I've been super into Dickinson lately," she says, flipping it open, typing, scrolling. "'*Because I could not stop for Death, he kindly stopped for me. The Carriage held but just Ourselves and Immortality.*' Ruth turned me on to her. She was obsessed with death and immortality—"

"Ruth?"

"Emily. Which makes sense when you read about everyone in her life who died young. When you're surrounded by death, it's hard not to consider living forever."

"I have a healthy amount of respect for my own mortality. The idea that death takes your all and makes it nothing . . ." My voice trails off as I realize how insensitive the comment is given the discussion around Stevie. "Shit. Sorry."

"It's fine. But just so you know, I don't think you're right about that."

"Yeah?"

"Maybe. I don't know. What do you think happens?"

Funny how a question can change depending on who's asking. I've thought about it before, obviously. Only now, I'm thinking something different. "I heard this theory once about the color blue. I'm butchering it, but the gist is, when you look back through literature, the word blue doesn't appear for centuries. It's not in any ancient texts or books. Whenever Homer describes the ocean, he uses wine as a comparison. It's like this thing that exists, but so far as anyone can tell, either people couldn't see the color blue or else they had no word for it. So then I think, maybe we had to evolve into seeing it? But if that's true, it's not like everyone on earth woke up one day and bam—there was blue. Which means there was a period in history when some people could see blue, and others couldn't. And the ones who could, they believed the color existed, didn't they? It was right there. But for the ones who couldn't, it was less a color, more a concept. An idea, like . . . true love. You believed in it, or you didn't. Maybe the afterlife is like that."

I feel the rhythms of Shosh's breathing, and I could lie here forever with her hands in my hair. "I know she's not here," she says. "But she's not nothing. And she's not nowhere."

When I ask for more Dickinson, she reads a few favorites, including one that makes me wonder if the old writers had their own Nightbirds:

"Hope" is the thing with feathers -
That perches in the soul -
And sings the tune without the words -
And never stops—at all -

After reciting this one, Shosh does this shruggy thing that makes me melt, and then our breathing changes, the air turns electric.

I don't know who moves first.

I sit up; she quietly shuts the computer, slides it to one side, and now her hands are on the back of my head, her eyes like soft fire.

I lean forward, our foreheads touch, galaxies collide—pasts and futures, too—all our ideas and dreams and fears made one.

"I'm a mess," she whispers, and I can smell her lips, but I wait.

Look down, lean away, just a little.

Her words could mean *slow*, could mean *no*, so I wait.

Then look up. Smile.

SHOSH
true blue

"NOBODY'S PERFECT," HE SAID.

"Some bodies are more perfect than others," she said.

Shosh blinked, a slow silence. And when they kissed, it was volcanic and molecular, fevered, a wonder both ancient and new. "I missed you," she said, and the kiss exploded, became many kisses, because she was right, it made no sense, but she was right. A gentle push, and she was on top of him now, and time was nothing, oceans and years were nothing, there was only Shosh and Evan, their mouths and tongues playing catch-up with their hands. Did he feel it? She hoped so. She kissed him harder to show him, deeper now, her hair falling on his face like the first leaves of autumn, her hips moving forward, backward, slowly forward, and backward, and then she stopped—sat up straight—pulled her shirt off over her head, and dropped back down onto him, kissing him on the forehead, kissing him on the neck, the cheek, the eye. "I believe in blue," she whispered, kissing.

EVAN
the thing itself

"SO, IN THE BROADER CONTEXT of 1950s Chelsea, when Mila Henry writes of 'exiting the robot,' what do we think she's really talking about?"

I cannot recall ever being this distracted in Mr. Hambright's class.

Which I'm sure has nothing at all to do with the events of last night.

"Clearly, she meant *fuck the patriarchy*," says a sophomore named Laura whose levels of thirst force me to believe she has never been quenched. "And, like, *pow*," says Laura. "Shots fired."

Hambright nods, goes full-on Hammy. "That is an answer, Laura. And I thank you for it."

Later, twenty minutes into a *cake* Mila Henry writing prompt, Hambright stops by my desk, reads over my shoulder as I write. "Hmm."

I set down my pen. "May I help you?"

"Is it your contention that *June First* was largely driven by Mila Henry's conflict—emotional and financial—as a stay-at-home mother?"

Yurt, behind me: "Is that your contention, bro?"

"No," I say. "It's my contention that *June First* exists *at all* because of Mila Henry's conflict—emotional and financial—as a *single* mother."

"She was married to Huston."

"Please. He wasn't around. She did it by herself."

"Hmm. So why do it at all?" he asks.

I can't help feeling he's toying with me. "Why do what?"

"By all accounts, her first book was an abject failure. No one read it—no one seemed to care. There was no looming pressure, no contractual concerns—"

"It wasn't about *commerce*. She had to write the book. There was value in the process, in the thing itself. Not just what that thing might become."

Hambright seems to consider, nodding slowly, and then— "Your mother tells me you let the Headlands deadline lapse."

I choke on my own saliva, then sort of casually look around the room to see who's listening. (Literally everyone.)

"No Glacier Bay?" asks Hambright.

"Uh, yeah. No, I mean—I decided not to go."

"That's too bad. I thought that program sounded right for you. Well, I'd love to read the application essays you wrote."

Pin-drop silence in the room.

"I didn't write the essays."

"Why not?"

"I told you, I decided not to go. What would be the point?"

Like a world-class chess player, Hambright never reveals what he's doing as he does it. You're just going along, everything's normal, and then *bam*—you're at the bottom of a hole you never knew you dug.

"I would have thought the point of an essay," he says, calmly, quietly, "was the essay itself, Evan. Value in the thing, yes? Not just what that thing might become."

SHOSH
ready, set, bake

WHAT WINTER WINDS STOLE—warmth, breath, the hum of life—
spring winds brought back in abundance. As if the air itself took a
different tack in spring, working with nature rather than against it.
As much as Shosh loved winter, as much as it felt more like home
than any other season, there was no denying the joy of a good thaw.

It wasn't here yet, spring. But standing at the window, she could
almost hear it coming. Certainly, she could smell it.

Or maybe that was the cake.

"Giuseppe made it look so *easy*," said her dad.

Shosh turned from the kitchen window to find him squatting
in front of the oven, staring inside, as if willing a suitable bake. "He
makes everything look easy," she said, pulling a can of Diet Coke
from the fridge. "Which is why he's gonna win."

"*Jürgen all the way!*" yelled her mom from the living room.

"Please," said her dad. "Crystelle is peaking at just the right
time."

The origin of their family's latest obsession rested squarely on
her father's shoulders. Somebody at his work had mentioned how
they'd gotten hooked on *The Great British Baking Show*, and that night,
when he'd turned it on, Shosh had plopped down on the couch
with every intention of mocking both the show and her dad for

watching it. Three episodes later, she felt roughly 400 percent more relaxed than when she'd entered the room. At some point, her mom joined them, and now they spoke this whole other language, full of soggy bottoms and stodgy bakes, sudden experts on things they'd never heard of before. It was a good show; Shosh couldn't deny it. But the show's quality had little to do with what compelled them to watch together so regularly, just as their reason for baking had little to do with the quality of their bakes.

Baking had never been a Bell pastime. And because they'd never baked as a family of four, it was the perfect hobby for a family of three.

"What's it called again?" Shosh asked, staring down at the mess of a cake her dad had just pulled from the oven.

"Amarena Cherry Gugelhupf," said her dad, consulting the printed-off recipe.

"I'd say it looks pretty Gugelhupfy."

"Maybe *too* Gugelhupfy."

"Well, how much Gugelhupf were you supposed to put in?"

"I don't know." Her dad smiled at her. "Maybe we should Gugel it."

She saluted him with her can, all, "Let's goooooo," and his smile changed, deepened. Like a spring wind, it brought warmth, breath, the hum of life.

Gently, he put both hands on her shoulders, and kissed her forehead. "We're gonna be okay," he whispered.

Later that night, after consuming one mediocre cake, and four extraordinary episodes of British broadcasting, they dragged their sugar-laden legs upstairs for bed. Pj's on, Shosh brushed her teeth, and when she stepped from the bathroom into the hallway, she saw something she hadn't seen in months: the door to Stevie's bedroom was cracked open, a sliver of light shining from within. Sock-footed, Shosh crept down the hall, peered through the crack. Inside, her mother was pulling things from Stevie's closet, setting them on the bed beside an open box. As she worked, she quietly hummed something vaguely familiar, something from when the girls were young; propped on the bed beside the box was Stevie's old ukulele, as if it had just been played yesterday.

Shosh smiled, turned for her room. Inside, she clicked the door shut, listened . . .

No songs. No Nightbird. Just the sound of a good thaw. Like prying boards from an old well or spreading a blanket in a patch of sunlight.

Without thinking too much about it, she pulled out her phone, and texted Evan: **Maybe we're wrong. Maybe it's okay to be okay.**

She tossed her phone on the bed, opened her laptop, and composed an email to an office she hadn't contacted in months.

EVAN
the ice queen

I HAVE TO READ THE email five times before I fully comprehend it. Even then, I'm not sure I do. In a daze, I walk to the kitchen—where Mom is prepping a taco casserole for the week—and hold out my phone.

"What is it?" she asks, wiping her hands on her apron.

"One of the students dropped out of Headlands. There's an open spot."

"Wait—" She grabs my phone. "I thought you missed the deadline?"

I tell her how Hambright prodded me to write the essay anyway, so I did. And how Shosh had sent a text out of the blue that made me think I should go ahead and submit the essay, so I did that too. "It was a late application. I didn't even think they'd read it."

"Honey—this is an *acceptance* letter."

"Sort of. They have that weird . . . contingency."

But it's too late. Mom's crying, covering her mouth with one hand as she rereads the email, and I wish more than anything that it could be real.

"Mom—"

Now she's wrapping her arms around me. "I am so proud of you."

"I'm not going."

She pulls away, studies my face. "If you don't go, I'm not talking to you for a year."

"Okay—"

"Forget Glacier Bay, it'll be the year of Glacial Mom. You *are* going."

"Do you really think—just because you don't let me come with you to the appointments, do you really think I don't know anything? You think I haven't read every article I can find, haven't memorized every blog post, that I don't google all of it? You think I don't know that thirty percent of breast cancer survivors experience recurrence?"

"I can tell you this. *One hundred* percent of my children who don't grab a dream when it's staring them in the face will be grounded for the rest of their lives."

"You'll never be *cured*, Mom. There's always a chance it comes back, and if that happens, I have to be here."

"Okay, listen now. Listen to me. If you ever decide to be a dad, you're going to be the best there ever was. Way better than your own, okay?" Upstairs, we hear Will reenacting the bike scene from E.T., running around his room like he's being chased by cops in suits. "You'll watch movies together, *make* movies together, build LEGO, and instead of Bubba Nights, you'll have Daddy Nights, and you'll wish it could always be that way. You'll watch your kid grow into their own person, and you'll be so proud, even though part of you is sad the old things are passing. Your kid will grow and change in the best ways, and maybe then you'll understand what I feel right now. That the only thing worse than watching your kid walk out the door is watching them quietly close it."

We're hugging now, both of us crying, listening to Will's beautiful racket upstairs.

"You are not putting your life on hold for me," she says into my shoulder, and I think hugging your mom is the best way to travel time; the places you've been, the people you've met, it's all there. "Now say, *Okay, Mom.*"

"Okay, Mom."

"*Ice Queen,* I'm telling you."

"I'm gonna pass on the obvious *Frozen* joke."

Mom laughs, wipes her eyes with the back of her hand, and only now—eyeliner smeared across her face—do I realize she's wearing makeup.

"Are you going somewhere?"

She mumbles something about a "meetup with a friend from work," turns back to the stove, continues prepping the casserole. Watching her, I can't help wondering if she had a Glacier Bay when she was younger. I can't help wondering if it was an open door she'd quietly closed.

"Mom."

"Yes, honey."

"If there's someone in this world who makes you happy—"

She stops moving but doesn't turn around.

"—I would love to meet that person."

A whispered "Okay," like a door, softly opening.

SHOSH
dispatches from in-between places

THE ONLY THING MISSING FROM Mavie's Oscar party was gin.

The theme was Old Hollywood, everyone dressed to the nines, mostly Roaring Twenties–style. The core group from Ali's kickback would be here, along with a number of faces Shosh didn't recognize, or barely recognized from her high school days. Screens were everywhere: a wall projector in the basement, one flat screen in the den, and another in the kitchen; on the back deck, a TV hung over a hot tub; there was even an iPad in the bathroom, so no one would miss a minute of Academy Award action. This party had it all.

Except gin.

The martinis were labeled "tonic and elderflower," whatever the fuck.

Shosh told herself she didn't miss drinking, but she did—a lot. The bottles in her house had been the manifestation of comfort, a truth she hadn't realized until those bottles were gone.

"Shoes at the door!" Mavie stood like a sentry in the spacious foyer, grilling everyone as they entered. Apparently, there was a walnut tree causing problems in the front yard. "You people will not be tracking old walnuts through my house. I will never hear the end of it."

"Hey, *Old Walnuts* was my nickname in high school," said Balding.

Mavie rolled her eyes. "You're in high school now, nerd."

Balding raised her bottle to some imaginary horizon. "There goes Old Walnuts, they used to say."

"Stop it. No one said that."

"Some people said it."

Mavie turned to Shosh. "Is Evan coming?"

Shosh sipped her gin-less martini. "His mom got off late, but he should be on his way."

"He better hurry if he wants to be in the ballot pool," said Mavie. "I don't fuck with late entries."

"Hey, *No Late Entries* was my nickname in high school," said Balding.

"Oh my God, why are you so gross?" Mavie could pretend all she wanted, rolling eyes and acting annoyed, but given the way she was currently wrapping her arms around Balding's neck, kissing her on the mouth like they were the only two people on earth, it was clear that Balding's brand of crude, corny wit was exactly Mavie's cup of tea.

Sara and Ali showed up together, and like clockwork, Yurt rolled in soon after. Roughly a half dozen others wandered in (dutifully removing their shoes) before Evan finally arrived, hair slicked back, fitted suit and tie, looking every bit like Leo DiCaprio's Gatsby. Shosh felt suddenly hot, her mouth suddenly dry, her whole body suddenly, suddenly.

"Hey," he said, standing in the doorway.

She opened her mouth, but nothing came out.

"Damn, son," said Balding.

Sara slow clapped. "Way to pull it together, Cervantes."

"*Shoes*," said Mavie.

After removing his shoes, Evan made his way over to Shosh. "You look . . . like . . ." was all he could manage, and she pretended not to be pleased—in her short flapper dress, sparkly headband, and smoky eye—but it was nice not being the only one at the party who couldn't find their words.

She did a mock twirl, and then another, landing on his chest. "You're a real looker, kid, and no mistake," she said, doing her best Katharine Hepburn, smoking an invisible cigarette. "The kid stays in the picture, see?"

Evan smiled. "You're gonna keep this up all night, aren't you."

"And how!" She stood on her tiptoes, kissed his forehead, then his lips, then ruffled his hair, and he just stood there smiling, ever the dapper Gatsby, and she wondered how in the world she was going to tell him she was leaving.

"Hey, that's what's-her-face. From *Hamilton*."

"Oh my God, it is."

"Dude, that is *not* her."

"It totally is."

"There's no way that's what's-her-face from *Hamilton*."

"Phillipa Soo," said Shosh, sipping her elderflower concoction. "Of Libertyville, Illinois. Julliard class of 2012. Has a dog named Billie. And a talent that won't quit." Shosh looked around, found everyone staring at her. "It's her."

"I *told* you it was her."

"It doesn't *look* like her."

"You're saying she doesn't look like *herself*?"

The room continued bickering until the next category came up—Best Supporting Actress—and Balding said, "Shosh, why aren't you up there?"

"What?" Shosh kept her eyes on the screen, wishing this moment away. "Stop."

"I'm just saying what we're all thinking. We've seen your plays." Balding pointed to the screen, where the nominees waited with bated breath as the envelope was being opened. "You've got what they've got."

"She's right," Ali said, and suddenly the room was full of nervously nodding heads.

Aside from Evan, she hadn't given much thought to these people knowing who she was before she'd met them. But knowing *about* a person was different from knowing them.

"You think you'll ever act again?" asked Sara.

"Come on, guys," Evan said.

"It's okay." Shosh put a hand on his leg, smiled at him, hoping he could see her thanks—as well as her apology for what was coming. "Yes," she said to the room. "I'm going to act again."

"Really?"

She nodded. "Actually, I emailed the USC dean of admissions a few days ago. Ms. Clark—my drama teacher—she's been talking with him too. The deadlines have come and gone, but given what happened, the circumstances last summer—he needs to talk to some people, but Ms. Clark says she's 'cautiously optimistic.' So we'll see, I guess—"

Shosh's shrug of a sentence was interrupted by an explosion of cheers. Yurt ran to the kitchen, came back with a tray of "Shosh shots," which turned out to be some kind of nonalcoholic oak-aged maple drink, so by the time Mavie informed Shosh she would be at UCLA next year—"LA or bust!" they toasted with another sham round—it took everything in Shosh not to grab Evan by the hand, pull him into the nearest bedroom, and have her way with him. Just to clear her head, to feel safe in what she knew.

"Well, I guess this is as good a time as any," said Yurt. "I didn't get into Duke." There was a scattering of sorrys and mumbled consolations, and then Yurt's face lit up. "So I'm going to Wake Forest. Got my acceptance yesterday."

The room erupted all over again. More gin-less toasts, hoorays and congratulations, and suddenly—out of nowhere—Sara tore across the room in a blur, threw her arms around Yurt's neck, and slammed him into the wall, where the two proceeded to make out for the next thirty seconds or so. "Heyyyyyy!" went the room, as Ali lifted a bottle of sparkling cider over her head, and eventually, when Sara pulled back, she wiped her mouth, looked around, and said, "Okay, then," to which Yurt said, "Okey dokey."

Sometimes, a room takes on the personality of the people in it. As each of them reclaimed their seats, turned their attention back to the TV, they tried to remember why they cared about the Oscars in the first place. Having tasted the sweet nectar of good news, the room was hungry for more, and so, a hushed expectation fell over them, as the room waited to be fed.

"I should hear from Georgetown in a couple of weeks," said Ali, a worthy effort, but nutritiously insufficient.

A few nods throughout the room, quiet words of encouragement—a growling appetite.

And because they all knew Evan had missed the Headlands deadline, when he calmly stated, "Well, I'm going to Alaska," the spirit of celebration was all the more jubilant for it. "Heyyyyyyy!" went the room again, hoorays and congratulations, and in the middle of it all, Evan and Shosh found each other.

She did another mock twirl. "You're going places, kid," a flat attempt to lighten the mood, as the literal interpretation sank in.

"You are too, sounds like."

On tiptoes again, she kissed his lips, rested her head on his chest. "And how," she said quietly, and they stood like that, the ravenous room celebrating around them.

Later, during a run of technical categories ("Can *anyone* tell the difference between sound *editing* and sound *mixing*?" asked Sara), Evan got up to go to the bathroom, only when he came back out, he caught Shosh's eye, and nodded to the back door. They stepped onto the deck together, and she thought she would live in that split second between the chattering crowd and the quiet stillness.

Outside, what had started as a light rain had become an even lighter mist.

"Hi."

"Hi."

"Didn't want to go the whole night without talking," said Evan.

Through the mist, the backyard loomed large, like one of those old English manors with manicured bushes and little pathways between gardens.

"Well-okay, Mavie," Shosh said.

"Yeah. Her mom has one of those jobs in finance that's even more confusing after she explains it." Evan cleared his throat. "She told you she's going to UCLA, yeah?"

Shosh nodded, and Evan said he was glad she would know someone out there, but his words were hollow.

"I've been trying to tell you," Shosh said.

"Me too."

"The kicker is, before I met you, I'm not sure I would have had the balls to reapply."

"Me neither."

Inside, the sounds of the party felt distant, boastful, as if showing them what kind of lighthearted fun they could be having. Instead, they stared out across a misty yard that suddenly seemed entirely too symbolic.

"USC could still fall through," she said.

"It won't."

"It could."

"Oh, I know. But it for sure won't. And, Shosh—I don't want it to."

She rested her head on his shoulder; this close, she could smell his smell, not a cologne, but the smell of his house, his hair, his Evan-ness. "It's like we found each other in this weird in-between time of life," she said. "Only you don't usually hold on to things from the in-between, so there's no protocol for what's next."

The logic was maddening: in finally getting what they wanted—and in helping the other do the same—they'd put their future together on the line.

"Shosh."

"Yeah?"

But there was nothing left to say. So they stood in the mist, wishing there were.

EVAN
time encapsuled

SEVEN BUBBA NIGHTS LEFT.

Not that anyone's counting.

When I first told Will the news of my impending departure, he retreated to his room for days. I tried to break it gently, but six months may as well be a lifetime when you're seven.

I watch him now through the kitchen window; he's reading a book under the apple tree, right around the spot where we buried that time capsule all those years ago. He stands, brushes grass and dirt from his jeans, then talks to himself as he walks around the yard, and I try to guess which scene he's reenacting from *E.T.*, which, as it happens, is cued up and ready to go as soon as the Jet's guy is here.

Part of my agreement with Will: Until I leave, it's Jet's and *E.T.* every Tuesday night. Mom even approved delivery *and* breadsticks.

I can't pretend to be annoyed, is how not annoyed I am.

In an effort to cut back on helicopter-parenting my brother, I decide to wait for the pizza out front. On the porch, I open my phone to an email I've reread so many times, I basically know it by heart . . .

Headlands has never accepted a late submission,
as doing so would be counterproductive to our core

code of community and responsibility. However, the
same morning we found ourselves with an unexpected
opening, we received your incredibly moving piece,
"Phone Home." Our team considers a wide array of
factors when choosing applicants, and while fate
certainly isn't among them, gut instinct is. And so,
I'm happy to say that we've decided to accept your
submission, and extend an invitation to this year's
program, under one condition . . .

I'd taken Ali's advice regarding the essay prompt—*consider a favorite book or movie and explain why it affects you*—and wrote about E.T. My opening line was, "My little brother and I don't watch E.T.—we speak it." I wrote about the language of movies, how the mutual love of a thing strengthens the bond between those who love it. I argued that movies were inert; they had no say in the lives of those who watched them. But when people sat down together to watch a movie, they entered the best kind of contract: the common pursuit of story. And sometimes, I wrote, that pursuit connected them forever.

Or something like that.

Honestly, I'm not sure what I said. I'd been in a fevered frenzy that day and wound up typing the essay straight into the online form. At the bottom of the page, when I saw the place to upload "supplemental materials," the fevered frenzy continued as I picked up my sketch pad and drew Will's head popping out of a giant refrigerator box (back when it was dressed up like E.T.'s spaceship). I drew his room the way I'll always remember it: a mess of stuffed animals, hodgepodge LEGO, scattered Minions, and Star Wars toys.

And I drew those two words on the wall, words that wound up being the title of my essay: *Phone Home*.

It's the last part of the acceptance email I can't get my head around.

> While you're here, in addition to your participation
> in regularly scheduled activities, we will require you
> to draw one fully realized sketch per day. The subject
> matter can be of your choosing, but we would love to
> see a few sketches of the local landscape. Call it an
> artist residency. No doubt, the first of many.

It's not the first time someone has referred to me as an artist. Just the first time I've considered the possibility they might be right.

Back inside, box of Jet's in hand, I'm setting up dinner on the coffee table when I hear it: not a scream or a yell, but a wailing cry from the backyard. I sprint through the back door, spot Will under the apple tree again, only now he's a muddy mess, face smeared in dirt and tears, and when I see what he has in his lap, something catches in my throat. "*Will*," I say, and because I need time to get myself right, I walk toward him slowly.

"Hey, Evan." He looks up at me through tears and pure light.

"Hey, bud."

In his lap, the rusted-out time capsule. "I dug it up," he says.

"I see that."

He wipes his nose, which just spreads the snot around his face. "Why does everyone leave?"

Breathe . . .

Just to breathe.

To feel myself existing.

I drop to my knees, hold his head against my chest, and rock with him back and forth as he cries. "You were just a baby when we planted this apple tree. It started rotting almost right away. Something in the soil, maybe we didn't water it enough, who knows. I remember Dad was *so frustrated*. He used to stand at that window and look down here, just staring at it, complaining it wasn't growing right. But he never did anything to make it better. I never understood him, even back then."

Gently, I put two fingers under Will's chin, lift his little face to mine. "Dad left," I say. "I may have to go, but I will *never* leave. I'll always be right here."

We hold each other in silence for a while, and when the tears are done, in the tired comfort that follows, we rebury the time capsule without opening it.

Next morning at school, I'm talking with Sara in the hallway when Ali walks up. "Hey, guys, I got a joke for you. What did one Hoya say to the other?"

"Wait—"

Her smile is bursting at the seams, and when it finally busts through, so do we, just all out going nuts right there in the hallway until a passing teacher gives us major side-eye.

"I can't believe I'm a Hoya," says Ali.

"What even is a Hoya?" asks Sara.

"I don't know. But I am one. Also, hey, let's not make a big thing of it, okay?"

Sara and I heartily agree not to make a thing out of it until Ali is well out of earshot, at which point we google the most crucial of questions: "Does Chili's take reservations?"

SHOSH
Ali Pilgrim, I don't know what a Hoya is

THE HOST STARED EVAN DOWN. "Really?" he said.

"Yes," said Evan. "We're a large party, so I thought it would be smart."

"Okay." He consulted a spiral notebook on the stand. "I've just never had anyone call ahead before."

"Well, Chili's doesn't take reservations, so."

Balding squinted. "You tried to make a reservation at Chili's?"

"Bro—" Yurt tapped Evan on the shoulder. "Do you know about Chili's?"

"Yeah, bro," said Sara. (Ever since tackle-kissing Yurt at the Oscar party, *she* was one step behind *him*.)

"I think it's sweet," said Shosh, to which Mavie agreed, at which point Evan said, "It's not *sweet*. It's Ali's special day. I wanted to make sure there would be room for everyone."

The host, who'd been listening to this little aside, did a slow half-turn toward the mostly empty dining area.

A distant cough . . .

The clink of glass . . .

"I think we can accommodate your party," he said, grabbing a stack of menus, and motioning for them to follow.

"Wait—what is everyone carrying?" Ali asked.

Everyone but her was carrying a gift bag.

"Please tell me you guys didn't bring presents."

"We didn't bring presents," said Evan.

Shosh reached for his hand as they walked through the restaurant. She found herself feeling a little clingy, partly due to his recent display of anal retentiveness—a quality she found surprisingly adorable—partly because their future was so up in the air, but mostly it was a memory of the last time she was here, when she accidentally ran into him and Will by the bathroom. Not her finest hour, perhaps, but there was something compelling about it, some measure of affection in returning to the early places of a shared history.

Unceremoniously, the host shoved two tables together, wished them "the loveliest of fine dining experiences," and disappeared.

"Is it just me," said Ali, "or is that guy kind of in love with us?"

After their waitress approached (a different server than Shosh's last time here, thank goodness) and everyone had ordered, Evan stood, tapped his spoon to his glass. "As you all know, we are here tonight to celebrate the incomparable Ali Pilgrim."

"Hear! Hear!"

"She cannot be compared to!"

Evan stumbled through the speech he'd prepared, barely reaching the end without crying, and when he was done, they all raised their glasses to Ali. And just as each of them had been instructed by Evan ahead of time, it was at this point in the proceedings when everyone lifted their bags onto the table.

"What is happening?" asked Ali.

Evan motioned for Shosh to go ahead; she stood, looked straight at Ali, and cleared her throat. "I have to admit, I was really nervous to meet you. But you've been so kind to me, exactly as awesome as everyone said you'd be, and I feel lucky to count you as a friend. Ali Pilgrim, I don't know what a Hoya is, but I humbly submit to you this bottle of very cheap vodka"—Shosh produced a bottle of vodka from her bag, along with—"and packet of red Kool-Aid, as Things That Might Be Hoyas. May your cup runneth over with Red Drink at Georgetown."

The table applauded as Ali got up and hugged Shosh.

"Balding, you're up," said Evan.

Balding stood, and from the moment she started talking, it was clear she was on the absolute verge. She told a story from a time in eighth grade, after coming out to family and friends, when someone had written in Sharpie on the bathroom walls, calling her all sorts of awful names. She then reached into her bag and pulled out a can of paint and a brush, and right then, Ali and Balding both burst into tears. "Ali Pilgrim, I don't know what a Hoya is"— and now they were laughing through tears—"but I humbly submit to you this can of paint, and this brush, as Things That Might Be Hoyas." A beat, as Balding wiped her eyes. "Just like you did for me, if anyone gives you shit at Georgetown—paint over it."

It wasn't the last tearful hugging of the night. Mavie's bag had a single note card inside—"Ali Pilgrim, I don't know what a Hoya is," she said, "but I humbly submit my grandmother's chocolate-chip cookie recipe, which you've been hounding me about for ages, as a Thing That Might Be a Hoya." Sara pulled a signed, framed photograph of Daniel Levy from her bag—"I humbly submit this autographed headshot of David Rose as a Thing That Might Be a Hoya."

Yurt's bag was full of DVDs—"I humbly submit all eleven seasons of *The X-Files*, and both movies, yo, as Things That Might Be Hoyas. I know they're streaming, but they take stuff down every month, and the truth is *always* out there."

When it was Evan's turn, having already given a speech, he said, "I don't know what a Hoya is, Ali Pilgrim, but I humbly submit the following three items as Things That Might Be Hoyas. First—" He pulled a knit scarf from the bag. "Mom never let me go with her to the hospital, so I had no idea, but apparently, there were a lot of waiting rooms, and she used that time to make this for you." When he held the scarf end to end, it read: HONORARY TAFT.

Just when it looked like Ali was done crying, she proved everyone wrong. Wiping her eyes, she grabbed the scarf and wrapped it around her neck.

"Second," said Evan, and when he pulled out a small stack of stapled-together pages, everyone knew immediately, this was the real prize. "A Will Taft original comic entitled *Oh Boy-a, It's a Hoya*—"

"No *way*."

"Oh yes. And lastly, my gift to you . . . you actually have to wait for. Until after we eat."

"It's a catamarangutan, isn't it?"

"Wouldn't you like to know."

"It's a catamarangutan."

"How would that even work?"

When the food arrived, everyone settled into dinner, and Shosh felt something she couldn't quite name. Was it *contentment*? Happiness in the now, even if a little fearful of the future? Whatever it was, she wanted to keep feeling it.

"Excuse me." She waved down their waitress, who was just old enough to want to prove her youngness, and whose eyes had lingered on their table all evening with a certain longing. Shosh lowered her voice, just a playful chat among girls. "Could I get a Tropical Sunrise Margarita? The big one, please?"

With a wink and a nod, the waitress disappeared.

EVAN
kids in parks

As opposed to Willow Seed, this park is pretty state-of-the-art: new equipment, a basketball court, pavilion with grills. Even though neither of us have been here since last year—that fateful night of Heather's party—when Ali and I climb out of the car, we know exactly where we're going.

"How you feeling?" asks Ali.

"I'm in the prime of my life. Why do you ask?"

"Just making sure your stomach's not eyeballing your throat's dick."

At the spot by the bushes, I look up at the tree where it all started: it's smaller than I remember, and not a bird to be found. "So," I say. "You're probably wondering why we're here."

"Is nostalgia not a reason?"

I point to the ground, where a newly planted bush sits tucked among the larger ones. "Ali Pilgrim, I don't know what a Hoya is, but I humbly submit this alpine currant as a Thing That Might Be a Hoya."

"What?" Ali bends down to inspect the little plant surrounded by fresh soil.

"Mom and I planted it this afternoon. The alpine currant is a very hardy shrub."

"Is it, now."

"So says the garden guy at Lowe's. If it survives its first winter, supposedly, you're home free."

"Well, that's good."

"We're calling it 'Ali,' for short."

No one hugs tighter than Ali, or with quite as much *umph*. "Thank you for my shrub," she says, and I say, "You're welcome," and even though a plant seems a silly way to thank someone for a lifetime of friendship, how else should a person show gratitude for such a thing? Do you know, Ali? Please say you do, because otherwise, this hug and this shrub are all I have.

"No one really gets us, do they," I say.

"No. But that kind of works for me."

Ali sits with her namesake shrub for a bit, introducing it to the things in life worth knowing: "So at the end of season seven, Duchovny *leaves the show*. I don't need to tell you what a shit-show the show became."

Eventually, we head back to the car, and apropos of nothing, Ali asks if I'm in love with Shosh, and I say, "I think . . . yes? Yeah, no, I definitely am."

She smiles. "I was gonna body-slam you if you said no."

"That's rather unsportsmanlike."

"You know I don't like being lied to."

I say, "Right," but really, I'm wondering if I'll ever have another friend who knows me better than I know myself.

We climb in the car; I turn the ignition.

"So," she says.

"Yeah."

"You guys are fucked, pretty much."

"That's the long and short of it."

Ali nods. "You could go to LA?"

I don't even have to answer. Not only has Shosh not invited me, but even if she did, I already have an LA, and it's called Glacier Bay.

"What are you gonna do?" asks Ali.

"Truth?"

"Yeah."

"I have no idea."

SHOSH
the worst scene in every animal movie

HER BRAIN WAS A SUN always rising.

And this was why.

To feel like this. The letting go of it.

Not just feeling everything, feeling the *most* of everything.

This was why she missed it.

"I'm worried about you, girl."

Through the window, so many cars passing, all these people, who were these people?

"You're too good for this world, Ruth Hamish."

"Look, I'm just gonna take you home, okay?"

"No. Do not do that. Please."

"Shosh. Hon. You can make just about anything look good, but *desperate* don't work for anyone."

"I'm not desperate."

"Last I checked, showing up at a boy's house after midnight, drunk off your ass, is the definition of desperate."

On some level, she knew Ruth was right. But the sun in her brain was so bright, its truth drowned out all others.

In the end, Ruth agreed to five minutes at Evan's house, but she insisted on waiting there, and taking Shosh straight home afterward. "And do *not* ring the doorbell," Ruth said. "You wake that little kid, his mother is coming after you."

• • •

She'd just about decided to start throwing rocks at the upstairs window when Evan finally answered her text. **Be right down.**

Only when he opened the door in his pj pants, hair all over the place, rubbing his eyes, did Shosh realize Ruth's sun was brighter than hers: she should have listened to her friend.

"Are you okay?" Evan asked.

Shosh pointed to his face. "A reasonable question from a reasonable boy."

Evan looked over his shoulder, then joined her on the porch, gently closing the door behind him.

"I'm breaking up with you," she said.

"Shosh—"

She tapped him on the shoulder as if knighting him. "I break up with thee."

"You're drunk."

"Not . . . a lot."

"How did you get here?"

She waved toward the street, where Ruth, clearly concerned, stood by her car.

"Where did you go after Chili's?" Evan asked.

"Where did *you* go after Chili's?"

"I took Ali to the park. You know that, we talked about it."

"Right, Park Boy. Well, I took Sara and Yurt to a bar."

"Okay."

"I used to go to bars. I know the ones that let you in." She poked him on the shoulder. "So, see? You don't know everything about me."

This was the part she always forgot. The part that came on the other side of need. The part of herself that she lost when she let go. And maybe she felt everything for a while, but everything includes *every thing*, even the parts a person isn't built to feel.

The sun that rose was the same sun that set.

She always forgot that.

"You need to go home, Shosh."

"It's like those scenes in the animal movies. Animal movies *always* have that scene at the end. Some dog that needs to be freed, or like—a fucking horse that needs to be wild, but it's an *animal*, Evan. It doesn't understand. All it knows is, it loves its owner, and then *that scene* happens where the owner has to yell at the dog to make it run away. And we're supposed to think it's noble, because how else does the animal get to be free? But it's not noble, it's just *mean*."

A deep sob bubbled out of nowhere, and Shosh was crying now, and Evan reached out, put his arms around her, and they held each other on the porch like that.

"Oh my God, what is wrong with me?"

"You're okay," Evan said.

"I am so sorry."

"It's okay." He guided her down the steps, toward the car.

"I don't want to break up," she said.

"Me neither," he whispered, nodding at Ruth as they neared.

"Oh God, I cannot believe I was going to throw rocks at your window. And I called you a dog."

"Okay, that's—not how I interpreted the story."

Evan helped her into the back seat of Ruth's car, where she

rolled down the window, and kept right on apologizing. "I am sooooo sorry, Evan."

He patted her gently on the head, then turned to Ruth. "You're taking her home?"

"Do one-legged ducks swim in circles?"

Evan squinted. "I don't know."

"Well, they do. And I am."

"Thanks. And hey—for my dad's girlfriend's son's girlfriend, you're all right."

Shosh chuckled from the car, eyes half-closed, chin resting on the open window. "That was a *lot* of words, just so you know."

Ruth smiled at Evan. "We can be friends, Evan Taft. Just don't go falling in love with me."

"Oh my God," said Shosh, "no one is *listening to me.*"

Evan ignored her, smiled back at Ruth. "If I fell in love with you, that would make me my dad's girlfriend's son's girlfriend's boyfriend."

"Pretty fuckin' presumptuous of you, Ev. Who said I'd reciprocate?"

"Hey!" said Shosh. "I *demand* to be taken *seriously.*"

Ruth turned to Shosh, reached down, and started rolling up her window. "Well, you should probably stop talking, then."

Indignant and intent on showing them, Shosh slapped the rising glass and was about to yell more, but her sun was almost entirely set, and she felt so tired, tired enough to fall asleep right there in the back of Ruth's car—

Late the next morning, after three Tylenol, two cups of coffee, and a solid hour of staring into oblivion, Shosh picked up her phone and called someone she'd only ever texted, but had considered calling many times.

"Hey, Sho."

"Hey, Mavie. Do you have a second? I have questions."

EVAN
proud glad sad love

I'VE BEEN SITTING IN THE same position for going on two hours when the text from Mom finally comes through: Almost home exclamation voice texting period sorry if it comes through weird smiley smiley heart

"Evan."

"Sorry." I put my phone away.

"It's okay," says Will. "The book says I should be patient with first-time models." He gets a look on his face like something just occurred to him. "Have you done this before?"

"Nope. First-timer."

He nods like a world-weary professional. "Yeah, I can tell."

Yesterday, Will came home from school with an idea. In art class, they'd been talking about how, before photography, people had gotten their portraits painted for friends, family, posterity, whatever. And he thought, what with my upcoming departure, he'd like a portrait of me. "To remember you by," he said, as if my six months in Alaska were the equivalent of being launched into space indefinitely. Alas, he was serious and I was game.

"Maybe someday I'll be as good an artist as you," he says.

Before I can figure out what to say to this, my phone buzzes again, and it's not that I don't fear the Wrath of William the Burgeoning Artist, but I need to know Mom's status pronto. "Hey, bud? Can we take a bathroom break?"

He sets the alarm on his watch. "Two minutes."

In the bathroom, I lock the door, but when I pull out my phone, the text isn't from Mom.

> Shosh: Hello. Hi. Good morning.
> I am truly sorry for last night
> Not that it makes up for it, but I want you to know
> Cliché as it sounds
> I think I have a problem
> I am getting help
> And I am really sorry

Before I have a second to respond, Mom texts: WE ARE HERE. In the driveway, ready when you are. Does W suspect????

Mind on overload, I respond to Mom: He has no idea!! One minute, we'll be right out.

Back on Shosh's thread, I reread her texts, and it's one of those moments when the English language comes up short. I'm proud, yes, but that word implies some measure of ownership in the thing, of which I can claim none. I'm glad she's working through it, but also sad that this is something she has to work through, and to top it all off, even though we haven't technically said I love you yet, for some reason, I've never wanted to tell her more than right now.

Proud glad sad love.

We need a word for that.

Instead, I go through and heart all seven of her text messages, tell her I accept her apology, and I'm here for her, whatever she needs.

Back in Will's room, he's sitting on a stool with his legs crossed, chin in hands, studying his sketch like some Parisian artist in the Louvre. "Ready?" he asks.

"Actually, can you come outside with me for a second? I need to show you something."

"What is it?"

"You'll see," I say, and he gets this intense look of curiosity, like maybe he can solve the mystery of what's waiting outside before we get there.

We're down the stairs in a flash, and when he starts to head for the back door, I say, "Front yard, actually," and now he's *seriously* curious. I go out first, position myself so I can see his face. Sure enough, the second he steps outside, he lights up like the North Star, his expression some combination of shock and joy and confusion, and I wonder how many times the English language is going to let me down today.

The dog looks just like his picture on the humane society website. He's medium-sized, dark brown, some kind of hound mix, and right away, you can see how playful he is.

"What do you think?" Mom says, all smiles, trying her best to keep the dog contained on the leash, but he is all over the place.

Will just stands on the porch, staring in shock joy confusion. "Can I keep him?" he asks, unknowingly joining a club populated by kids across the known universe.

"He's for you! Well—us." Mom heads toward the porch, gently pulling the dog along. "His name is Abraham Lincoln, but he's pretty young, so they said we could probably change it if you want."

There are moments in life that none of us deserve: weddings, childbirths, lovers reunited after years apart. But I think the most spectacular undeserved moments creep in the back door when we least expect them.

The moment Will and the dog find each other is an image that will be burned in my brain for the rest of my life, a vision of two wandering souls finding their way to each other. As they roll around on the ground together, each getting lost in the joy of the other, Mom and I lock eyes, and she smiles, and I know our family is going to be okay.

Will names the dog Elliott.

OSLO

· 2109 ·

EIVIN'S LIFE WAS A DEDICATION split two ways: to an overly needy Siberian cat called Yuri and to a job that required more hours per day than purring Yuri would have preferred. But Eivin wasn't lonely, or he didn't think so. He was, quite simply, bored of everyone he met. He'd go on dates, only to have his mind wander to the stack of art books waiting at his bedside, the warm bath he would run later that evening, and he wasn't sure what was sadder: that he went home alone most every night or that he was glad about it.

If youth were a ladder, Eivin had a white-knuckled grip on the bottom rung. He was of an age where one friend's wedding became five friends' weddings, and his life suddenly felt like a celebration of other people's love. When that season ended, the season of babies began, families burgeoning in litters, and before long, the lives of his friends were filled with a promise of the future; on that time-line, Eivin was history.

Mostly, he liked to paint. Just for himself, nothing too involved. Clear nights were rare, but when the stars were out, Eivin would carry his easel to the back patio, and there, as Yuri brushed his heels, he would paint the starry sky. And sometimes—on occasion—he would wonder if he'd missed his chance at love.

· · ·

As a child, Søl had dreamed of nothing but space. As a teen, she'd studied only space, and as an adult, she'd committed herself to the rigorous training of the kosmonaut at the Norwegian Space Agency. So intense was her desire for interstellar travel, she rarely acknowledged her fellow humans, and found the basic premise of love to be useless. But now—a hundred days into a three-hundred-day solo flight aboard Norwegian space station *Nima II*—what had started as a crack in her psyche had become a gaping chasm she could no longer ignore: Søl was terribly alone. When she wasn't conducting biological research, sleeping, eating, exercising, she spent her time at the station window, singing songs from her childhood just to hear the sound of a human voice. As she sang, she stared into the cold vacuum of space, and that rolling blue sphere she'd so longed to leave, and sometimes—on occasion—she wondered if she'd missed her chance at love.

Everything tells a story. The world speaks of motion and mystery: hurtling through the cosmos, we feel stagnant; surrounded by people, we feel bored; we are but fleeting subplots in the spinning yarn of the universe.

But even subplots have a story to tell.

On her 101st day alone in space, Søl was singing in her window when she saw something strange: a sequence of floating lights drifting across the expanse, arranged in the shape of an enormous hexagon. At first, she thought it was a trick of light, the orbital sunrise playing games with her vision, but no, there it was, a towering hexagon, each bulb slowly pulsing in synchronized rhythm as it soared through space—dimming, then brightening; dimming, then brightening—*like wings flapping*, she thought. Her best guess was that the hexagon was somewhere between thirty and fifty meters tall, roughly a ten- to fifteen-story building. Later, the obvious would occur to her—that she should have grabbed the onboard camera *pronto*—but for now, all she could do was stare in wonder.

As Søl stood mesmerized in space, Eivin stood in the bathroom at work, studying his eyes in the mirror. He'd had migraines before, but this was something new: minutes ago, an aura had appeared in his field of vision. The pain was minimal, but the aura was enormously distracting—he could hardly see out of his left eye. He splashed water onto his face and, trusting the headache would resolve itself eventually, went back to his chair, where he heard the beep of an incoming holograph from *Nima II*.

Søl waited by the onboard holo-cam, desperately hoping someone at NOSA Mission Control could confirm what she'd seen. When a controller finally answered, she described the hexagon of lights in detail, and when she was done, the controller calmly asked her to repeat the story.

From his desk in Oslo, Eivin listened in stunned silence as this kosmonaut in low-Earth orbit perfectly described his current aura.

Everything tells a story. Some use simple mechanics: *this* connects to *that* to make *the other*. But stories are notoriously unreliable machines, and when the higher-ups at NOSA asked Søl to prove what she'd seen, she could not give them *this*, *that*, or *the other*. As for the machines at NOSA Mission Control, none of them had clocked the supposed "hexagon of lights," and so, with nothing but the word of a single kosmonaut—whose mental stability was now firmly in question—the account was disregarded as unverifiable.

Søl herself might have questioned what she'd seen were it not for three words she'd heard from Mission Control that day: "Jeg tror deg," Eivin had said, quiet, firm, final.

I believe you.

For the next two hundred days, the controller and the kosmonaut spoke as often as they could. She was a little older, had always known what she wanted; he was younger, only knew what he didn't want. She counted down the hours between transmissions; he was her tether to reality, the only person to whom she'd ever craved connection. On his days off, he made up excuses to come to work; she was the only person whose company he preferred to that of a good book in a warm bath.

From his patio at night, with Yuri at his heels, Eivin worked on a series of paintings entitled *I Will Find You.* They were all variations on a theme: the *Nima II* soaring through space, Søl's face peering out from a little window, as if searching for Eivin in the vast expanse. And in those moments, Eivin's mind wandered the hallways of their possible futures together: the children, the years, the Yuris. He pictured them at parties, telling the story of how they met. *The original star-crossed lovers,* they would say, and their friends would think them the happiest people on earth.

From the *Nima II* window, Søl stared at that rolling blue sphere, and thought of him down there, believing her. She sang songs of the past, the doors each of them had walked through that had led to each other, and for reasons she could not explain—whether from the dusky blue glow of the planet, or the idea of believing in the absurd—a hollow phrase rang like a bell in her head: "Jeg tror på blå," she sang over and over again. *I believe in blue.*

PART
SEVEN

CODA

SHOSH
happy bird-day

ACCORDING TO CHARLIE, THE THEME of his fourth birthday party was "may da forth be wid you," which was both adorable and confusing: adorable, because his lisp turned *force* into "forth," and he insisted on informing each guest who arrived, in hushed and urgent tones, what the theme was, as if the Death Star balloons, light saber streamers, and Threepio cake hadn't tipped them off; it was confusing because (a) it wasn't even May yet, much less the fourth, and (b) the pun *would* have worked, given that it was his fourth birthday—and indeed, his mother had tried to explain why it would be ever so clever to have one's birthday theme match one's birthday age—but young Charles would hear none of it.

The business of birthdays—and of Star Wars—was no joking matter.

When Shosh arrived that morning, Charlie ran to hug her. "It'th my *bird-day*, Thoth," he said, chin down, eyebrows furrowed.

"I *know*," said Shosh, doing her best to match his solemnity. "Which is why I brought you this." She held out a medium-sized gift; urgency melted into joy as Charlie took the box, turned, and ran for the living room.

Shosh took off her coat, hung it on a rack, and found Ms. Clark in the kitchen with a slew of doe-eyed kids and tired-eyed parents, none of whom she knew. For a fleeting moment, she longed for her trusty flask. But she was a different person now, or at least, she was trying to be. Hence, attending a "bird-day" party for a kid who could probably land a triple-axle before properly pronouncing her name.

"You came!" said Ms. Clark, wrapping Shosh in the most legit of hugs. And like that, the group—composed mostly of neighborhood friends, and families from Charlie's preschool—welcomed her into the fold. It reminded her of Ali's Holiday Kickback: friendship by transitive property. Everyone here loved Charlie and Ms. Clark, and so everyone here loved each other.

For most of the party, Shosh kept to herself, just happy to be there. At one point, Ms. Clark pulled a guitar out of nowhere, handed it to Shosh, who pretended she hadn't seen this coming. In actuality, she'd prepared a little something—a "Happy Birthday" remix set to the tune of "The Imperial March"—which went over like gangbusters.

"Again! Again, Aunt Thoth!" And so Shosh played it again, and the kids went nuts.

Later, after the cake had been cut and served, Shosh found herself alone in the corner of the kitchen with Ms. Clark. She flashed back to that day in the police station, FaceTiming with Ms. Clark and Charlie as they baked together in this very room. At the time, she'd longed to be part of their tiny, beautiful family, and only now did it occur to her that, in a way, she was.

"Thank you," she said, wondering how to repay this woman who'd changed her life on an elemental level. "For everything."

Ms. Clark turned from the bustling kitchen to Shosh. "You're gonna bring down the goddamn house, kid. I can't wait to see it."

• • •

After cake, it was time for presents, an announcement that set the kids off like a cannon of confetti. As Charlie unwrapped boxes and opened bags, Ms. Clark sat next to him, reading each tag aloud so Charlie knew who to thank. Shosh stood near the back of the crowd, her face sore from smiling so much.

"Let's see now," Ms. Clark said when they reached the gift Shosh had brought. "This one is from Aunt Shosh."

Before he even opened it, Charlie said, "Thankth, Aunt Thoth," and the room giggled.

As he unwrapped the box, Shosh kept smiling to push down the tears she knew would win eventually. "The first one's kind of weird," she said, and as soon as Charlie pulled out the record, Ms. Clark put a hand to her mouth.

"What ith it?" asked Charlie, handing it to his mom.

Ms. Clark smiled, swallowed. "It's a record, honey. A band called the Beach Boys." But Charlie's attention was grabbed by the second gift in the box.

"A guitar!" he said, pulling the ukulele from the box.

Stevie had never learned to play, not really. But that hadn't stopped her from constantly tinkering with it. Shosh could still see her, sitting on the edge of her bed, strumming the same sad chords over and over again, singing her heart out. "That used to belong to my sister," Shosh said, and even though the gift was for Charlie, she was looking at Ms. Clark: teacher, friend, swan. Both of them were crying, and before Ms. Clark had a chance to ask, Shosh said, "One thing about her—she loved music."

EVAN
folie à deux

MAYA SAYS SHE'S PROUD OF ME.

"For what?"

"Seriously? You haven't had a storm in months. You're graduating high school, embracing the gap year in Alaska. Look, part of my job is helping people recognize when things aren't well—but there's just as much value in recognizing when things are."

The truth is, I'm going to miss Maya. She says she'll be here when I get back, and we have six calls scheduled—one for every month I'm away—though those are likely in flux until I have a better idea what my schedule at Headlands will look like. But I can't deny the quality of my life now versus what it was before I got here.

Hot take: if therapy were a universal mandate, the universe would be improved by orders of magnitude.

She asks about Mom, and I update her on the hormone treatment. Yes, there are hot flashes and mood swings, but all in all, things are good. "I think the thing now is just . . . what if it comes back?"

Maya says sometimes fear is logical so long as it doesn't run the show.

That's all—she doesn't go on and on about it. And I think how I'll miss this shorthand, whole sentences in a single nod.

I tell her about Elliott, how he's a handful but worth it, how he follows Will from room to room, the two completely inseparable. We talk about Mom and Neil, how it's kind of weird to have him around, but nice, too. He helps out with Elliott, he builds LEGO with Will, and most importantly, he makes Mom smile in a way I haven't seen in years, if ever.

"You think she loves him?" asks Maya.

"If so, she's not the only Taft in love."

Maya smiles. "The Tarantino film?"

"Yeah, but now I know her better, that doesn't seem right. I think she's more of a Sofia Coppola."

"And does Ms. Coppola feel the same about you?"

"I think so. We haven't—like—said *the words*, but—"

"You feel it."

"I can't decide if it was good luck or bad that we found each other when we did. Each of us needed the other. And part of the people we've become—the me who decided to give Alaska another shot, and the Shosh who decided to reapply to USC—we only became those people because of each other. So in a way, the very love that drew us together has now conspired to keep us apart."

"Six months." Maya snaps a finger. "Over before you know it."

"Okay, but like—she's *going* to be a movie star. Like, it's a done deal. And I know that sounds *whatever*, but when you meet her, you know. She radiates that kind of otherworldliness. Everyone in the room feels it."

"So?"

"So what, I'm going to swoop into Hollywood, fresh out of rustic Glacier Bay, and marry a movie star?"

"Well, I imagine there would be a few steps in between."

"I'm serious," I say.

"So let's talk seriously. You told me you love her."

"Yes."

"You think she loves you?"

"Yes, but it can't be that easy."

"But what if it is."

"It can't be."

"But what if it is."

"So what do I do?"

"Have you talked to her?"

"It can't be that easy."

"Yes, but what I'm proposing is"—Maya leans forward—"what if it is?"

Willow Seed looks different in the middle of spring. It's still got the minimalist thing going for it, but it's somehow less cozy, as if the swings and slide were designed to be covered in snow. Short of that, the place feels incomplete.

"Maybe we went temporarily insane," says Shosh.

"Simultaneously?"

"Doesn't seem likely, does it."

"Plus, we heard the same lyrics. Hard to imagine two strangers sharing a specific hallucination."

Just like that fateful night last winter—after chasing Nightbird to this park, to each other—we lie on our backs on the merry-go-round, spinning slow circles, eyes on the sky. It's the time of year when warm afternoons turn to crisp evenings, the air pleasant, the stars bright, even if our mood is anything but.

Shosh sings a chorus from one of Nightbird's songs: *From the Seine to the sea, your voice is in me. In the madness of two, I will find you.* Then, quietly, she says, "Folie à deux."

"Folie . . . ?"

". . . à deux," says Shosh. "It's a condition. Shared psychosis. But I think it's mostly within families, or people who already know each other. They transfer the delusion. I'm not sure how I know that."

Shared psychosis might explain some things, but still doesn't seem right. We talk for a while about how Nightbird might be French: aside from folie à deux, there's the reference to the Seine, as well as a certain line in "Division Street" that has me blushing in the dark. "*Je t'aime, je t'aime, je t'aime,*" sings Shosh, the translation hovering like a prize in the air.

I take a deep breath, let it out. "I keep coming back to this: We heard the same lyrics, the same melody. Shared, yes. But a delusion? I don't buy it."

"Maybe"—Shosh turns onto her side, rests her head on my shoulder—"we stop questioning. Maybe it's enough that she led us to each other."

"Just in time to say goodbye."

"Goodbyes are a gift, Evan. Don't ever be sad you get a good-bye." She tilts her head, her lips so close to my ear now I can feel each exhale. "Anyway, meeting in time to say goodbye means we met in time to say hello."

I could live a thousand lives and never meet anyone who sees the world like Shosh Bell. The inches between us go electric, and it's not our final kiss, but it is our goodbye kiss, full of all the things we don't know how to say, all the possible roads ahead we're too afraid to name. And I don't know if Maya is right—I don't know if being with Shosh is as simple as loving her, but if this is how it ends, I want to make it count.

Do you understand, Shosh? Please say you do. Please say you see the value of us, not just what we might become.

SHOSH

madness of two

DID HE FEEL IT? DID he feel how much she would miss him? She hoped so, but just to be sure—

She kissed him deeper, slower, to show him. And the feeling of his being, of his body against hers, became again both ancient and new, and how to explain that for as much as she would miss him, it was nothing compared to how much she already *had* missed him? She had no answers, was tired of looking, and in the absence of reason, she offered what she could: she kissed him until they lost themselves in each other, until it was impossible for one soul to tell the other apart.

FOUR MONTHS LATER

SHOSH
LA

Shosh was folding laundry, listening to a podcast called *Dead Eyes,* when her phone started chiming like a pushy guest at a motel desk. The podcast—which was either one man's attempt to get answers from Tom Hanks or an exploration of failure in the arts— had become an obsession of late. Intent on not interrupting, she let the phone chime until she could let it chime no more.

Kendra: GUYS. Josh's band is playing open
mic at the kibitz room tonight

Court: 💀💀💀💀

Ross: OMG what time

Kendra: Starts at 10 but we should get
there early

Roo: I'm in!!

Court: This will be hilarious
And by hilarious, I mean "fun"????

Kendra: I mean the band is called Big Spicy
Beefs, it's not like they *don't* want laughs

Roo: Canter's tuna melt FTW

Ross: That tuna melt is LIFEGIVING

Kendra: OMG with the tuna melt, how good
could it possibly be

Roo: SACRILEGE

Court: I vote Kendra out of the group

Kendra: I was gonna DD, buuuuuuuuut

Court: NVRMIND

Ross: You can stay!

Kendra: 😩😩😩😩
OK, everyone Uber there, I'll drive after
We can see what's up elsewhere

Court: Kibitz at 10?

Kendra: Kibitz at 10!

Roo: Holla

Kendra: You in, Sho?

A quick Google search and Shosh was staring at a dive bar with a little stage and tables, a full cocktail menu on display. The Kibitz Room boasted quite the history of performers through the years, from Joni Mitchell to Guns N' Roses; it appeared to be attached to a deli called Canter's whose tuna melt was, arguably, a cut above.

She flipped back to the thread, fingers hovering over the screen, considering . . .

"Shit."

Back to messages, she clicked to a different thread, and typed:

This is wayyyyyyyy complicated

Seconds later, her phone rang. She answered: "Hey."

"Where are you?" asked Mavie.

"My room. Knee-deep in laundry."

"*Dead Eyes?*"

"*So good.*"

"Told you."

"Reminds me a little of *Mystery Show*, RIP."

"Starlee Kine is a national treasure."

"She is at that." Shosh cleared her throat. "You remember at lunch yesterday, I mentioned my theater group?"

"From the intro class."

"Yeah, so we have this group chat, and they're all going to this show tonight, and I'm just like—I don't know if I can?"

"You should avoid places you can't handle."

"Right, but like—how do I know what I can handle?"

"It took me a while to figure out how to be social without drinking. So like, for me, anything in the family of a rave is off limits. The whole EDM club scene, I go in thinking I'm hot shit and I wake up two days later in the next town over. Can't do it. But different people have different parameters."

"Right."

"What's the deal with this place tonight?" asked Mavie.

"It's like—a deli?"

"The fuck?"

"But there's a bar attached, and like, a stage—"

"Oh, you mean Canter's?"

"Yes! Wait—have you been?"

"I know, right? A month at UCLA and my primary education has been where to eat. Look, if you want to go tonight, I can handle Canter's, no problem."

"You'd come with?"

"Luckily for you, delis are nowhere near the rave family. Plus, it's like twenty minutes from me, and I could kill a tuna melt right now."

The Kibitz Room was exactly as advertised: dive bar but make it charming, with photos of rock stars lining the walls, and a mural onstage of the iconic Rolling Stones tongue logo attacking the winged Aerosmith logo. There were button-leather booths and neon Budweiser signs, and it was weird not drinking in a bar, but with Mavie around, Shosh felt okay.

Their group occupied one of the tables nearest the stage; they ate, drank (sodas for Mavie and Shosh), and cheered far too vigorously for bands who were far too unskilled. Before long, it was Big Spicy Beefs' turn to play. In keeping with the night, the band was also exactly as advertised: goofy as shit. But they had fun with it, and so did the room, and when the set was over, the band joined them at the table. The bass player, a six-and-a-half-foot kid named Seth—whose nickname was Really Tall Seth—took a quick shine to Shosh. "You're like a prettier version of that musician chick in New Girl."

Shosh was familiar with the Really Tall Seth prototype, a factory build that required little imagination. There were approximately one billion Really Tall Seths in circulation.

"Zooey Deschanel," she said.

He took a long gulp. "Is that where you're from?"

Looking at him, all she could see were elbows and knees. "Yes. I'm from Zooey Deschanel."

"Dope," he said.

Her kingdom for a beer.

Across the table, there was talk of some new club in Echo Park. "I hear it's fucking edge," Josh was saying, and before the next act had finished their set, the group was done with Kibitz, ready to head out.

As the band gathered their stuff, Mavie searched the new place on her phone. "Ouf. You wanna go, you're on your own."

"In the family of a rave?"

"A mother of a rave, looks like."

Whether from her current caffeine blood level (Diet Coke, as it turned out, much better on tap), the joy of time spent with Mavie, or a desire to distance herself from people whose extremities were so defining as to require they include them in their name, Shosh didn't have to think twice. "You guys go ahead," she told the group. "Mavie and I are gonna stay and catch up. Illinois contingent only."

"You sure?" asked Kendra.

Really Tall Seth leaned his really tall torso over the table. "You should totes come. Everyone says it's fucking edge."

"I don't know what that means," said Shosh, who then proceeded to slurp the hell out of her Diet Coke.

After they'd left, Mavie said, "Do you think Seth wanted you to come?"

"I just wish I knew what he was thinking, you know?"

They laughed and watched the next act—the night's first solo artist—tune his guitar.

"He was cute, though," said Mavie.

Shosh huffed. "All eight feet of him."

There was something in Mavie's nod, like she wasn't agreeing with Shosh so much as consoling her.

"What?" Shosh flagged their waitress, pointed to her empty cup. "You think I should go out with Really Tall Seth?"

"I don't know." Mavie set down her phone. "Don't listen to me. I'm the last person to give dating advice."

"How is Balding?"

"Balding is . . . lovely. And infuriating. She is infuriatingly lovely."

"Okay."

"First two weeks, we pretended it was no big deal. FaceTimed every night. She was all, *the trees, the mountains, the maple syrup*, and I'd joke about the smog, or the traffic, because jokes are what you do when the truth is hard, but I mean—*Vermont?* I keep thinking I'm gonna end things, but then she'll say something about best practices for making the perfect peanut butter sandwich, and it's like—I can't quit her, you know? It'd be easier if she sucked, even a little."

"Alas, Balding does not suck," said Shosh.

"Not even a little."

Being seen and feeling seen were not the same things. Ever since moving out here, meeting new people, trying to find her place in a place so crowded she could hardly breathe, Shosh had been thinking a lot about the difference between the two. All her life, people had seen her: from the stage to the hallways, her hair, her clothes, driving trucks into pools, or just sitting at a table, watching mediocre bands. Some people went their whole lives without ever being seen, and Shosh was careful never to complain about having the opposite problem, knowing how privileged she was to not be invisible. But in the end, it all added up to being seen.

Mavie's words took root, found fertile soil in Shosh's heart, and for the first time since leaving Illinois—since saying goodbye to Evan—she felt seen.

Onstage, having finally tuned his guitar and adjusted his levels, the next act stepped up to the microphone.

"This guy looks hella jittery," said Mavie, and Shosh was about to tell her how much she appreciated her coming tonight, how glad she was that they both landed in LA, when she heard it—

The song was just as fragile as she remembered, flittering and airy, a billion dust particles in sunlight, only something was different, something was wrong.

"I can't tell if I like it," said Mavie, staring at the stage, and when Shosh turned, time slowed to nothing, as if she'd woken from one dream to find another waiting for her.

"*Take me for a fool or lose me for good*," sang the man onstage, and Shosh watched in a trance ("*I don't care if you can, I care if you should*"), hearing live for the first time a song she'd heard many times before ("*You got blood on your hands, a bird would be better*"), and she wondered what other unreal things might be made real. "*I wrote it in a song, a book, a letter.*"

"Shosh—you okay, girl?"

"Yes," she said, but she couldn't stop staring, listening . . .

I'm a crooked painting of unknowable place
With hands constructed to frame your face
There is a place we like to go
Where secrets hide in trees of snow

Breath becomes smoke, the inside wants out
Choke down a scream, whisper, don't shout
From the Seine to the sea, your voice is in me
In the madness of two, I will find you

Without meaning to, Shosh had constructed a portrait of Night-bird in her head: a youthful woman in flowy-white clothes, long blond hair, likely singing barefoot by a river, or atop a snowcapped mountain, some mystical milieu befitting a woman whose voice broke the laws of physics. And now here was this man—midforties, white, bearded, flannelled as all hell—singing those very songs in the back room of a bar known the world over for a tuna fucking sandwich.

Surreal wasn't enough; this was entirely unreal.

When the song ended, he introduced himself as Neon Impos-ter. She'd seen a lot of fidgety hands and nervous twitches through the years—the stage had a way of eroding confidence in otherwise confident people—but she couldn't remember the last time she'd seen someone so entirely uncomfortable in the spotlight. "This next one, I usually do on piano," he mumbled. "So—bear with me if it's a little off," and her mind continued to bend as he dove into the song Shosh had heard most frequently: *"Please don't ask why I never try."* The lighting in the room dimmed, the mural onstage lit up, and the way Neon Imposter was positioned—the winged Aerosmith logo on the wall directly behind him—it looked like he'd suddenly sprouted giant feathered wings.

The only thing she wanted more than a drink right now was to talk to Evan.

• • •

"I don't understand," said Mavie.

"That makes two of us."

"Okay, but I have classes in the morning, so."

"I just need a minute. Promise."

This part of Fairfax was classic LA: streets lined with palm trees, traffic and nightlife all around, and she knew it was silly, but Shosh preferred Los Angeles after the sun went down, the gritty Hollywood tableau of it all (even in parts of town that weren't very Hollywood).

She and Mavie had been standing on the sidewalk outside the Kibitz Room waiting for Neon Imposter for a half hour, and just when Shosh was about to call it, there he was, guitar in hand, exiting the building.

"I'm here if you need me," said Mavie, pulling out her phone, retreating into the background. And Shosh found herself face-to-face with the bearded manifestation of a voice she'd once called a ghost.

He had his phone out, looking up and down the street, clearly waiting on a ride.

"Hi," she said.

He turned, smiled. "Hi."

"Sorry, I was just . . ." She stood there, struggling to find the words. "I was wondering where you got your songs?"

"Where I got them . . . ?"

"Right, like. Where you heard them? Before you started playing them."

"They're originals. I didn't hear them anywhere. I wrote them."

He looked back at his phone, then up the street again.

"I realize how strange this sounds. And I'm not, like, trying to bust you. I won't tell anyone, but"—Shosh leaned in, smiled a little, as if they were in this thing together—"we both know you didn't write those songs."

And thus, the air deflated, and his friendly tone with it. "Okay. This is weird now."

"I know those songs, man. I've heard them before. I could sing them for you."

"*Cool,*" he said, the word lathered in sarcasm.

Shosh felt her chance slipping away. "Look. Let's start over. Can I buy you a coffee or something?"

"This has been fun and all? But this is me." Just then, a car pulled up. He opened the back door, pushed in his guitar, and climbed in after.

"Wait—"

But he didn't, and as the car disappeared into the night, Shosh felt herself melt into the gritty Hollywood tableau, wishing she were someplace else, someplace cold, someplace north.

EVAN
Glacier Bay

NOTHING ABOUT THIS PLACE IS what I thought it would be.

Online, photos of endless forests and snowcapped mountains present the very picture of serenity. In reality, endless forests and snowcapped mountains are beautiful, yes, but it's a beauty more akin to sharing a coop with a full-grown elephant: wild, captivating, potentially very dangerous.

I'd read the first paragraph of the website so often, I had it memorized: *Headlands provides an immersive educational experience in which students live together for six months, concentrating on academics, democratic self-governance, community life, wilderness exploration, and on-campus labor. Whether paddling icy fjords, building chicken coops, participating in rigorous academic courses, shoveling snow, or making venison sausage, students in our program will learn the importance of interdependence between ecosystems both human-made and natural.*

No objections, really, except they left out the part where you lie in bed every night convinced your muscles must have passed through the sausage grinder right along with the venison. Alaska is wilder, harder, wetter, bigger, prettier than I could have possibly imagined. And I'm loving it.

"You okay, Ev?"

"Yep. Just waiting for my body to regain its bodiness. You?"

"Next time they say 'optional excursion,' remind me to opt out."

I've never met anyone prouder of where they're from (rural Kentucky), what they believe (democratic socialism), what they sound like (a person from rural Kentucky), or what they want to be (president, as in, of the United States) than Reese Jones. In fourth grade, when Mom asked why I was failing math, and I said it was because math was boring, she said, "There are no boring subjects, only boring teachers." When we first got here, no one was sure what to make of Reese, but I think at this point, he could suggest an afternoon of long division, and we'd all lean in eagerly.

It's late by Headlands' standards—after nine p.m.—but having just returned to the bunkhouse from a two-day wilderness excursion, mostly in kayaks, I imagine the rest of the cohort looks a lot like Reese and me at the moment: wiped, achy, too exhausted to sleep.

In the bunk above me, Reese plays music on his phone; I lie on my back, flipping through my sketch pad. When I first got here, I was so compelled by the landscape, all I could draw were mountains and lakes, wildlife, and plants I couldn't name. Eventually, I shifted into portraits of Will, Mom, Ali, Shosh, as if the souls of those I loved were trapped inside my pencil, and it was up to me to sketch them free.

As it turns out, theirs aren't the only souls desperate for escape.

A few days ago, new images blossomed as I slept: a woman playing a piano with a large bird perched on the edge; two men in the middle of a bridge staring out across a river, a bird soaring above them; a portrait of a girl with freckles and flowy hair held back by a thin band with wings; and most perplexing, a woman standing naked in an open window, giant feathers growing out of her back. "Birds are the real deal," Reese said once when he saw my dream-sketches. "If they ain't on the hunt, they're on their way home. In a way, you always know where they're going."

Strangely, something about these dreams has always felt unsafe. Like I'm cutting too close to a truth I'm not supposed to know.

Either way, Nightbird has clearly worked her way into my permanent subconscious, so . . . yay me.

"Dude," says Reese. "You gonna get that?"

"Get what."

"Your phone is buzzing."

Completely distracted, when I reach for my phone on the bedside table, I wind up knocking the photo of Will and Elliott to the floor and dropping my sketch pad in the process. Eventually, I wrangle the phone into bed with me to find a string of texts from Shosh. The first few are catch-ups and I-miss-yous, but the final one lands hard: I know you have limited access, but call when you can? Not an emergency, just need to talk. 🩶

"Looks like you should call your girl," says Reese, head dangling over the edge of the top bunk.

"I would, but your mom's on eastern time."

He throws a dirty sock at me, I throw a pillow at him, this is the way of things.

"I'm gonna see if I can find a signal." It takes everything in me to swing my legs onto the floor; luckily, when I crashed earlier, I'd been too tired to remove my boots.

"Henry said he got a strong one by that big spruce."

"Which one?" I ask.

"The one you can see from the window by the woodstove. Facin' the mountain."

I put on my coat, hat, gloves. "She's not my girl, by the way."

Reese has a way of shrugging with his eyes. "Y'all text enough," he says.

"We're friends."

He glances at my journal, still on the floor where it fell, its pages open to an especially warm portrait of Shosh's face.

"Mm-hmmm."

Turning for the door, I can't help smiling. "I'll be back."

The bunkhouse is a small two-story deal: bedrooms with bunks upstairs, mudroom and living room down; the whole place is warmed by a woodstove, which we take turns stoking through the night. I make my way downstairs, and out into the chill night air.

Sometimes—usually during one of the more menial tasks, like chopping wood or planting kale—I'll look up and see the sky, and I could swear I'm in a whole other world. Alaska calls into question the idea that all things bend toward atrophy. At the very least, it calls into question the idea that atrophy is a net negative. Maybe atrophy is necessary; maybe it's what comes after that counts.

Either way, this place puts the wild in wilderness.

On my way out to the spruce, I dial Shosh's number, but it doesn't take. A few tries later—the mountain ahead, the spruce behind, my view of the bunkhouse completely blocked—it rings . . .

"Hey," she answers, and I have a sudden urge to reach through the phone and hug her.

"Hey."

"Wow."

"I know."

"Feels like . . ."

"Yeah."

"Where are you right now?"

"I am . . . outside. By a spruce. Looking at a mountain."

"This feels peak Alaska. Wait, isn't it like—daylight there?"

"Not this time of year. It is regular night right now."

. . .

. . .

"We just got back from a wilderness excursion."

"You couldn't be more Alaska if you tried."

"I thought of you, actually. We passed this old cabin. Reminded me of your couplets. You still do those?"

"Right now, with classes, there's not much time . . ."

"Right."

. . .

. . .

"It's good to hear your voice."

"Yeah."

. . .

. . .

. . .

"Listen. I'm not really sure . . ."

"You okay?"

"Yeah, I just—have you heard of a musician called Neon Imposter?"

"I don't think so."

"Neither had I. But I was at this show with Mavie—"

"How is she?"

"So great. Struggling with the whole Balding-in-Vermont thing, but I think it's good we have each other right now."

"So you guys were at a show . . ."

"Yeah, some friends of friends are in this ridiculous band, but after their set, this other artist went on."

"Neon Imposter."

"Right, but, Evan—he's Nightbird."

. . .

. . .

. . .

"What do you mean?"

"I mean I'm talking with Mavie when I hear the songs. Like— *our songs*. Only they aren't coming out of nowhere, they're coming from onstage. From this forty-year-old bearded dude."

. . .

. . .

"I don't understand."

"So when the show ends, I confront him. I mean, like, in a nice way. But I asked him about the songs, and he swears he wrote them. He's on Spotify and everything."

"But we searched online—"

"He's only been at it for a few months. His earliest online presence is well after we'd stopped searching. Even now, it's pretty minimal, but get this—instead of giving any credentials or background, his bio just says '*Neon Imposter writes what he dreams*.'"

. . .

. . .

My eyes are on the mountain, even as my mind flies back to the bunkhouse, up the stairs, into my room, straight to the open journal on the floor.

I can see the sketches now: the woman playing piano; the men on the bridge; the girl with the winged headband; the woman in the window, wings sprouting from her back. And I can't say what's more disturbing: the specificity of each image or the creeping sensation that I know the faces in them.

. . .

. . .

"I know how this must sound. But I can't shake the feeling she was there last night. In the club."

"Nightbird, you mean."

"Like that guy was just a conduit."

. . .

. . .

. . .

"The songs stopped after we got together. Almost like—"

"She was leading us to each other."

"And now we're apart again . . ."

. . .

. . .

There is no shortage of birds in Alaska. This one must be big, given the distance and time of night. I watch it rise over the mountain, imagine it soaring through the outer reaches of space, all the way to the moon, alone and asleep, and it's the most peaceful thing.

"Shosh."

. . .

. . .

. . .

"I feel it too."

"Yeah?"

"Mostly, when we're close. Like . . . physically."

"Same. And it's like—"

"I was looking for you."

. . .

. . .

. . .

The bird is gone now.

But that's okay. I know where it went.

LOFOTEN ISLANDS

· 2066 ·

THEY WATCHED FROM THE PORCH as the gull flew across the fjord, distant memories of youth flitting between them. It was cold out, they were bundled, so it went.

"Hope is the thing with feathers," he said, and she imagined this gull soaring through zero gravity all the way to the moon.

"Would you go to space, if you had the chance?" she asked.

He considered. "I don't think so. You?"

"Definitely."

Norway was no whim. It was the fantasy they'd danced around for years, whispered about in secret, not wanting to scare off. They'd ogled photographs online, read firsthand accounts of the Reinebringen, of the northern lights and polar night, of life within the Arctic Circle. "Someday," they'd always said. And then Shosh's headaches. And then the doctors: emergency, primary, specialist. Eyes down, voices down, all these doctors like a garden of wilted flowers. Results became consultations, which eventually became a realization: there was no such thing as someday; there was only today.

They booked the dream. Ten days in Lofoten. "A temporary retreat," they told friends, trying not to say what it really was: a final adventure.

Upon arrival, they found their cabin small but sufficient, nestled among mountains and fjords, tucked in the world's most magical wrinkle. It was red, it was wooden, it was perfect. A hiker's paradise, a fisherman's delight—but they hadn't come to *do*, they had come to *be*, and there was no kind of being like being together. Together, they spent their nights under the dancing lights of the aurora borealis, its shivery green blaze a herald of science and wonder. In the afternoons, when some majestic tern or gull swooped low, carrying memories like fish in its beak, they pondered their bodies in quiet bewilderment: *Surely*, they thought, *the vessels that carry our everythings should be more durable than this.*

Alas, all things bend toward atrophy. And though atrophy was unstoppable, when Shosh smiled at Evan, he saw it for what it was: defiance and acceptance in equal measure.

She may be dying, but she would not be bitter about it.

In the upstairs loft, canvas and paints were scattered everywhere, an easel set up at the foot of an enormous window overlooking the fjord. Even now, when he painted her, the contours of her body came alive in his brush. Sometimes, she would open her mouth and a quiet song would fall out, but mostly, they sat in the comfortable silence of each other. And on the ninth day, as they were packing to leave, she said, "Ten days really isn't enough, is it," and without a second thought, he said, "I'll message the owners."

Ten days became two months, and together they witnessed the midnight sun, when daylight left its stubborn foot in the door, and the sun hovered low in the mountains like a simmering wildfire. In the mornings, they greeted their neighbors with a friendly

"Hej," and when Shosh felt up for it, they walked to the market in the afternoons. Eventually, two months came to an end, and she said, "Not nearly enough time," and he said, "I'll call them," and this time, rather than extend the stay, they bought the cabin outright.

Lofoten was home in a way home never had been. Painters and poets often visited, musicians and writers seeking northern inspiration in the vivid colors of the cold: the wild white mountains, the dusty green northern lights, and the blue hour of polar night, that time of year when the sun was never far but never present, as if waiting backstage for its cue.

"I believe in blue," they would say.

Here, it was hard not to.

In time, having found home, they felt the urge to explore. "You sure you're up for it?" he asked, and she answered with a look that reminded him what people did when they were alive: they lived.

They saw the Ice Domes in Tromsø, then flew to Stockholm, where Evan cried in a half dozen art museums. In Oslo, at the newly renovated Norwegian Space Agency, Shosh imagined herself soaring among stars; at the Konserthus (a modern work of art in its own right) a piano concerto stirred their souls in strange ways. They moved slowly throughout the trip, took things at their own pace, and when, one night, Shosh said, "I think I'm done," Evan said, "Let's get you home."

On the flight back to Lofoten, they glimpsed the distant Shetland Islands, and Evan said, "We'll go there next," knowing full well they would not. At least not together.

• • •

Back in Lofoten, on the drive home from the airport, they stopped in Svolvaer to see the statue called the Fisherman's Wife. But it was farther down the coast, at the foot of a different statue, where they felt a true sense of finality, as if they'd come to the end of a very long journey.

Half the size of the Fisherman's Wife, this statue depicted a striking young woman in tattered clothes, long hair whipping around in the wind off the harbor. In one hand, she held a knife; in the other, a bird. There was a large plaque at the base of the statue, and because their Norwegian was still elementary, they used their phones to translate:

SOLVEIG: DAUGHTER OF THE SUN

In 1798, the future king of Norway married Désirée Clary, who had once been engaged to Napoleon Bonaparte. Known as a protector of orphans, Queen Désirée took special interest in a child named Solveig Bonnevie. Bonnevie would later be imprisoned for murder on the fortress island of Røstlandet, only to escape in 1832, hijacking a boat to Lofoten. Here, history gives way to speculation: it is thought by some that Solveig Bonnevie—commonly known as Sølvi the Dreadful—was nothing less than the illegitimate child of Queen Désirée and Napoleon Bonaparte.

Depicted here with a knife and a bird, holding guilt and innocence in equal measure, she represents the duality of the Lofoten spirit: polar nights and midnight suns; chilly climates and cozy hearths; from fjord to mountain, landscapes both perilous and nurturing.

Sølvi the Dreadful was last seen in this very spot.

• • •

The drive back to the cabin was quiet. It was late, the aurora borealis on full display. As Evan drove, he reached over, took her hand in his. Shosh felt tired in a way she never had, as if her bones had folded in on themselves. She leaned her forehead against the cold glass, stared up at the dancing lights, and saw her life in pieces: the people she'd loved, the people she'd been. She saw her sister, sitting alone on a rock in a river, waiting for her. And she wondered what else was waiting there, hoping it was something beautiful, hoping it was something.

"I'll find you," whispered Evan.

Shosh squeezed his hand, one thing became seven, memories multiplying like the evening's first stars. Then she closed her eyes and moved on.

ACKNOWLEDGMENTS

LIKE EVAN, I TEND TO avoid talking about my own therapy. Not out of shame or embarrassment, but out of ownership and privacy. In the book, Evan bemoans those who wear therapy as a "badge of honor," and I have to admit, I've occasionally felt this way too. But in the wise words of Maya, "Some people need a badge," and so here's the truth: I've had seasons when anxiety was an unshakable shadow, when panic attacks were the organizing principles by which I governed my life. And so it's fitting, in a book (at least in part) about someone whose therapist guides him through dark days, that I should thank my own therapists—as well as doctors, friends, and family—for guiding me through the same.

My second batch of gratitude goes to a woman I've never met: my grandmother Lakie Boggs, who died in 1975 after a ten-year battle with breast and bone cancer. Lakie's musical skills, sense of humor, and enormous heart live on in my own mother (a kind of reincarnation itself). In this book, Mary Taft's experience with cancer differs drastically from my grandmother's—we've come a long way since 1975—and so, while this storyline was inspired by Lakie, I needed more than inspiration to write it. I needed help. To that end, I am forever indebted to Lauren Thoman and Stephanie Appell for graciously sharing their stories with me, for reading early drafts, and for offering invaluable insight. This book wouldn't exist without the two of you, and I could not be more grateful. Thanks also to my mom, who never shies away from sharing a story about her mother, and in so doing, shares the woman herself. I never met her. But that doesn't mean I don't know her.

Thanks to my incredible team at Penguin, especially: my editor, Dana Leydig, for all the phone calls, the brainstorming sessions, and the *Schitt's Creek* GIFs; the wonderful Ken Wright, who never fails to email at just the right times; Theresa Evangelista, who consistently designs the greatest covers ever, and Sam Chivers, whose illustration is the perfect match for this book; Lucia Baez, for the gorgeous interior design; Marinda Valenti, Jackie Dever, Sola Akinlana, Krista Ahlberg, and Kaitlin Severini, for their shrewd copyediting prowess; Lathea Mondesir, Jen Loja, Felicity Vallence, Jenny Bak, Tamar Brazis, Carmela Iaria, Venessa Carson, Emily Romero, Alex Garber, Brianna Lockhart, Christina Colangelo, Ginny Dominguez, Gaby Corzo, Shannon Spann, and James Akinaka; Julie Wilson, Todd Jones, and everyone at Listening Library; and a huge shout to the good folks in sales, so often the unsung heroes.

Thanks to my ever-intrepid agent, Dan Lazar, and the whole gang at Writers House, especially: Victoria Doherty-Munro, Cecilia de la Campa, Alessandra Birch, and Sofia Bolido. Thanks to my UK editor, Emma Matthewson, and everyone at Hot Key. And a big thanks to Josie Freedman and the whole crew at CAA.

Many thanks to: Court Stevens, Becky Albertalli, and John Corey Whaley, for the early reads, insights, and friendships; the editorial team at Salt & Sage Books, especially Sachiko Burton for her acumen, expertise, and generosity of spirit; Jasmine Warga, Adam Silvera, Jeff Zentner, Emily Henry, Bri Cavallaro, Justin Reynolds, Silas House, Gwenda Bond, Christopher Row, and everyone at Lexington Writers Room; Nina LaCour, David Levithan, and Steph Perkins, for the lockdown zoom sessions that kept me sane; Nathaniel Ian Miller, for the top-shelf virtual drams; Jen McNely and Brian McNely, for their help with French and Norwegian sections; Pål Stokka, for further assistance with Norwegian translations, and Alison Kerr for further assistance with French translations; Lauren Redford, for some sound early advice; my brother, AJ, for lending his expertise in a few key places; Caroline Reitzes, for theater terminologies; longtime creative partner and friend Trevor Nyman (aka Frogers), without whom the songs of Neon Imposter would not exist; Ryne Hambright and Ashley Balding, for letting me steal their perfect names; and to the good people of Lucignano, my home away from home—especially the whole beautiful Malberti clan, Simone Brogin and Enrico Battelli at Caffe del Borgo, Anselme Long, and Margherita at the wine shop—grazie mille.

Thanks to Julianna Barwick, Sufjan Stevens, Alaskan Tapes, and William Basinski, whose music can be found hovering in/around/through/over every page of this book. Thanks also to David McCullough and Peter Davidson, whose books—*The Greater Journey: Americans in Paris* and *The Idea of North*, respectively—had a profound early impact on this book.

At some point, it occurred to me that even though I fell in love at a young age, I'd never written a true love story. This was my chance to rectify that in my own strange way. Steph, thanks for hanging with me in that park back in the day, and a million parks since, and for always being you when you were what I needed. I am baffled and grateful that you continue to walk through doors with me. I love our life (lives?) together.

This is the second book I've dedicated (at least partially) to my son, but it's the first one where I need to thank him for his help. Wingate, thank you for setting me straight in all Star Wars and *Nightmare Before Christmas* references, and for rekindling my love of E.T., and for that time we walked into a public restroom and you said, "It smells juicy and exhausting in here," and for that card you made for me that said, "my hart glos to you," and for the brilliance of your book *Wingate's Question*, all of which is used in this book with your gracious permission, and really, literally, thanks for everything. You're the best kid I know and I'm so glad you're mine.